LAST SINNER

EMMA LAST SERIES: BOOK SIX

MARY STONE

Copyright © 2023 by Mary Stone Publishing

All rights reserved.

No part of this book may be reproduced in any form or by any electronic or mechanical means, including information storage and retrieval systems, without written permission from the author, except for the use of brief quotations in a book review.

❦ Created with Vellum

This book is dedicated to all who hold faith close to their hearts. May we always remember the power of belief to unite, heal, and uplift. In a world of diverse convictions, let us find strength in our shared humanity.

DESCRIPTION

Hate the sin. Kill the sinner.

Special Agent Emma Last knows that Leo Ambrose is watching her closely. Her fellow agent suspects she's different, that something strange is happening to her. She can feel his questions in the air between them. She's not ready to answer them, though, and is happy when a new case diverts his attention.

It's a bad day when blood and death is easier to discuss than the truth.

A bar owner and a bartender, embroiled in a secret affair, are found shot execution style shortly after closing time. Security footage reveals the perp forcing his victims to their knees before taking their lives. With only a Bible verse left behind, the religious undertone is unmistakable.

Another zealot making an entire faith look bad.

The message is impersonal, self-righteous...and indicates the killer isn't done. Now Emma and the rest of the team must find him before he leaves his next blood-spattered clue.

When the gunman's signature is found at a nearby mosque, Emma thinks he's marked his next location. Her hunch proves wrong, though, and he had a different location in mind, executing two more victims.

With a body count of four in just a day, the urgency escalates.

As this killer becomes more unhinged, nothing can prepare Emma for who and where he strikes next.

***Last Sinner** is the sixth book in the Emma Last series by bestselling author Mary Stone. As the pages turn, prepare to pray for mercy.*

1

Jeff Glanton rubbed his cramping hand and flexed his scrolling finger before settling his palm over the mouse again. He should've quit after that last game of Solitaire, but no way was he leaving the Lost Highway Tavern's little back office.

Hidden back here, he could wait out the clock without being bothered by any stragglers begging for one more drink after last call. His closing bartender, Stephie, was more than capable of wrapping up. And once the place was locked up, he'd be wrapping up with her. After tonight, he wouldn't see her again until Thursday.

Five days without that sweet honey is too long to wait.

The thought of going home to his wife barely crossed his mind. Now that football season was over, Jeff didn't have an easy excuse for coming home extra late. Linda would be expecting him no later than three a.m., but that would still give him and Stephie enough time for a quick one.

Jeff's fingers twitched at the idea of her smooth, dark thighs gripped in his hands and him holding her ass up against the old wooden tavern bar.

Brushing down his mustache and beard, he glanced once more at the wall clock.

Eureka...two a.m. on the dot. Bar's closed, folks. Stephie's legs, open for me only.

He shut down his computer mid-game and tucked his button-down back in, happy to show off the twenty pounds he'd lost in the months since he'd had Stephie's kisses for inspiration. Why she'd fallen for a man near twenty years her senior, he couldn't say...but he wasn't about to complain.

Outside his office, he leaned against the bar proper and enjoyed the view of Stephie ushering out their last patron, old Rodney Cambers.

"You go on home, Rodney. Take it slow, and don't go trying to sleep in our doorway again, you hear?"

Rodney patted at his coat, mumbling something about his phone. "Where...where'd I put it? Gotta call...call a cab."

"You want me to call one for you?" Stephie was patient as the day was long.

Still fumbling at his pockets, Rodney turned to face her. "No, no, you go...you close up, Stephie. Pretty Stephie, you just do what you gotta do. I'm sure I got my phone somewhere."

"Okay, then. We'll see you again. Maybe tomorrow night."

The old soak staggered to one side, then made it to the coatrack near the front door. Stephie waited, arms crossed, making her breasts nice and perky. If she intended for any man to get a move on while striking that pose, she was sorely mistaken. Rodney cast an appreciative eye, and Jeff frowned at the man.

No question about it, Stephie was the centerpiece of the place. His place. The long line of booths along his left seemed more luxurious, the shining bar to his right more dapper, just because Stephie Jones was centered right between them. She looked extra good tonight. Tight, high-waisted jeans that were acid-washed in a way that took him right back to his heyday, and a V-cut sweater that might just be deep enough for him to...

"Hey, Jeff, I thought you'd left." She offered a half-cocked grin as Rodney took his sweet time buttoning up his coat. "Weren't you here at opening too?"

He sucked in what remained of his gut and made eyes back at her. "Couldn't leave without saying good night to my favorite bartender."

Stephie's skin was too dark to show a blush from where he stood, but her cheeks appled up in pleasure. To hurry Rodney along, she pressed the door open, letting the cold air in. Their last patron was still a little too focused on Stephie's cleavage to avoid fumbling his coat buttons.

I don't blame him, really. I sure can't resist her.
But he needs to get the hell out.

As they released Rodney into the D.C. night, Jeff felt the blast of cold from outside and couldn't help thinking about Linda, no doubt nestled up in their big bed back home. Asleep, utterly trusting, and still in love with him. He loved her, too, he honestly did.

But Stephie was something else. Whether he called it a midlife crisis or a lapse in sanity, either way...he just couldn't resist the girl. How many forty-five-year-old bar owners got the chance to have sex with a hot girl in her mid-twenties?

Hell, he owed it to other middle-aged men to take advantage of the opportunity and score one for his kind. Every chance he got.

Plus, she'd come on to him.

That was how he remembered it, at least.

Stephie flipped the dead bolt and turned around with an exaggerated shiver, lips pursed to blow some of her soft brown curls out of her face. "You should be home. You know I can close up for you."

He shrugged and moved sideways to begin wiping down the bar, plucking a rag from the end rack. "Two sets of hands make light work. And besides, if we finish fast…"

"Oh…" Her smile faltered, one red nail scratching at her temple. She moved over to pick up glasses from one of the booths. "I ran into Linda at the store a few days ago, and I just…" She glanced at him over her shoulder but didn't meet his gaze. "I feel terrible about what we've been doing."

Hearing Linda's name out of Stephie's mouth was about the last thing he wanted, but Jeff forced himself to keep wiping down the bar. Sure, he was an idiot to be screwing around with an employee, and it would blow up in his face at some point…but not tonight.

Please, to all things good and holy remaining to middle-aged men who need a break in this life, not tonight.

"Stephie, honey—"

"No, Jeff, seriously." She bustled over with the glasses, dropped them into the sink, and went back around the bar for another armful. "I still love you. That's not the problem. I do. But seeing Linda, having to smile and pretend like I wasn't just using her man for some sweet loving the night before…I don't know what to do."

The little tremor in her voice shouldn't have made his dick harder, but it did. He dropped the dish towel and went around the bar. Without giving her time to argue, he took the glasses from her and set them back down in a booth.

"Stephie, honey, things have a way of working themselves out. Let's just be together tonight." He twisted some curls away from her face, back behind her ear, and let his fingers trail down the dark stretch of her neck to the edge of her sweater. "How about we go in the back and—"

"Would you leave her?" She lifted her chin. "For me?"

He blinked. "What?"

The overhead amber lights of the bar glowed a little

brighter around him, serving as a spotlight on her impromptu interrogation instead of as ambience. He clicked his teeth together, fussing with her hair.

She wanted him to leave Linda. For her.

Man alive, was she serious?

"I can't keep sneaking around like this." Stephie's eyes went a little wider, and one of her hands trailed along his arm. She was doing it on purpose, he knew, but that didn't make her easier to resist. "Seeing you mostly after hours or on the occasional lunch hour before my shift. And if we love each other…"

Jeff's mind sputtered, but he aimed for distraction, one hand sliding under her sweater above her hips. *Her skin is so fucking smooth. Don't let this end yet.* "Honey, you're not making this easy on me." He pulled her in closer, breathing into her ear in the way that drove her crazy.

She shivered in his hands, giggling. "Jeff, come on. Seriously. You must've thought about it."

A loud knock sounded at the front door—probably Rodney coming back to ask them to call a cab after all.

The knock came again, louder and insistent. If it was Rodney, well, he'd get a cab along with an earful from Jeff for interrupting his and Stephie's conversation.

"Hold on, honey. That's gotta be Rodney come back for a cab."

This'll give me time to think too, so maybe I owe Rodney some thanks instead of a kick up his backside. Leave Linda? Fucking hell.

Any other night, he would've yelled out that the Lost Highway Tavern was closed and told the guy to get lost, and then he'd have pulled Stephie back to the couch in his office and gotten cozy. But she didn't seem up for cozying tonight—anything but, if her mind was on love, dammit—and he could use the distraction of whatever this was.

Rodney knocked again as Jeff approached.

Behind him, Stephie asked, "Are you sure we should—"

"It's okay," he waved a hand behind him, hushing her, "he probably just remembered he left his phone at home."

On the other side of the stained glass, Rodney leaned heavily against the door and banged on it again with a fist. The pounding just about jarred the picture beside the door loose from the wall, jiggling it on its nail. A real annoyance crept into Jeff now.

Damn drunk. Even if he's our most regular of regulars, I might need to ban him for a week. Wake his dumb ass up that we aren't his damn servants.

Sighing, Jeff flipped the dead bolt back and opened the door several inches. "Rodney, give it a rest will—"

The man shoved open the door. Jeff stumbled backward, the momentum nearly knocking him on his ass. The vagrant —definitely not Rodney—was inside and closing the door before Jeff could think to say anything.

Behind them, Stephie was hollering about them being closed and for the guy to get the hell back out on the street.

The stranger muttered something, stumbling a few steps closer and weaving a bit on his feet. Drunk or dazed or high or something. But his face was distorted, weirdly obscured.

Fucking hell. He's wearing a ski mask. A beige ski mask that Jeff had mistaken for pale skin in the dim light.

Jeff's heart stuttered a beat, his feet growing leaden where he stood. "Man, whatever you want, whatever it is you're here for, let's don't—"

The man's muttering got louder, and the stranger swayed on his feet, stuffing a hand into his coat pocket.

Jeff shuffled backward and bumped into Stephie.

He darted a glance over his shoulder. She stepped back against the tall barrier between two booths, hugging herself. "Get him out of here. The dude isn't right."

"It'll be okay, honey." He turned back to the intruder. "Hey, man. We're closed. As in shut down for the night. You need to leave, or I'm calling the cops."

The guy was within arm's reach now, and some of his muttering became clear.

Bible verses? Guy pushes in here at two a.m. to spout Bible verses? This fucking city, man.

Jeff's fists clenched. He'd thought the man's mask meant something nefarious, but it didn't. This guy was probably just one of those religious nuts who came to town in a tent and caused trouble. He'd come to the wrong place tonight.

"I know the scriptures, man." Jeff held his hands up in a loose boxer's stance, ready to snap out a jab if it came to that. He stepped closer. "No need to preach to us."

The guy kept going, over and over with the same lines of verse. Jeff recognized it finally.

"That's the one about false prophets, right? Prophets who show up in sheep's clothing but are actually wolves? That what you're doing here? Coming in to be a wolf? You picked the wrong bar, man, so get the fuck out."

Jeff shot out a hand at the guy's chest, open-palmed to shove him backwards. But he was weirdly fast and dodged to the side, twisting away from Jeff's reach.

The guy growled and lurched forward. "*Ravenous* wolves."

"Same difference, bozo. I said get—" Jeff's words died off at the sight of a gun.

The guy waved it between them, swaying on his feet again. Stephie shrieked and cried Jeff's name.

Now or never, old man. Prove you still got that football energy.

Jeff lunged with the intention of tackling the man to the ground and taking the gun.

The thunderclap of the weapon firing nearly ripped away his hearing.

Stephie's screaming fought to be heard over the gunshot.

Jeff's thigh burned with an agony that beat the time he'd popped a knee out of place. He felt like his leg was being clamped down in a vise, and he was on the ground without any way to get back up or defend himself.

Clutching his thigh, he let a roar rip from his throat as blood covered his hands, the sticky liquid already spreading on the old hardwood flooring. Sound was all muffled, a mix of thumps and Stephie's shrill screaming. Another gunshot broke the air, and Jeff sensed her land on the floor beside him, crying out in agony.

He shot Stephie. Dammit, he shot Stephie.

Jeff released his thigh and tried to pull himself backward, crabbing his way toward her, but his blood-slick hands slipped on the floors.

The man stepped on his ankle, stopping his awkward attempt to get to Stephie.

"Turn around. And then kneel."

This can't be happening. This cannot be happening.

"Mister, you don't—"

"Turn now. Kneel."

The second command hit Jeff in a way the first hadn't, and he forced himself to turn around, spinning in the slippery trails of blood.

He stared back toward the office where he had a pistol in the top drawer of his desk. That was where he kept it because he didn't trust his other idiot bartender not to drop it and shoot his foot off. But even if it had been behind the bar, that would've been too far off as well.

No way could he get to it in time. Not with a gun already pointed at his back.

Fuck, but this can't be happening. Not like this.

"You too. Let's go."

And there was Stephie, sobbing and with one arm hanging limply by her side. She did as the stranger said, both of them kneeling now. Jeff was emotionally numb, but his leg screamed for attention.

"Close your eyes and pray." The voice behind them was a little clearer now, as if the speaker had gained some focus in the time it had taken for them to kneel.

Jeff's thigh throbbed, pulsing hot, and he imagined the stranger's command vibrating through his bloodstream, pushing more and more blood out until he had none left.

Nearly entranced, Jeff gazed down at the floor where Stephie's blood—his sweet, hot Stephie's crimson-red blood—was *drip-dripping* onto his own, mingling, the puddle expanding, soaking the knees of their jeans. Someone could've been sawing his leg off right now, and it wouldn't have hurt more.

Beside him, Stephie had one hand balled up in front of her chest, while the other hung uselessly. She was praying, "Hail, Mary..." like a good girl.

But Jeff couldn't form the words himself, only stare. This couldn't be happening. Not in his own damn bar beside his own sweet Stephie.

Another heavy footstep signaled their stranger stepping closer, and Jeff was just about to give him the safe's combination, before the man screamed. *"Get behind me, Satan!"*

Linda's face appeared in his mind. *I'm so sorry, sweet—*

The world exploded, burning like fire, then all went dark.

2

With one foot stepped forward and her back heel pressed into the mat, Special Agent Emma Last tightened her core and lifted her arms skyward like she was directing an airplane to its arrival gate. She faltered, nearly toppling sideways as she overcompensated, toes clenching on her yoga mat.

The warrior one pose was killing her. So much for being a modern-day warrior for the FBI. Barefoot and swaying side to side against gravity's pull, Emma focused on her breathing. Her fellow practitioners all stood so firm and steady, Emma swore she was the only one struggling.

Or there's an earthquake happening under the little square of floor I'm on and nowhere else in here.

She knew that wasn't it, of course. Her inability to avoid wobbling every which way was just due to her being a novice. *Suck it up, Emma girl.*

It was also because of her inner turmoil, she knew. Why had she developed the habit of talking through her problems out loud? At the office? Where Leo could hear every damn word?

Breathing deeply, she attempted to erase the memory of Leo's face as he overheard her talking about her dead mother and the Other.

Seriously? How could she be so stupid?

Maybe it was because she hadn't spoken to Marigold in close to a week. The Other occupied more of Emma's attention than she'd like, and talking to the psychic was like opening a valve, releasing the pressure.

You gotta call her soon, Emma girl. Or you're going to end up falling on your ass on this yoga mat and making even more of a fool of yourself.

"Remember your power," Oren said, returning her focus to the present.

Oren, Yoga Map's owner and most sought-after instructor, looked damn good rotating into warrior two, presenting his chest to his admiring students. He spread his arms straight as rails and gazed out over his forward hand. Oren's unruly brown hair was tousled in a way that Emma imagined it would look after sex.

They hadn't, of course, had sex. They hadn't quite gotten that far. Not with her work schedule.

"Focus, everyone. Deep breath in, settle into your stance. If you're struggling to stay balanced, concentrate on opening your hips. Use your core to lift your torso upright and press into the mat with your feet."

He turned his head so he could examine the room, checking each of his students in turn. His gaze spent a bit more time on Emma's form, and she blushed. She also attempted to open her hips by tightening her core, lifting her chest, and digging in with her heels and toes on the mat.

"There you go, Emma."

Oren's words of encouragement nearly toppled her all over again, but she held firm, letting a smile curl her mouth.

Emma breathed deep alongside Sandra, the redhead to

her right, and possibly the only other student who had trouble staying steady. Oren relaxed from his pose and began roaming the room, guiding them all to move from warrior two into triangle pose.

Here and there, he stopped to offer adjustments or suggestions. Emma swiveled into the new pose, reaching out with her upraised hand and pressing down with both feet. She closed her eyes—taking her view away from her handsome man for a few seconds—and worked to clear her head. Steadier in her pose, she tried to focus on her breathing as Oren coached them all to stay still, stay centered.

I can do this. Just gotta practice relaxing.

Not that having her legs spread and her arms perpendicular to the floor felt *quite* relaxing. Yet. But she was getting there, with Oren's help.

For him, she could even ignore the ghosts lurking around the studio, popping in from the Other. For Oren, she could get used to anything.

Oren moved sideways out of Emma's vision. "Focus on your breathing. Ignore me."

Breathing deep, Emma fought to center herself on her mat, doing her best to ignore Oren's steady pacing through the room as he adjusted everyone. All she had to do was breathe and concentrate. And ignore the grouchy old ghost in the corner.

Unable to help herself, she glanced Grumpy's way. His one pleasure in the Other seemed to be giving her the evil eye. Always there in his garland pose, scowling and sometimes even growling. She'd almost have preferred it if the old grouch just cursed at her or at least told her what his problem was. Instead, he just acted like Yoga Map's own personal gargoyle sent to put a damper on her morning.

One of these days, I'll have to tease his identity out of Oren. Without making myself look the fool if at all possible.

Oren's voice rumbled over the room, coming from the back now. "Let's move through a *Vinyasa* into child's pose now. Remember to be gentle with yourself. Good. Now lower your knees to your mat and stretch your spine but be aware of your limits. Be gentle. Gentle like a parent with a child."

Emma could manage this transition just fine without the benefit of an extra concession made for her relative beginner status. But once she had her face to the mat, a pleasant ache spread across her back and into her arms as she stretched her hands forward.

As Oren went on about the elasticity of a child and the safety of a parent's loving arms, Emma couldn't help thinking about her mother.

Every night, her mother's warning echoed in her head. She couldn't walk across her apartment without hearing that still-so-recognizable shrill cry. *"Get out of here! She can see you!"* Even now, just the thought of the panic in that voice left Emma's throat dry.

Her mother's panic bleeding into her own—

"Breathe, Emma." Oren's hand came down on Emma's back. "Slow and steady. Whatever you're thinking about, let it go. Focus on breathing."

His hand was warm against her cotton top, calming. She nodded, doing her best to follow his instructions.

Channeling her mother's panic wouldn't do anyone any good.

As Oren moved on, Emma allowed her focus to split, because despite how she was supposed to let the outside world go when she entered this studio, the Other didn't want to give her any breaks. The real world with its guns and criminals around so many corners wasn't forgiving either.

The problem was, Emma had no earthly—or *Otherly*— idea of who "she" could be. Her mom's warning had been maddeningly unspecific, despite the desperation. And why would some random ghost have it out for Emma anyway?

Not like the ghosts will tell me either.

Emma hadn't given up on demanding answers from residents of the Other, but she was getting close to doing so. The ghosts who'd intruded on their last case by spouting tattoo stories had, arguably, been helpful, but only in a way that suggested they'd also been bending over backward to be cryptic. And Emma and her team could damn well solve cases without ghosts chitchatting in riddles at every turn.

She couldn't stop herself from tilting her head, glancing toward the grouchy old man lurking in the corner once again. This was the ghost she'd seen her first day at Yoga Map, but his demeanor hadn't changed. Unlike the majority of ghosts she met, who just seemed terrified, Grumpy was pissed, ready to blow. Ironic, given the environment.

And no way did Grumpy McYoga seem like he'd help her navigate her issues with the Other.

"All right, everyone." Oren had landed back at the front of the classroom. "We're nearing the end of class for today. When you're ready, lift yourself out of child's pose and come up to kneeling, then slowly lie back into a healthy corpse pose."

Finally.

Despite the name, Emma loved the final resting pose. Lying flat on her back, letting all the stress and strain slip away from her, *Savasana* was its own special type of perfect.

After what felt like only a minute of lying still, a quiet chime sounded from the front of the room, signaling ten minutes had passed.

"Great work today. Remember, your yoga practice doesn't have to end when you leave the studio. Keep breathing and stay hydrated."

Oren held the door open as his students departed one by

one, taking their rolled-up mats with them. Just over two dozen women had shown up that day, most of them pretty advanced and all of them making googly eyes at Oren. But unless Emma started splurging on hiring Oren to do private yoga sessions in the middle of the night, which she actually might consider, this class suited her schedule the best.

Emma lingered behind, taking her time rolling up her mat. She met Oren near the front of the studio where she'd dropped her water bottle and shoes next to his duffel bag. He squinted at her a bit too knowingly. This close, she could see the lightest sheen of sweat on his forehead.

"You're doing well, but your breathing was pretty heavy in child's pose. Everything okay? Another case?"

Oren had asked the last bit more softly, clearly offering an ear more than demanding answers. For once, though, she could answer in the negative. And with a smile. "Not yet. Just...my brain. It's been racing since the start. Isn't this supposed to be meditative?"

He grinned, winking at her as if he could read right through to her thoughts on midnight yoga sessions—very *intimate* midnight yoga sessions.

Emma's cheeks warmed, but she shook off the blush. Now was *not* the time, not with another class coming up in just a few minutes. Students had already begun arriving and rolling out their mats in a grid pattern.

Oren sipped his water, eyes remaining on hers long enough to heighten the blood in her cheeks. "Don't be too hard on yourself. Quieting the mind takes practice."

And probably a simpler life too.

Not that there was any chance of that happening anytime soon.

Oren chuckled, then sighed right along with her when her phone pinged from the bench.

She picked it up to find what she'd known she would...

Jacinda's serious face above a text telling her to get to the office. They had a new case to greet the new week.

"Before you leave…" Reading the moment, Oren had turned away to reach into his bag, interrupting her excuse before she could make it. "Tell me what you think of the new flyer?"

He held up a sheet of paper featuring his own smiling face. Below his image, it read, *Blaze a trail to your inner spirit at the Yoga Map.* The address and website for the studio were just below that, but it was Oren's smile that made the flyer a standout.

Emma gazed back at him, unable to hide her own grin. "You look great, Oren. I'm sure you'll bring in lots of," she paused playfully, "*students* with that smile."

The man had the grace to look embarrassed. "Well, I'm glad you like it."

Emma came perilously close to giggling before holding up her phone. "I'm sorry, really, but no matter how handsome you look, I've got to go."

He leaned in a bit, speaking more softly. "I understand. I'm just glad you found the time to come to class this morning. Perhaps we'll get to meet somewhere else."

"And see each other soon regardless." Emma smiled, making sure he heard the sincerity in her words before she slipped on her shoes and turned away. Butterflies tickled her stomach in a manner that hadn't happened in ages.

One way or another, this guy was far too good for her, and she intended to find a way to keep him in her life. If anything, or anyone, could force her into figuring out a better work-life balance and making room for a future for herself, it was Oren Werling.

My very own handsome yogi. Now to solve this case and make some real time for him. And then maybe solve the Other and figure out my team, at which point we'll be all set for all sorts of midnight yoga sessions.

Very, very private yoga sessions.

Emma blushed from the images in her head, not the cold wind, as she let the door to Yoga Map close behind her.

3

With half his mind still on Denae lying in his bed, Leo lingered in his kitchen and poured his coffee, debating about going back to the bedroom. He'd had a hard time not waking her up the instant he'd roused that morning. Thirty minutes later, it wasn't getting any easier.

Wearing one of his ragged Iowa t-shirts, she could make his old university Hawkeyes a top-recruiting school. She looked so good in the dang thing.

But she'd needed sleep, just like he had. At least one of them ought to enjoy his bed.

Leo swirled more cream into his coffee, promising himself he'd abstain from doughnuts and pastries if anyone brought them into the office.

Still leaning against his kitchen counter, he tasted the brew, crooked an eyebrow at the cup, then added just a bit more creamer. It wouldn't kill him.

Unlike lack of sleep.

Sometimes, coffee calmed him while also keeping him awake, and Leo could only hope today would be one of those days. After another night of insomnia, he still felt restless.

But at least he couldn't dream when he remained awake. The wolf dreams kept coming, and though they were getting old, that didn't make them any less terrifying.

When it came to choosing between the unearthly howls in his dreams and exhaustion by day, he honestly wasn't sure where he stood. Especially on a Monday morning, when the Violent Crimes Unit awaited his presence.

The water in the bathroom sink sounded through his small home, and he put his coffee down on the counter to pull out another mug.

Unlike him, Denae had slept like a baby.

Just as she slipped into the kitchen, still wearing that t-shirt featuring Herky the Hawk, Leo turned her way and held up the mug. "Coffee?"

"My knight in shining armor." She took the mug and practically purred when she sipped from it. "You made it strong, the way I like it."

He grinned, both of them knowing that he wouldn't have made it nearly as strong if he'd just been making it for himself. "Do you want me to make you breakfast also, or just pour you a few more mugs of brew?"

"You kidding?" She slipped onto a stool and perched there with her hands wrapped around her mug. "Go ahead and give me a show in your kitchen, if you please."

Truth be told, he'd gotten up early enough that their breakfast was already well-prepped, and he'd been counting on that answer. After putting some bacon on to fry in an already-burning-hot pan, he began pulling bowls from the fridge. Red and green bell peppers, onions, the tiniest bits of broccoli, and freshly shredded cheddar.

"Leo! When did you do all this?"

He leaned over the island, pecking a kiss on her forehead. "I wanted to surprise you."

Mostly the truth. He might as well have been cutting up veggies if he wasn't sleeping.

Behind him, Denae murmured something about him surprising her in more ways than one.

"I was thinking I'd cover some of the black beans left from last night in shredded cheese and *pico* as a small side instead of making potatoes. Sound good?"

She harrumphed what might have been a curse, and he chuckled at the stove. "Leo, are you trying to turn me into a fat, spoiled housecat?"

"Me? Never. Besides, you're so fit, it'd take more than one breakfast to do that. You should stay over more often." He flipped the bacon, deciding to give that another minute or two before bothering to get out the eggs. He came back to the island and rested on his elbows, sipping his coffee and enjoying how companionable their silence was. More time for him to wake up too.

"Leo? What is it?"

He'd been staring at her, and apparently, the look on his face had been less adoration than he'd aimed for.

"I...just a rough night's sleep. That's all."

"More wolf dreams?"

Leo jerked upright and nearly dropped his coffee mug. "How did you know?"

"Sometimes, you mutter under your breath when you get out of bed at two in the morning. Sometimes, you talk in your sleep."

The acid from the coffee curled in his stomach. "What do I say?"

"Nothing that makes much sense. I mean, that's dreaming in a nutshell, right?"

He laughed and settled back onto his elbows. "Yeah. It's just dreams. Nightmares, I guess."

"About what? Just wolves?"

Yep. Just wolves. Nothing at all to do with them hunting Agent Emma Last while I'm powerless to help.

He nodded and sipped his coffee. "It's…sometimes, it's the wolf. Just one. Then, sometimes, it's just howling, like a sound I can't escape. I know it means something bad is going to happen, but I can't see where it's coming from or what's making it. I know it's a wolf, but knowing doesn't help. It's still terrifying, and I wake up and can't get back to sleep no matter how hard I try."

The truth was, it hadn't really been the wolf howls in his dreams keeping him up last night. Not entirely. He couldn't seem to stop going over the things he'd heard Emma saying from the break room. If only he could talk to Denae about it…but he wouldn't be the one to give up a team member's secrets.

Not unless their life depended on it, anyway, and that wasn't the case here. Certainly not yet.

Leo hadn't been able to make anything meaningful out of Emma's muttering, and it was driving him up the wall. She had definitely mentioned "the dead," a place she'd ambiguously called "the Other," and said something about her mother, who died when she'd been young. Emma had been younger than him when he'd lost his parents, which meant she'd likely been too young to remember her mother at all.

He put down his coffee and pulled eggs from the fridge. Leaving the bowl for their contents, he cracked them on the counter just like Yaya had taught him—all the better to crack them cleanly—then pulled forth a fork to begin whisking. Denae muttered something about how she ought to help him, and he exaggerated a glare that sent her back to her caffeine.

"Enjoy your coffee." He winked over his shoulder, hoping he looked as carefree as his words sounded. "And enjoy the view."

She giggled, cheeks darkened from either the flirtation or the coffee. The sound almost made him wish they were open about their relationship in the office. Almost. They'd agreed to try things out on their own and avoid the gossip train that Vance and Mia had started up for themselves. For now, having fun like this was more than enough.

Especially while there are secrets in the air between us. Even if they are mostly Emma's.

And then there are the wolves. Can't forget the dang wolves.

All of it sounded crazy, even in Leo's own head. He'd never been the spiritual type to look at symbolism and delve into dreams. And, hell, he never would've pegged Emma for the spiritual or occult type either. But that was kind of what her mutterings had sounded like, and his own thoughts on dreams and symbols put him in the same category.

"Leo?" Denae waved her hand off to the side, catching his attention. "What are you thinking about?"

"Hmm?" He shrugged, still stirring the eggs that were well past stirred. "Nothing."

Denae's lip quirked in suspicion. "Well, Mr. Nothing, I think the bacon's about to burn."

"Shit." Leo spilled coffee on himself as he whirled back to the stove and attacked the frying pork, flipping the strips before anything more than his shirt could be damaged. "Sorry."

"Hey, I like it burnt." Denae paused, the mug clicking onto the counter. "You didn't sleep again. It's okay."

"I slept enough." He mixed the cheese into the eggs and poured the mix over the softening peppers, adding the other veggies as a sprinkle. "Maybe you just need more sleep than me."

A touch of guilt tickled at him for brushing off her concern, but he wasn't ready to play all his cards yet. And the last thing he wanted was for his interest in Emma to come off as romantic, which it very well could if he wasn't careful. He couldn't chance that, not when things with Denae were going so well.

He pulled the remaining beans and *pico de gallo* from the fridge, opting to nuke the beans so that everything would be ready at once. While they heated, he pulled out plates.

Denae opened her mouth like she might ask him another question, but he made a show of fixing their plates in order to hold her off. And, as planned, the display left her in awe. Almost perfectly fried bacon, a picture-perfect veggie omelet, and shiny black beans with a splash of pico and cheese.

Not a bad spread if he did say so himself.

He pushed a plate across the island. "Want some more coffee?"

She opened her lips to answer, but the buzzing of their phones on the island cut her off.

He pointed his fork at their ever-present devices. "How dare she."

"You called it. Jacinda." Denae lifted her phone so he could read the SSA's text directing them to come in for a new case briefing. She forked up a large bite of beans even as Leo bit into a piece of bacon, enjoying the crunch. "Man, this is delicious. But we better eat and run."

4

Emma grabbed her bag from the passenger seat of the Prius, bracing herself for the cold. Somehow, the parking garage's recesses always seemed colder than even the outdoors in winter.

Better to hurry. Hold onto some of the heat I picked up from Oren, with any luck.

A touch later than usual, she didn't expect to run into her teammates as she headed inside. She passed behind Leo's truck and took a quick step back when a shadow leaned out from around the cab. Was he just getting there too? She hadn't heard the door open or close, and Leo was the last one she wanted to see alone. Half thinking about ducking out of sight and giving him a head start, Emma hesitated.

Mia came out from between the truck and a car parked beside it. Before Emma could react, Mia's eyes narrowed on her. "Emma? What's up? You look like you've seen a ghost."

Emma almost rolled her eyes, but her friend looked so serious, she only focused on steadying her breathing. "Sorry." This was so *not* the way to start off a Monday morning. "I thought you were Leo."

Mia had started to turn to lead the way toward the door but waited for Emma to catch up instead. "Is there really that much stress between you two? You seem to be working together great." Confusion laced her voice, which bundled Emma's nerves even tighter.

Forcing a laugh, Emma could only keep her gaze ahead. "I'm just not looking forward to talking to him. He overheard me, uh, talking to myself about the Other and Mom's warning when I was at my desk on Friday. I tried to play it off, but there's no way he bought it."

Mia's lips were pursed, but a smile seemed to be brewing. "Well, are you going to tell him the truth?"

Holding the door open for her friend, Emma paused to unbutton her coat now that they'd reached the warmth of the building proper. "I don't know. I mean, yeah, I will eventually, but I'm not ready. It took a lot for me to tell you, remember?"

"I remember." Mia sighed, gazing up the one flight of stairs that led to the VCU's floor. "Look, Emma, I'll be there to back you up whenever you're ready. But remember, Leo's a good guy. Nobody ever won any battles by turning away allies."

On that note, Mia started up the short flight of stairs, leaving Emma frozen on the bottom step.

Battles? Who said anything about battles?

It's Mom's warning. She's expecting me to be in for some kind of fight.

"You coming?" Mia peered down at her from up the stairs, already holding the doorknob.

"Yeah. Yeah, I just...never mind." Emma inhaled and headed up after her friend. "But speaking of colleagues, before we go in there, how are you and Sloan doing?"

Mia's cheeks dimpled as Emma reached the landing. "Operation Friendship Repair is in full swing. We even went out for drinks over the weekend. It's a little awkward, but not like I would've thought. We're going to start looking into Ned's death more seriously as soon as we get some time."

Emma shifted her bag onto her shoulder and gave Mia a quick hug before pulling back. "I'm so happy for you two. I'm sure Ned would be thrilled."

Mia's smile trembled, but she nodded. "Yeah, he would be. If you see him, you tell him, okay?"

Emma forced a smile, trying not to show how very much she did not want to see Ned again. "Promise."

The man was running around with a transparent head, for crying out loud, having lost his in the auto accident that killed him. She could handle gruesome ghosts, but seeing that level of trauma attached to features that were so similar to Mia's was something else.

"I'll tell him you're looking into his old boss, Arthur Roberts. I don't know if Ned suspects him of being involved in the car accident, but he deserves to hear about it." Emma trailed off and shifted toward the wall, allowing someone to pass them by on the landing. "And Roberts has got some explaining to do for why he disappeared so suddenly."

"Right? His right-hand man and his own wife and brother go down in separate accidents, and he's arranging to go off the grid." Mia sighed, pulling open the door and speaking more quietly as they stepped inside. "I'm hoping this case won't require more sixteen-hour days. If we get a normal workweek for once, maybe we'll be able to track him down."

"Oh, to have a normal eight-hour day." Emma's joke made Mia chuckle even as they walked toward the VCU. But secretly, she felt a tinge of jealousy.

Mia glanced over her shoulder at Emma as they approached the glass doors of the VCU headquarters. "Heads up, Emma. Good luck!" And with that, Mia offered none other than Leo Ambrose a quick hello before heading on over toward her and Vance's desks.

Leo gentled the door shut after Emma. "Got coffee going for you and Mia and put it on your desks. Jacinda's already in the conference room getting set up for the morning briefing."

"Thanks." Emma settled her bag into her seat and just barely made herself shift her coat off her shoulders before reaching for the steaming brew. "You didn't have to do that."

"Not a problem." Leo shrugged and leaned against his desk with his arms crossed loosely. "You have a good weekend?"

This man's not any better at small talk than I am, charmer or not.

"Fine, and I fit in some yoga this morning." Emma sipped at the coffee, humming her approval. "I don't know if I'm getting better, but I'm falling on my ass less."

Leo's smile was a little too wide for the joke, betraying the tension between them. And the fact that he held no coffee in his hand could only mean he'd already had more than his fair share.

Still, Emma did appreciate him not bringing up Friday right off the bat.

"Listen..." Leo ran his hands back through his hair, a lick of his lips betraying the nerves he felt. Emma could understand that much. Her own anxiety was roller-coastering through her stomach. "Whatever's going on, Emma, I just want to help. That's it. I know what it feels like to lose family, so if I can help Mia, or you, I'm here. No pressure to let the skeletons come out to play, though."

The nerves she'd felt building collapsed in on themselves. So this wouldn't be an interrogation. Not yet anyway.

She didn't have to force a smile this time when she thanked him. What else she might've said next, she wasn't sure, as Vance called from the side of the room that Jacinda was ready for everyone.

"Time to go." Leo muttered something else to himself, plucking a bottle of water from his desk.

Before he could step away, Emma grabbed his elbow, holding him up. "Life's crazy right now, but I really do appreciate it. I'll fill you in when I can."

Leo grinned, nodding so fast that the bangs he so often brushed away fell right back into his face. "I'm looking forward to it, but I can be patient. I'll tell you this, though…" He trailed off, making sure her gaze met his before he continued. "When you're ready, I will be too."

5

Walking into the briefing, Leo made sure to hold a smile on his face. On the inside, he was boiling with frustration. His hands itched to drag Emma back to their desks, handcuff her to her chair, if need be, and demand to know the truth about what was going on.

The wolf had howled her name to him in his most recent nightmare. It had sounded an awful lot like her name anyway. Going on his third night of almost no sleep, everything sounded like either a wolf's howl or someone's name being screamed into his ear.

Emma took a seat across the table from him, offering a friendly smile that suggested she'd taken his promise of patience to heart. He'd offered, hadn't he? And he'd make good on the offer, as long as she broke down and told him what the hell was happening sooner than later. He could play the good guy and let her choose the time and place to spill the beans, especially since pushing her seemed unlikely to get him anywhere.

But he'd keep his eye on Emma. Something very weird

was going on—had been going on for a while—and Friday had proven it.

For now, though, they had a case. Denae lounged in her chair beside him, one leg crossed so that the heel of her boot nudged the side of his pants. He tilted toward her just a touch, adding to the contact and taking a hint of the stress away. At least he didn't have to worry about her not being what she seemed.

At the head of the table, Jacinda began. "First things first, it's great to have the whole team together again." She schooled her expression, narrowing her dark-brown eyes on each of them in turn. "Nobody, and I mean nobody, better get sick this week. Understood? Enough of that. You get sick, and I'll make you homemade chicken noodle soup myself, and that's something you *do not* want."

Vance coughed out a surprised laugh and sat up straighter, adjusting his overpriced suit jacket. "Noted."

"All right, on to the case." Jacinda hit a button on her computer, and two images popped up on the screen at the front of the room. One of a pretty Black woman with a wide smile and a short, coiled afro. The man in the other picture was older, white, and red-cheeked with short brown hair.

Leo pulled out his iPad to see if the files had already been sent to him. They hadn't. He pulled out a pen and paper instead.

"Meet Jeff Glanton and Stephanie Jones, deceased bar owner and bartender of the Lost Highway Tavern. Both victims died of gunshots to the back of the head, execution style. The kill shots were taken after wounds that were meant to either disable or scare them, one to Jeff Glanton's thigh and another to Stephanie Jones's shoulder. The shooting seems to have happened just after closing last night. No witnesses known."

Leo jotted down the bar's name and then glanced back to

the photos. "He's what, in his forties? And she's in her twenties?"

"Good eye." Jacinda referenced her notes, reading out loud. "Stephanie was twenty-six. Jeff was forty-five."

The government ID shots disappeared to be replaced with two bodies sprawled forward side by side on a dark hardwood floor. Blood glared red around the bodies, splashed up on the surrounding booths and barstools.

Jeff had landed on the right side of his face, revealing a gruesome bubble of bloodied brain matter poured from his forehead. Stephanie had gone down face forward. Her curls —thankfully—hid her killing wound. With her arms splayed out, though, a separate wound showed in one arm that bent at an odd angle. One of Jeff's thighs was also painted red, with a patch of semi-clean floor breaking up the blood pools between his thigh and his head.

The shots were gruesome, especially close-up and enlarged as they were.

Mia sighed, leaning forward toward the screen. "He's wearing a wedding ring. There's a spouse, so that's one person we need to talk to. You said there were no witnesses?"

"Not that we know of." Jacinda glanced around the table. "But we do have security footage. Everyone ready?"

Emma rolled her finger in a scrolling motion. "Let's play it, Boss."

The video feed was darker, and Leo found he was thankful for that much. The opening of the recording showed Jeff and Stephanie embracing in the center of the bar, Jeff nuzzling her neck.

Leo laced his hands behind his head. "*They* weren't married, right?"

"Not to each other, no." Jacinda referenced her tablet. "Stephanie was single, so we have an affair, or the beginnings of one at least, and it looks mutually accepted."

Jeff and Stephanie playfully pawed at each other, but their dialogue was too soft for detection. A loud knock at the door broke them apart. Jeff opened it and was pushed backward by a figure whose face appeared blurry. It took a moment for Leo to determine the individual's face was deliberately concealed by some kind of light-colored mask.

Despite the mask, Leo felt confident they were watching a man enter the bar. He was dressed in a dark overcoat, heavy-duty-looking jeans, and a dark-colored sweater or sweatshirt. He could've been any of a million men on the D.C. streets at night, but for the mask and the slight sway to his walk as he moved forward.

"Intruder looks about the same height as the bar owner," Vance looked back to his notes, "whose ID reads six-two."

Jacinda eyed her notes and jotted something else down. "That puts the perpetrator between six feet and six-four, loosely."

Across from Leo, Emma leaned far over the table toward the screen, her face scrunched in concentration. The camera microphones were clearly not up to par. Static buzzed beneath the scene. Emma apparently couldn't hear what the man was saying any better than Leo could, and a quick glance around the table suggested none of his colleagues could either.

Jacinda read their looks and pointed to the screen. "I know, I can't understand him either. Keep watching, though."

The masked man came farther into the bar, backing Jeff up. In another second, he had a gun out, and in the next moment—seemingly without provocation—he shot Jeff in the leg, Stephanie in the arm. And then they were kneeling, turned away from him with their heads down.

"It's like they're praying," Leo breathed out, "only to be—"

The second round of gunshots cut him off. Jeff fell forward, then Stephanie beside him, blood spraying out across the floor and ahead of them, garishly red even in the video's cheap feed.

Jacinda froze the video there. "It isn't clear if the kneeling...and praying, if Leo's guess is correct...is by force or choice, but we have reason to believe that religion is involved. I'll forward these images and video to your tablets."

"Do you mean," Emma gestured to the screen, "that there's reason to believe religion is involved?"

"I'm getting to that." Jacinda pulled her red hair back from her face, frowning. "The Metropolitan PD received a shots-fired call around three this morning from a neighboring business. Before you came in, I'd just gotten off the phone with the local precinct's chief of police, and he's requested our assistance in—"

"Wait," Denae sat up straighter, "this is D.C.? They've got plenty of cops on hand. Why do they want to bring in the Feds for a bar shooting? That doesn't make much sense."

"As I told Emma," Jacinda shot her a *please be patient* look, "I'm getting to that. And the religion. You've all had too much coffee and need to stop interrupting. Look at the screen, folks."

Jacinda turned back to the screen along with the rest of them, and a tap of her finger switched the view to the next slide, which showed a bloody piece of parchment-like paper with what looked like a partial fingerprint on it. Leo breathed in, seeing exactly what Jacinda had been talking about with the religious element.

On the paper, one line was written. *I am the Way. You are the Lost.*

Everyone remained silent for a few seconds, as if the words needed their own space in the room. Around the parchment, blood was spattered on the wood.

"Capitalization like out of the Bible." Leo copied the

message directly into his iPad. "For emphasis instead of labeling. The note was on the floor? By the victims?"

Jacinda nodded. "In Glanton's hand."

"Makes sense. I didn't think we'd get that lucky with that partial."

Denae dropped her pen to the table with a clatter. "Dammit. Another cult?"

Leo sympathized. Memories of that religious community they'd encountered in Little Clementine, Maryland, were more than fresh enough.

He hated when these crazies made the entire Christian faith look bad.

"The first part is from a Bible verse. John 14:6. 'I am the Way.' Followed by 'I am the Truth. I am the Life.'" Jacinda used a laser pointer to circle the second sentence. "But this is new. This 'You are the Lost' bit. Generally, a killer leaving messages for the police or detectives means one of two things. Either the murders are personal in nature, or there are more murders already planned and coming. Given the general nature of this message, subject-wise, the chief is speculating that our killer isn't done. He's leaving messages. I'd rather us be safe than sorry, which means I'm ready to follow along with the chief's suspicion that we need to catch this guy before he kills anyone else."

Vance unwrapped a stick of gum. "Guessing he didn't do us any favors by leaving fingerprints behind? I couldn't tell if he was gloved in the video."

"He was." Jacinda flipped back to the last still image that showed his hands in the video and zoomed in. Sure enough, the man wore gloves. "Forensics is investigating the scene for clues, but his head was fully covered and, as you can see, so were his hands."

Emma nodded. "So all we have is that, by the looks of it, he's male, of medium build, and around six feet tall."

"Any video cameras on the street outside?" Mia typed into her phone, looking for the bar's address and nearby traffic cameras, if Leo had to guess. "Other businesses' cameras, maybe?"

"Patrol cops are looking into that possibility, but I doubt it." Jacinda pulled up a map of the neighborhood and pointed to a square marked as the Lost Highway Tavern. "This is the grid for that area. This tavern is a neighborhood place, about three blocks off any main road and four blocks from a stoplight. There's plenty of parallel parking, but also plenty of buses. Businesses are scattered, and generally low profit, so they don't bother with outside surveillance. We're probably lucky this place had a camera on the inside."

"And if it was past closing," Vance tapped his pen on the table, frowning, "that probably means buses weren't running. Not in that neighborhood on a Sunday night. So the chances of anybody on a bus seeing anything are low, if not nil."

"Who found them?" Emma asked.

Jacinda closed her laptop, shutting down the overhead screen. "MPD say a regular patron returned to collect a phone he'd left behind last night. He's being held on scene at the moment. Now for assignments. Emma and Mia, you two check out the crime scene and surrounding areas. Talk to our man with the phone while you're there."

Leo cursed under his breath. He'd hoped to be partnered with Emma. Maybe she'd finally talk to him if they were stuck together in a car.

Emma looked relieved with the pairing. "Yes, ma'am."

"Vance and Leo, the two of you go speak with Glanton's wife and learn what you can. Stephanie doesn't have family in town, but she does have a roommate, Jessica Wren, so you can talk to her too. Denae, you and I will talk to owners and employees of nearby businesses, especially bars that might still have been closing up shop when this happened. Everyone ready?"

Leo pushed back from the table. "I'd say so. We have a killer to stop. Let's get to it."

Ideally, before this guy drops any more twisted interpretations of religion for us to find, blood-spattered or otherwise.

6

The cots at the shelter were so awful. Springs dug into my thighs and back no matter which way I shifted. It wasn't like residents could be picky about comfort in homeless shelters, but I would've done better on a sidewalk.

Except for the icy cold. The shivering. So cold I can't focus on God's voice.

Not that I could do that any easier inside this shelter with all its noise and disruptions to my peace.

The man on the cot beside me rolled over and kept snoring. I glared over his lumpy form at the woman still rambling about aliens from Jupiter as a shelter worker gently encouraged her to get in line for breakfast. Finally, the lady got up from her cot, but she kept up her blabbering.

I'd seen her kind before, those clanging cymbals in the streets. I knew she was high on something.

For a Christian shelter, this place houses too many sinners.

God had told me I'd be safe here, despite being among them. And it wasn't like I had the money for a hotel.

I stretched, holding my breath until I could wrap my

hands over my nose against the overpowering stench of air freshener and sweat.

The man in the cot behind mine shifted, and the scent of drink poured off him.

My coat smelled familiar at least, like the pines near my home. That was why I used it as a pillow.

God had plans for me to return home someday, I knew. But I had to earn that reward first. It was important not to linger, so I would get breakfast and go. The Lord's voice filled my mind as I stood, freezing me in place.

"You do honor to your Father, my son. Those sin-peddling adulterers were creating 'holy diversions.' They and their poisoned works have no place in my Kingdom."

Two fewer sin peddlers remained on this earth, setting up innocents to be wooed by the devil over glasses of alcohol.

And, of course, they'd been sinning in more ways than one. If God had told me of their adultery beforehand, I might've lingered and made it clearer to them why they had to die. It had been such a surprise. I'd recognized the man's wedding ring glinting against his blood, while the woman had worn no ring herself.

From outside, I'd seen them kissing.

Their lives had been built on converting others to sin through the temptation of drink, then celebrating with sins of their own.

The shelter was such a mess of chaos, I chanced whispering to God out loud. "They won't be taking any more of your lambs, neither through alcohol nor any other means."

"Yet more remain who would soil this Paradise I have given to them."

God's voice ceased, and I quickly made to leave the dormitory area, aiming for the refectory where workers were serving breakfast. A line of residents already protruded from the entrance.

I joined in, inching forward behind a woman who smelled like cats and mints. She muttered a prayer beneath her breath, and I silently thanked the Lord for granting me a reprieve from the company of sin in which I found myself.

I focused on the words of prayer instead of the smell.

Ahead of me, the shelter had laid out a stack of cafeteria trays, bowls of soggy oatmeal, and sweet baked goods. Some brown-spotted bananas sat heaped at the end of the line. Most of the sinners here ignored the oatmeal, instead choosing the miniature sweet buns and muffins. Only one or two chose a banana.

The praying woman and I each took a bowlful of oatmeal. I craved anything hot, tasteless or not. The coffee stand had sugar I could add to it.

A fat priest giving out blessings with the food reached for my hand after I'd set my oatmeal on my tray. I forced a smile of greeting.

The condescending priest raised his cross, a prayer slipping from his lips before he met my eyes. As if this man, who freely housed sinners and the saved alike, knew anything about God and prayer compared to me.

"Good morning, my son."

"I'm God's son."

The priest flinched at my snarling tone.

"We are all God's children." The loftiness in his voice was maddening.

My feet itched to run, even without eating, but I made myself nod. "Thank you, Father."

I had roused the old priest's suspicions—and in expressing them, he unwittingly revealed himself a sinner. I wanted to flee, to escape this brood of vipers.

"Patience, my son."

I'm doing my best, oh Lord. I am. Bless me.

"You are blessed."

God's grace warmed my chest as I picked up a banana. A woman from the shelter staff brought out some apples, and I took one of those as well. She smiled at me like I was her grandchild, and I smiled back. I'd always found it easier to deal with her than the hypocritical priest.

I couldn't trust priests anymore. Not since my childhood priest, Father Maxwell, betrayed me.

He called my faith *false*. I confided in him about how God spoke to me, and Father Maxwell accused me of being mentally ill. He told me I had no special connection to God, no particular understanding of what God's intentions for sinners should be.

A spike of deep hatred ran down my spine, stiffening me in place. The shelter worker stopped stacking apples and stared at me.

"Are you all right, dear?"

I should've answered, but I was caught by the memory of a sinner's vile deeds and how they'd hurt me. I looked away and forced myself to keep moving, aiming toward a corner table where I could enjoy some privacy, joined only by God as I ate my meal.

Falling into despair from my hatred for Maxwell wouldn't get me anywhere. I knew God would want me to deliver Maxwell's punishment, but now was neither the time nor the place, and, of course, God understood that.

Maxwell's betrayal still burned, though. Father Maxwell was the one person who should've understood how special my connection with God was.

Instead, he'd reacted as if I'd sworn allegiance to the Beast himself.

Maxwell said I needed help from a *professional*, that God would never suggest I enact violence on His behalf. The priest needed to read his Bible to remind himself of the God he supposedly worshipped.

If the heinous attack me, they will fall, and they will perish! It tells me so right in the Old Testament, you stupid sinner. Or maybe Maxwell really is an instrument of the devil. Attempting to convert God's faithful toward doubt, toward sin. Wouldn't that explain things?

I skinned open my banana and tore off one strip, pretending it was Maxwell's brightly colored stole. Then I twisted the strip around the banana like it was Maxwell's neck, pulling until the top portion popped off, as if his head were falling from his body. Plucking the severed head from my tray, I crammed the banana chunk into my mouth.

Throughout my imaginings, God voiced no disapproval.

How could He, when Maxwell's words still echoed in my head? *"My son, that's not how we commune with God."*

That he would say such a thing only proved how much holier I was. For him to denigrate and belittle my Lord talking to me—acting like I didn't know what I was saying—was a travesty. Blasphemy. The old man didn't recognize his own God's actions.

I spooned up a bite of oatmeal. I'd forgotten to visit the coffee station for sugar, so the meal was hot but tasteless.

As tasteless as Maxwell's understanding of the world.

I couldn't help grinning at the thought, and when the shelter priest's eye caught mine, I nodded and gestured with my spoon. As if the bland oatmeal were making me smile, rather than my joke about Maxwell.

My only regret was that I hadn't killed that old man before leaving Woolward. He deserved it. When I'd attacked those other boys on God's command, Maxwell hadn't even backed me up. Not for a breath of prayer, even.

"I have other plans for you, son."
I know you do, God. Thank you.

And it'd all work out. God had promised me I'd get Father

Maxwell eventually. After I completed my mission and proved myself.

I popped a ball of sweet cinnamon dough into my mouth and couldn't help thinking of my grandpa.

This had been Grandpa's favorite flavor when it came to doughnuts. Cinnamon-powdered, and surprisingly, these weren't stale. When the powder sprinkled onto my sweatshirt, I pictured Grandpa bleeding out in his bed, blood tracking down his chest with his face and hands coated in cinnamon and sugar.

The doughball tasted good but had a sting of guilt in the aftertaste. It was false guilt, though, trying to trick me away from God's path. He warned me that might happen.

I roughed my tongue against my teeth, trying to get rid of the last bits of cinnamon, and took another spoonful of oatmeal.

Grandpa said I was crazy. Wanted to sever my connection to God through some unholy treatment he'd talked to Maxwell about. They discussed me behind my back. Made plans behind my back, as if they knew me better than God.

This ability to hear His words directly was a gift.

I'm a saint. Or maybe a saint in training. And they're jealous.

"A saint in training." I liked that. On the way to being a real saint. "I am the Way. You are the Lost." There was only one way to reach the Kingdom of Heaven, and it was my duty to remove those who'd seek to divert others from the Path.

"The bar was a good start, my son. And yet, there are far more nefarious sinners that distract from the Holy Path."

It was so good to hear God's voice speaking to me. He'd been talking to me more and more since I'd made D.C. my home. That was proof. I was on the right track, obeying His Word.

God, I am your tool, but I don't understand. Help me see who deserves your wrath.

"Seek charlatans who steal spiritual pilgrims from the Holy Path. They tempt with the promise of alternatives to the Word. But they are the Lost. There is only one Way."

False prophets and promises, pulling innocents away from God's flock. "I understand, oh Lord, and I will obey."

And I would. Soon, I would teach more of the Lost. Oh, how I would teach them. And here and now, in this humble space, I could not only hear God, but also sense His smile shining upon me from Heaven.

"Eat your breakfast, son. Take your nourishment. And then, do your work."

7

Emma kept her head down and her eyes peeled for ghosts as she and Mia trekked toward the Lost Highway Tavern. Local police had set up an outer perimeter at a wide radius from the bar, hoping to snare the perpetrator before he left the area.

So far, based on the expression on every cop's face, they'd had no luck in that department. Two uniformed officers stood behind a strip of police tape up ahead. Emma and Mia flashed their badges and were waved under, with one officer holding it up for them. After weaving in between press vans and passersby for two blocks, they'd finally reached the inner perimeter, just a few yards from the bar's entrance.

Faces turned their way through the windows of the neighboring diner as Emma and Mia passed, but Emma did her best to ignore them. One benefit of it being cold was that the lookie-loos who'd come out for the spectacle were quickly lured indoors by the temptation of coffee and a hot breakfast.

Mia stepped to one side, allowing a uniformed officer and plainclothes detective to pass by. Emma joined her on the sidewalk outside the bar, taking a moment to catch her friend up on developments with the ever-inquisitive Agent Ambrose.

"Leo just said he'd be patient." Emma spoke lower as forensic technicians exited the bar, carrying evidence bags in their gloved hands.

"Patient?" Mia kept her voice low too.

"I don't understand the Other myself, even interacting with it. And I have no idea what Mom's warning is meant to communicate." Emma sighed, watching the breath plume out in front of her. "The hell with Leo being curious about what's happening. *I'm* curious about what's happening."

Mia turned to face Emma, her elfin features more serious than usual. "We're going to figure this out. If you're not comfortable telling Leo, that's up to you. But don't doubt yourself. You've got this, and I'm here for whatever you need. Leo will be, too, if you let him in."

Emma gave Mia a fast, heartfelt hug, ignoring a gory ghost observing her from across the street, highlighting just how difficult all this was. "Thank you. But if we're done with the therapy session, let's get inside, okay? Before I freeze?"

Mia pulled back and led the way with a smile. "As if I'd let you."

Nudging her with a shoulder, Emma followed as they finished their trek to the bar.

Chuckling, Mia withdrew her ID as they approached a young, uniformed officer standing at the entrance. Flecks of ice glittered in his woolly curls. "I'm Special Agent Mia Logan, and this is Special Agent Emma Last. We're—"

"I gotcha. Name's Officer Dante Spriggs, and I'm at your service." The cop waved over one of his buddies and then pulled the door open, allowing them to enter the bar first.

Forensic technicians remained inside, scouring every surface. Blood splatter marked the center of the floor, radiating out from where the two victims had fallen. Coroner staff had already collected the bodies, but Emma could swear they still filled the center of the floor. She didn't feel the Other's icy chill or see any ghosts. She just saw the space they'd once occupied, surrounded by pools of dried blood.

As she and Mia took in the scene, Officer Spriggs came up behind them, bringing the door to a quiet close. "We got two bodies and a real big mess. Victims are the owner and a closing bartender named Stephanie—"

"Officer Spriggs, thank you," Emma held up a hand at chest height, halting him mid-sentence, "but we've been briefed."

"Oh. Sorry to interfere with y'all. I'll be outside if you need anything." With his gaze dropping in such a hangdog reaction, Emma almost felt bad for the young man.

Mia's cheeks dimpled, always ready to take the sting out, and Officer Spriggs perked up just like that, his face brightening with a smile before he turned to leave. Once the door closed, Mia gave Emma a slap on the shoulder. "Be nice to the rookies, and they'll be nice to you."

"Or you and Leo can use your charm, and I'll keep up the FBI's old and angry reputation, eh?" Emma grinned at Mia's pursed lips, but the expression faded as they rotated back to the scene inside the Lost Highway Tavern.

Just like they'd seen in the video, a line of booths ran up the right wall of the shotgun-style establishment, and a long oak bar ran along the left. Framed posters from punk bands and signed photos of rock stars littered the walls above both, with an impressive run of beer taps displayed along the bar. The exterior might have seen better days, but the owner of the joint had taken great care with the upkeep on the inside.

She walked up to the former location of the bodies as Mia discussed the scene with the nearest tech. No new information beyond what they'd seen in the video came up, though, and Emma focused instead on taking in what she could of the surroundings. Some of the chairs were up on tables, but one had not been bussed. Their victims must've been in the middle of cleanup when the perpetrator entered.

Conned his way in the door maybe? On the video, it looked like Glanton had unlocked it.

Mia stepped in by her side and gestured toward the cash register. "No sign of a burglary, even though you'd expect someone coming in at closing to be after the money."

Emma frowned at where the bodies had lain, wrinkling her nose against the metallic smell of blood drying around them in the cold air of the bar. Even inside, the February chill had slowed the drying process enough that larger pools of blood were still liquid at the center. "Could've been a crime of passion. If he knew them, maybe he felt cheated."

"Jilted lover?"

"Maybe. Stephanie might've dumped him before starting the affair with Glanton, seeing a business owner as a safer bet than whatever her ex may have done. But we won't know for sure until we get more details on the victims' histories."

"You don't sound convinced, even though you're the one coming up with these ideas. What else are you seeing?"

Emma faced Mia and shook her head just enough to confirm the only thing she'd seen so far was the aftermath of two senseless deaths.

Mia stepped closer, lowering her voice. The forensic team was off swabbing and dusting the bar and the door to a small office at the back of the space. "Okay, then. No ghosts. At least, not yet."

"Nope, nobody here but us chickens. Scout's honor." Emma held up her right hand and wiggled it.

Mia sighed, stepping carefully around the blood splatters as she moved deeper into the bar, following the line of booths. "Officer Spriggs was right. We do have a big mess.

No obvious motive or known connection between the perpetrator and his victims. Nothing here at the scene that tells us anything new. We could all be chasing our tails for weeks and still come up empty."

Emma's frustration equaled Mia's, but she put it aside as best she could and focused on what they did know, or could reasonably suspect. "Jilted lover or an abusive ex might explain it. Except a crime of passion wouldn't be accompanied by a weird religious message."

"Unless they were all members of the same church. But even then, it'd have to be a seriously intense church to inspire the kind of thinking that leads to double homicide."

"We know churches like that exist, but this doesn't look like a religious killing...except for that note. Zealots who are this offended by people having an affair or drinking alcohol? Christ got angry with money lenders, not adulterers or bartenders, correct?" Emma mirrored Mia's movements, edging around the techs near the bar.

That was when the air went cold, thickening around her. She stopped moving as soft crying reached her.

Mia had joined a tech heading toward the back office.

Emma waited until they'd gone inside before she followed the crying around the edge of the bar. The techs had finished back there, leaving Emma free to explore.

When she rounded the counter, Emma found the ghost of Stephanie Jones curled down low on a rubber mat. The ghost sat hunched over, hugging her knees and crying into her jeans. Shadows cast by the beer taps above lanced across and through her figure, and blood dripped onto the mat from her bloodied arm.

Glancing at the techs, who were gathering their equipment and making a slow exit, Emma decided to chance it. She crouched beside Stephanie, bracing her lungs against the cold and thickened atmosphere surrounding the Other. This was just another tortured ghost, she had to remind herself. Not an angry attacker and not a threat.

Or at least not a threat beyond your teammates deciding you've lost your marbles.

"Stephanie." Emma waved her hand near the ghost's knees as she whispered. "Stephanie, can you talk to me? Do you know who did this?"

The ghost's pretty curls, soaked in blood where they framed her face, shook as she continued crying into her knees, rocking against the open shelves at her back. Pint glasses and tumblers sat in orderly rows.

"Stephanie, can you hear me?"

The ghost wavered, then went still. She rotated her head to look in Emma's direction. "Said we were lost."

Emma scooted backward, just catching herself before she crashed into a shelf of pint glasses. A few teetered at the edge, and she steadied them with her forearm before they hit the floor.

Stephanie's ghost went back to sobbing and rocking in place, as if Emma weren't even there. But her expression had been a shocking sight.

"Emma?" Mia's voice sounded over the bar counter. "Emma, where'd you go?"

Emma took a second to collect herself, breathing in deep before she stood.

"Sorry, Mia, I'm here. Find anything?"

Mia frowned, tugging disposable gloves from her hands. "Not much. Bar office is just what you'd expect, if a little bit neater. We can go through receipts, but unless we get some evidence that the guy was a patron, I don't—"

She was cut off by the front door opening in a rush, letting in a blast of cold that competed with the Other. A bleary-eyed man in a hunting cap entered, clapping his hands together for warmth.

Officer Spriggs followed behind him, hustling to catch up. "Sir, I told you to wait outside until the scene has been cleared."

The man stumbled backward directly into Spriggs, who nearly fell out the door from the weight of him.

Mia and Emma hurried their way.

Up close, Emma smelled a heavy reek of alcohol hanging around the man like a cloud. "Sir? You can't be in here. This is a crime scene."

The man nodded, and his gaze slid to the right, looking past Emma's shoulder at the bloodstains.

"Sir, you shouldn't be in here." Officer Spriggs had a hand on his shoulder, tugging. "Let's step back outside, okay, Mr...?"

"Cambers. Rodney Cambers. I left my phone here." Rodney Cambers raised a shaky hand and pointed beyond Mia and Emma at the blood splatters. His bleary eyes widened as two forensic techs emerged from the back office. "I was just here last night."

"I'm so sorry you had to see this." Emma put a hand on his other shoulder, half afraid the man would collapse. "You shouldn't have been allowed in here. Let's go back outside with Officer Spriggs, and you can tell us what you saw last night."

Emma waved Spriggs forward, and they made a small escort for the bar patron, ushering him outside and to a nearby patrol car. Spriggs opened the back door, and their shell-shocked wanderer perched on the side of the seat.

Cambers's feet rested on the curb next to a chalked note on the concrete.

J146.

"Mia? Is that from the utility company or something?" Emma pointed at the note. Sometimes utilities would mark spaces they needed to service, but this didn't look like that kind of thing.

"I don't know." Mia, apparently thinking along the same lines as Emma, pulled out her phone and snapped a shot.

"Let's scoot down the sidewalk a bit so we don't disturb it."

Emma offered a hand to Cambers, guiding him up and around the marking. They took a few steps down the street with Mia following.

When Spriggs kept hovering, as if to participate in the interview, Mia caught his eye before Emma could chase him off. "Officer Spriggs, why don't you go check with one of the techs and get them to photograph that chalk mark. Then see about whether there's a lost-and-found box behind the bar? Maybe they'll be able to release this man's phone if it's there."

Spriggs nodded as if he'd been given a top-secret mission before heading off.

Biting back a smile, Emma returned to their witness. "Do you come here often?"

The man shook his head, corrected himself, and nodded. He stared back toward the bar. "Been coming here for eight years. Long time. Known Jeff a long time."

"And you said you left your phone here last night?" Mia asked. "How late were you here yesterday?"

"Right up 'til closing. I'm a late drinker. Come in early and stay late on Sundays, usually. My wife does choir practice, and she and the girls go to someone's house for wine after, so I stay here. Think I left my phone in the head. If Jeff found it, he'd know it was mine because of the new cover I got. Has the Marine emblem and a photo of my dog on it." Tears began leaking down the man's stubbled cheeks. "Poor Jeff."

"Sir?" Emma placed one hand on his shoulder. "Did you happen to notice anyone strange lurking inside or outside?"

Rodney shook his head, muttering to himself.

Mia leaned closer. "I'm sorry, Mr. Cambers, what did you say?"

When Rodney coughed, she handed him a tissue. "I thought I saw a sad old drunk when I left, but I was just seeing my reflection in the windows. Least they died together."

Well, that's one response.

Emma shifted beside Mia, trying to catch the man's downward-cast gaze. "Can you tell me what you mean by that?"

"I shouldn't speak ill of the dead, but I guess I'm not, if they were happy." He rubbed his arm against his face, drying his tears as they fell. "The two of them, Jeff and Stephie, they were a couple of lovebirds, you ask me. I could see it in how they looked at each other. Say what you want, I guess, but age don't make no difference. Heart wants what it wants."

Emma leaned back on her heels. If the affair had been this visible to drunken regulars, there was no telling who would've known about it, which definitely meant it could be their perpetrator's motive, religious weirdness aside.

Pulling out her tablet, Mia began taking down Rodney's information as Emma glanced back toward the bar. Spriggs had been distracted from his chore by some press who'd moved up to the inner perimeter line. But he was also defending the *J146* marking. No telling yet if the techs had found any fingerprints or how close they were to clearing the scene.

Promising to help Officer Spriggs look for the man's phone, Emma stepped away. If the phone hadn't been left behind, maybe their regular had come back to involve himself in the investigation.

Anything was possible, yet with the way this man had reacted to the sight inside the bar, she doubted they'd found a potential suspect. Killers often returned to the scenes of their crimes, but Rodney Cambers didn't strike Emma as anything other than a man who'd lost a friend today.

Passing by the techs at the door, Emma spotted Officer Spriggs wearing nitrile gloves and poking around behind the bar. Gingerly, she sidestepped the sobbing ghost of Stephanie and joined him. "Any luck?"

"Not a bit. Bar's pretty clean back here, but I ain't seeing a lost-and-found box or anything."

Emma squatted and examined the storage areas behind the bar, finding nothing but glassware, bar rags, a bucket of oily water, and rolls of receipt tape. As she stood, Emma spied a phone peeking from beneath the register.

"Got it. Can you fish that out, Officer Spriggs?" Emma leveled a finger at the phone while taking her own phone out with her other hand. She snapped photos of the device while he held it up. The phone's custom cover featured a rotund golden retriever puppy beneath the Eagle, Globe, and Anchor emblem of the Marine Corps.

She waved at a tech filling out some forms on his tablet at the end of the bar. "Okay to give this item back to the owner?"

He waved her off. "Let me dust it first." He pulled out dust, brush, lifting tape, and a card from a box beside him. With a practiced flourish, the tech collected prints from each face of the phone while Emma stood by.

Officer Spriggs motioned toward the door. "Looks like you got this? Imma step outside unless—"

"Thanks, Officer. Appreciate the assist."

As he departed, the tech finished his task. "Okay, you're good to go." He passed the phone back to Emma.

Peering out a window, she saw that Cambers had given in to tears and was sobbing into his shirt. Since the man didn't seem ready to go anywhere, she took one more moment for herself and pulled out her own phone.

The religious note might have been a decoy, except that the phrasing was fervent enough for Emma to lend weight to its relevance. Still, either Jeff or Stephanie could've had a former partner who was highly religious and angry enough to commit murder to satisfy their indignation at being passed over for someone else. That in mind, she texted Leo.

Be on the lookout for a scorned lover. Even the regulars knew Jones and Glanton were an item.

That done, she headed back around the bar with Rodney Cambers's phone in hand. Stepping past Stephanie, she fought down the urge to say, "Excuse me" as she passed. The woman remained curled up there, crying into her arms all but silently. Grief over her own death clung to her, but she belonged to the Other now, and Emma could do nothing for her but find the man who'd sent her there.

8

Leo slid his phone back into his pocket after giving Emma's text a thumbs-up, confirming he'd received her message. Beside him, Vance gazed over the dashboard for another second as Leo relayed the message and got them moving down the street.

"I'd be a little surprised if Glanton's wife matches up with the figure we saw in that video."

Leo thought back to the recording and had to agree. "Her having a lover might be one angle, though."

"Sure, but if she's got her own lover, why wouldn't the unhappy couple just split up and go their separate ways?"

"Maybe one of them had the money, and the other wanted it. That's usually how it goes when one spouse kills the other."

"The guy owned a little dive bar. How much money could he possibly have?"

"He owned a little dive bar in D.C., so I'm guessing he had plenty. At least enough to keep his business in business."

"Fair point. But if the killer is on the wife's side of things,

I can't see him caring enough to go all Holy Avenger on the husband. Talk about the most obvious motive, right?"

Leo knew they'd exhausted that thread of possibilities, despite lacking any firm evidence. Even without hearing exactly what the killer had said, Leo recalled the man's hushed voice, almost steady enough to have been a chant.

Thinking about it made him shiver. The tone and cadence had been so fervent, so full of righteousness, like their perpetrator believed every word he said and was killing for his own reasons, not to mollify a needy lover.

"I don't think this is a crime of passion." He pulled to a stop at a light, tapping his hand against the steering wheel. "That message found in Jeff's hand feels too impersonal. Too…I don't know. Driven? Self-righteous? Plus, it sets up more potential murders, assuming we're reading it right. Crimes of passion are usually one and done."

"So something for the back burner." Vance fidgeted with the seat belt across his chest, adjusting it downward. "Unless the wife sets off any red flags."

The light turned green, and Leo eased into the intersection, taking his time. He would never get used to D.C. drivers, even the ones who didn't drive like Emma Last. "No quip about me driving too slow? You didn't even bust my chops for making the coffee too strong this morning."

Vance chuckled. "You do that for Denae. Your brew's nearly as bad as hers lately."

"That's my point." When the other man didn't respond, Leo glanced sideways, but his partner only focused out the window. "I'm the new guy. You're the old guy. You bust my chops."

"I'm not old."

Leo grunted. "You know what I mean. You've been distracted. What gives?"

A shrug.

Perfect. I've only got so much patience to go around, and Emma's monopolizing the shit out of it.

"Vance, come on. What's up? You and Mia doing okay? Is that the issue?"

For a second, Leo thought he'd get another shrug, as Vance just kept staring forward. Finally, though, he shifted in his seat. The hesitation alone said it all.

"We're doing fine, but..." Vance trailed off, running one hand through his too-perfect hair. "Mia seems distracted lately. Distant. She's been spending a lot of time with Emma, and now Sloan, and I can't get past feeling like they're talking about me. But things were going just fine between us until recently. *Great*, even."

He would *think her being distant is about him.*

Tempted to make fun, Leo held himself in check despite this being Vance. If the situation had been reversed and Denae grew distant, he might take it personally too.

"For what it's worth," Leo slowed, turning into the Glantons' neighborhood, "Mia seems to really like you. For *some* reason. I'd say she'll come around. Every relationship has its lulls, and with Sloan and her being friendly again, I bet that's brought up a lot of feelings about her brother."

Vance nodded, and Leo might have imagined it, but his shoulders relaxed a touch too. "I hadn't thought about that. She's mentioned Ned more than usual lately, so you're probably right." He stretched his hands, seeming to shake off whatever worry he'd had. "And what about you and Denae? Doing well?"

The question startled Leo. He didn't think anyone on the team had known, or seen, or *thought* about Denae and him together. "How did—"

"We're FBI agents, genius. But a blind person could've spotted you two." Vance grinned. "I can't believe I'm on a team where we've got two couples paired off already. Feels like a Hollywood screenplay."

Leo had thought the same thing when he'd realized that his and Denae's date hadn't been a one-off. "I think so. We're taking it slow, especially since we work together. Kind of a weird thing, ya know?"

Vance didn't prod for more information, thankfully. Leo had no desire to say more than he already had. Hell, if Vance had prodded, he might've hit the gas for real and done Emma's bellyaching proud.

The neighborhood they'd entered was on the edge of what could be considered D.C. proper, but the homes were well taken care of. An HOA hard at work, Leo guessed. The Glanton home was no different.

Leo pulled up to the curb in front of a house, as the driveway was already crammed with five other vehicles. Some dogwoods scattered shade over the yard, even without their leaves, and a wind chime clanged about with the breeze, hanging near one of the rockers on the front porch. "Looks like they got new siding pretty recently."

"And those are top-of-the-line windows," Vance pointed at the new-looking facade of the home, "so either the bar's doing well…"

"Or money's coming from somewhere. Maybe we take 'crime of passion' off the back burner after all." Leo climbed out of the car, but rather than focusing on the house, he thought back to the bar they'd seen via video feed. It had looked pretty nice for a neighborhood place in a not-great neighborhood, on the inside at least. That wasn't an easy thing in this economy.

They climbed the front walk to a sheltered porch with two wicker rockers framing an arrangement of potted plants. When Vance knocked on the door, a burst of voices responded from inside, then a man answered.

Older, gray-haired, and definitely not the grieving wife of Jeff Glanton. He glanced between them with a frown. "Yes, can I help you?"

Leo held up his badge and introduced himself and Vance. "We're looking for Linda Glanton. Is she here?"

"She's my daughter, and she's had a shock, so—"

"We're here about her husband." Leo leaned in, speaking more quietly. "I know she's grieving, but we need to speak with her. I promise we'll keep it brief as can be."

The man nodded, his features softening. "I'll get her. Try to be quick. This life's not fair, is it?" Without waiting for a reply, the man backed off and shut the door behind him.

Vance leaned one hand against the porch pillar, a twitching curtain nearby drawing both of their gazes. "Least she's got family to support her. I hate going to question a widow and finding them alone."

The comment sounded more like something Mia would've said. Maybe she and Vance were better suited than Leo'd guessed. The door cracked before he could offer a response, though.

Linda Glanton's face was red from crying, her brown eyes shining with moisture even in the dry air of winter. She'd pulled her long brown hair into a tight bun, but strands frizzed out from every direction. Leo could easily imagine her family's fawning and hugs having that effect, but somehow, it made her look all the more grief-stricken. She hugged her sweater around her, and nearly stumbled coming out the door.

Vance and Leo both moved to catch her elbows at the same time, and she nodded without speaking as Leo guided her to the nearest wicker rocking chair, taking the other for himself.

She clearly wanted to talk to them outside. Shoeless,

wearing only her socks, and not dressed for the cold, she didn't even seem to care about the temperature.

"Linda Glanton," Vance confirmed needlessly, "I'm Special Agent Vance Jessup, and this is my partner, Special Agent Leo Ambrose. We're investigating—"

"Jeff's death. Of course." Linda gazed at the brick beneath their feet. "Thank you for coming."

"We're sorry for your loss, Mrs. Glanton." Leo exchanged glances with Vance. "We'll make this as fast as we can."

Still not looking at them, she began rocking in the chair. "I know. Thank you. For being here. Investigating."

Leo tried to catch her eye, and mostly failed. "Mrs. Glanton, can you tell us if you noticed anything strange about the way your husband was acting lately? Or if you know of him being in contact with anyone unusual?"

She shook her head. "Not really. We had the siding redone a few months back, and the contractors hung around an awful lot, but that's the last time anyone out of the ordinary was here."

There's my opening.

"It looks good. Must've been expensive, the way things have been lately with supply lines."

Another shrug. "It was, but my dad paid for it. He's always trying to give us money. Loves supporting the bar. Doesn't believe my nursing and the bar could bring in enough, but you'd be surprised."

Well, that explains that.

"Everything's been normal, on autopilot." Linda rocked harder, the back of the chair hitting a porch post as she became more anxious.

"And, uh," Leo quieted his voice, worried the widow's father might be listening in and try to chase them off the property if he heard this part, "did you have any concerns about Jeff...was he acting out of the ordinary in any fashion?"

Linda frowned at her knees, still rocking. "Jeff was Jeff. Easy. Working hard. Same as always. He shouldn't be gone."

"What I mean is," Leo glanced at his partner, but Vance offered no help, "did you have any reason to suspect Jeff was, uh…distracted?"

The widow before them kept rocking. "By what?"

Vance eased out a breath. "By someone else, maybe?"

Linda's piercing eyes went wide and met his. "Are you joking? How dare you ask me something like that!"

Inching a touch closer, Leo cut in. "Ma'am, we have to—"

"No!" Linda stood, knocking the chair against the porch as she came to her feet. "Jeff was loyal. We are…" she clamped her lips shut, and swallowed hard before continuing, "*were* a good Christian couple. That you'd insinuate anything less is an insult to my husband."

Leo bit back a sigh as he stood. "I'm sorry, ma'am, but—"

"But nothing." She placed her hand on the door handle, focusing on Vance after cutting Leo off. "I think we're done. My family's here for me. I hope you'll be there for Jeff. If you need anything, after you've started *investigating the crime* instead of Jeff, please let me know."

After another furious glance at Vance, she yanked the door open and stepped inside, slamming it behind her.

Vance raised one eyebrow, waving at a window as a curtain was pulled shut. "You sure have a way with women, Ambrose, I'll give you that."

※

THEIR NEXT STOP was the home of Stephanie Jones, a decent-sized duplex as far as D.C. rentals went. Unlike at the Glanton home, Leo and Vance wouldn't be traversing any bricked walkway to a covered porch complete with outdoor seating. There was not an ounce of curb appeal, and the building needed work.

Vance climbed out of the car and left Leo to follow him.

Coming up to the front door, Leo stepped over a pile of bricks that was once the step onto the tiny porch. He was about to knock when the door opened, revealing a brown-haired twentysomething in an oversize sweatshirt.

She eyed them both. "You're here about Stephanie?"

Vance pulled out his ID. To her credit, she took her time examining his badge, despite being almost sickly pale and gnawing on her lower lip. Leo figured she'd rather be doing anything other than standing up, much less talking to federal agents.

"Agent Jessup," the young woman looked up from the ID to Leo, and he showed her his, "and Agent Ambrose. I was Stephanie's roommate, Jessica Wren. Come on in."

She backed away from the door, letting it hang open, and led them into a little living room featuring an oversize sectional that had seen better days. In one corner, a standard poodle lay curled up and staring at them. When a low growl greeted them, Leo paused.

"Hush, Pepper." Jessica waved for the agents to sit and settled herself right next to the dog. "He's just grumpy about his nap being interrupted."

Leo sat on the opposite side of the sectional, kitty-corner to Jessica, and Vance lowered himself down beside him. He'd learned well enough in college that you didn't trust a woman's dog when you were an unknown man, well-intentioned or not. "Your dog or Stephanie's?"

"Oh, he's mine." She patted Pepper's head, and he lowered his muzzle to his paws with a huff. "Just a grumpy old man now. I've had him since college."

She seemed to nod at herself, more controlled than she'd

been outside, and Leo took that as his opening. "Is that when you and Stephanie met? You look about her age."

"Oh, gosh no." Jessica shook her head, leaning back into the couch and letting her fingers wind within the poodle's curls. "I mean, yeah, we're the same age, but we only met recently. I really don't know her that well."

Vance pulled his iPad out and leaned forward. "But you were living together?"

"Just roommates." She met Vance's eyes, then Leo's. "We weren't a couple. I'm not even into girls."

Leo cleared his throat, nodding at Vance to indicate he'd take the lead on their interview now. "Ms. Wren, how did you and Stephanie meet?"

"I'm kind of a regular at the Lost Highway. I go for a beer after work most days, though I don't stay late."

"And where do you work?"

"I'm a part-time letter carrier. For the post office."

Vance coughed. "A fellow federal employee. Thank you for your service."

Jessica rolled her eyes. "Sure. Anything to pay the rent, ya know?"

Sensing the tension between Jessica and Vance, Leo sat forward. "Ms. Wren, we were talking about when you met Stephanie Jones. How long ago was that?"

"About six months back. I was at the Lonely Highway, Stephanie was saying she needed to find a new place, and I already knew she liked dogs."

"So she moved in."

Jessica shrugged. "We got along fine. It's good to have someone who works nights and likes dogs around. Means Pepper isn't alone as much as when I'm out delivering mail. I'll have to start looking for someone new soon."

Leo nodded in sympathy. Dogs were great, but they wanted to be around people, and good roommates were hard enough to come by without adding a large canine to the mix. "And was Stephanie seeing anyone?"

"No, and before you ask, she didn't have stalkers or creepy exes or anything. Not acting strange lately or talking about anything weird either. To answer your next questions."

Vance barely held back a laugh. "You must watch crime shows."

Jessica didn't react, focused on the dog. "In my experience, two women living together can't just be roommates, or have nothing other than a basic need, like paying rent, to bring them together. There's always some other reason in people's minds. Crime shows don't reflect reality as much as you might think. But I figure a fellow federal employee would know that."

To hold Vance back from responding, Leo put up a hand. Jessica continued to stroke her poodle, giving him a scratch under the chin as he flopped onto one side and stretched his legs.

"Any more questions, Agents, or can I get back to enjoying my thoroughly restful day off before I go looking for a new roommate?"

Vance spoke up first. "Was there a chance Stephanie was having an affair with someone at work?"

"You mean Jeff." Jessica sighed. "Yeah, I'd say so. I mean, I don't know for sure, but I suspected it. I thought I heard his voice one night coming from her room when I came home, and the way they looked at each other at the bar…yeah, they were a thing. Probably."

Pepper grunted in his sleep, and Leo muffled a laugh with a quick cough. The dog could've been commenting on the relationship, that noise had been so well-timed.

"And was Stephanie religious?" Vance twirled his pen as he spoke, continuing when he only got a shrug in response.

"Maybe you heard her praying or know of a church she belonged to?"

"Not that I know of. I mean, you can look around her room, I guess. It's my name on the lease, so it's my call, right?"

Leo nodded. "That would be helpful."

"I'm sure she'd want me to help however I can, considering what happened. But I never heard her praying, and she definitely didn't attend services anywhere regularly, or I would've known. She'd usually get home so late Saturdays… from work, I mean…that she'd sleep 'til like one in the afternoon most Sundays."

Leo hadn't expected anything different. "You don't mind if we see her room, you said?"

Jessica shook her head and eased up from the couch, disengaging from the dog, who only raised his head to gaze at them suspiciously as they left the room.

She opened one of two doors in the hallway and waved them inside. "Just let me know when you leave, okay? And don't take anything unless you tell me about it. I'm gonna box it up and send it to her mom down south."

There wasn't much to search, as it turned out. No surprises in the bureau or nightstand drawers. The only pictures showed Stephanie with an older couple, who Leo guessed must be her parents. A shelf of novels sat above a desk. Vance picked up the laptop for forensics to search, and they gave Jessica a number to call about retrieving it or having it dropped off later in the week.

"Nothing to signal a motive or suspect." Leo clicked the door shut behind them.

"And nothing out of the ordinary." Vance shifted the laptop from one arm to the other, keeping his eyes on his expensive shoes and the scattered patches of mud as they made their way across the yard.

"So we're back at square one. Do either of us actually think this was a crime of passion?"

"No way in hell."

Leo sighed. "Whoever killed these people, I don't think he knew a thing about them. Although, maybe he thinks he does."

9

Mia adjusted her laptop so she could view the screen from beside the conference room table. Reaching her arms toward the ceiling, she stretched to one side and then the other. And repeated the move again. Eyes still on the screen, body twisting and turning.

Anything to keep herself awake and aware at this point.

Emma had talked her into fried calzones for lunch. The marinara and dough and cheese might as well have been a Thanksgiving feast, the way she felt. It didn't help that the security footage of the street outside the Lost Highway Tavern, courtesy of a nearby bookstore, was about as exciting as a documentary on tax code and making her sleepier.

The conference room door banged open. Sloan Grant dashed inside so fast she nearly tripped.

Mia lunged to catch the other woman's laptop before it fell from her hands, but Sloan juggled it down to the table safely.

"What are—"

"You won't believe this, but I think I found him!" Sloan

raced around the table and tugged at Mia's arm, angling her toward the laptop.

Gaping, Mia fought to catch up. "You found...you mean Ned's old boss, Arthur Roberts? How?"

Sloan patted the laptop as if it were a beloved dog. "You recognize this old thing yet?"

Recognize it?

Mia turned her attention to the machine and realized it was indeed old. The brand hadn't been manufactured in years. A faded band sticker took up the lower corner by an internal CD-ROM drive.

"Ned's computer. I kept telling him he should get a new one—"

"But he loved this one. Trust me, I *know*." Sloan shook her head, obviously having had the same conversation with him. "I've held onto it since his death but never looked inside until we started talking. I mean, why would I?"

Mia was stunned Sloan had kept her brother's laptop. "Why didn't you tell me you had this?"

"I..." Sloan faltered, diverting her gaze from Mia's, one hand combing through her strawberry-blond hair. The gesture betrayed her nerves.

Mia found that she didn't care if she made Sloan nervous.

"It was just his work computer, Mia. You never asked for it—"

"I figured our parents had it, Sloan." Scowling, Mia leaned back in her chair and crossed her arms. "Because why wouldn't they?"

"It was old. And I knew he had pictures of us, so I didn't think to say anything." Sloan tapped at the track pad, bringing the screen back to life. She blinked fast, holding back sudden tears. "I still have some of his old clothes too. I'm sorry. I guess I should—"

"Forget it." Mia placed her hand on Sloan's shoulder. "I'm

an ass. I'm sorry. He'd have wanted you to keep his things to remember him by."

Sloan squeezed Mia's hand. "I miss him."

The simple words hung in the air over the whirring of Ned's old machine. Pictures of him and Sloan scrolled by as the screensaver activated. Ned and Sloan taking selfies on the Capitol Mall. The two of them sitting on a dock fishing, then walking shelter dogs together, and finally Sloan with Mia and her family around the dinner table at Christmas.

She would've been my sister if he'd survived. The least I can do is stop acting like I've got some claim on Ned that she doesn't.

"We're gonna get justice for him." Mia gripped Sloan's shoulders before releasing her. This time when she caught the other woman's eyes, she smiled. "We are."

Sloan swiped moisture from her face, taking a deep breath. "Ned would be happy we're working together."

"Hell, he'd be happy we're talking without sniping at each other." For a moment, Mia imagined he was watching them inside this very conference room. She was thankful Emma wasn't there to tell her otherwise.

"I should've said something when we realized Ned's death wasn't an accident." Sloan hesitated, frowning at the laptop. "But I guess I didn't see how this thing could contain anything useful after all this time."

"I get it." Mia tamped down the lingering annoyance at only having just been told about the laptop. "Just promise not to hold anything else back."

"Promise." Sloan reached for the laptop, her fingers skating across the keys. "And meanwhile, you need to see this."

Ned's personal email account was open, revealing an message from a Slate House Rye showing today's date. "I don't understand. Ned's got a delivery coming today? What is this?"

Sloan grinned. "Whiskey."

"You're making about as much sense as a drunk. *Have* you been drinking?"

"Funny." Sloan's lips quirked in a proud smile. "It's for Ned's boss. Arthur Roberts is a whiskey snob. Ned always bought him the same brand from this place, Slate House Rye. I once found an entire case of the stuff at Ned's and asked him what the deal was because—"

"He hated whiskey." Mia remembered, taking another glance back at the computer. "So you think the case on order is for Roberts?"

"Right. Ned told me it was tradition to give him a bottle every time they closed a big deal together and Arthur cut him a fat bonus check. When business started picking up, Ned bought a whole case straight from the source, getting a discount for buying in bulk. So fast-forward to today. I was looking through his email, and this message shows up."

"Ned's been dead three years. Kind of odd he's got a delivery of his old boss's whiskey coming to him today."

"To be delivered by seven p.m. And the package is actually addressed to Ned." She clicked on the invoice attached to the email. "I've been digging in his emails the last week, just in case I could find mention of some vacation home or something where Arthur could've disappeared to. I found a conversation where Ned jokingly gave Arthur his account information for Slate House because he thought Arthur should order it himself. So I'm thinking the man must've kept ordering through Ned's account."

Mia frowned. The invoice sat right in front of her, clear as day. "But, I mean, why? Wouldn't it be just as suspicious to use Ned's name as his own?"

"Unless Arthur's not worried about the whiskey company being suspicious. He's worried about staying off someone else's radar."

"Unbelievable." A flutter of hope built in Mia's chest. "This guy's taste for whiskey could lead us straight to him."

Sloan pointed at the address on the invoice. "I already looked up the address and P.O. box. Mooreshire, Virginia is a tiny town near the West Virginia border. It's only about an hour and a half away."

"You think he'll be there?" Mia glanced guiltily at the security footage frozen on her own computer. "If we're fast, we could grab takeout and eat in the car on the way after work, if you're up for it."

Sloan grinned. "Oh, I'm up for it. But to answer your question, no, not really. If the guy's hiding, really hiding, he's probably off the grid. But there's a hell of a lot of off-grid land near there. I'm thinking he must've set up a P.O. box to pick up supplies, including this whiskey. This stuff's valuable, so he'd want it picked up tonight. If he doesn't come, he'll send someone to do it for him. We follow them, we find good old Arthur Roberts."

The possibility hung in the room, clouding over the security footage and everything else. Despite knowing she ought to hold onto a dose of skepticism, Mia couldn't quite do it. After all this time, they finally had a lead on Ned's killer.

She gripped Sloan's hand.

One way or another, they were going to catch this guy.

For Ned.

10

Emma stared at the full text of John 14:6, which she'd written down on her trusty legal pad. She tapped her fingers on her notepad as she read the quote from the King James version of the Bible for the hundredth time.

"Jesus saith unto him, I am the way, the truth, and the life: no man cometh unto the Father, but by me."

Her desk blurred around the pad until her eyes watered with the effort of maintaining focus. After nearly a full day's work and nobody coming back with any new leads, she'd decided to do a deep dive on the only real lead they had, which was the note the killer had left behind.

She had it memorized at this point, for what good that did her.

As far as Bible verses went, she'd quickly discovered that this one was weirdly controversial. Critics called it rigid and arrogant, arguing that it was dismissive of all other religions, implying that Muslims, Jews—and, in fact, all non-Christians—were damned for following the wrong religion.

Others claimed that if Jesus was truly God, then he could potentially be saying that the only way to Heaven came through "God" in a more generic sense, leaving the door open for other monotheistic religions that worshipped the same god in different ways or by different names.

Too bad the Bible doesn't talk about the Other. If I have to learn theology, it'd be nice to put it to use for my own ghosts, holy or not.

Emma huffed and drummed her nails over the notepad again, wondering if she might finally wear through the pages to the desktop beneath. She had so many questions with no answers, and the unhelpfulness of the ghosts was really starting to get to her. Especially when she came to work and got bombarded with more riddles.

"I'm so tired of cryptic killers."

"What's that?" Leo offered a half smile, heading over toward his desk with his laptop tucked under one arm.

"Nothing." Emma waved her notepad at him. "I'm just tired of riddles. I've been reading up on the verse our perpetrator quoted, and it's not getting me anywhere. Our unsub's addition isn't helping either."

"Right. 'You are the Lost.'" Leo perched on the side of his desk, reading over Emma's legal pad and the notes she'd taken on the controversy while she held it up for him. "You're thinking he was playing off these ideas? The other religions being shut out?"

"Hell if I know." Emma sighed, glancing back to the pictures of Stephanie and Jeff she'd left open on her computer screen. "And I mean, in what way were they lost? We were told that Jeff was a Christian, and apparently a 'good' one, if we can trust what you and Vance got from his widow."

"She seemed sincere. It's hard to fake that level of indignation without giving away a guilty rage underneath it. I almost thought she was on the verge of quoting scripture herself."

"She's still gotta be suspect number one until we rule her

out." A thought occurred to Emma. "Unless her indignation was genuine for a different reason, like you were disturbing her when all she wanted to do was forget about Jeff and celebrate her newfound freedom."

Leo gave a slight shake of his head. "Mrs. Glanton insisted Jeff was a good man. I doubt she had a clue he was in bed with his bartender, and she might still have defended him even if she had known."

"How so?"

"From what I could see, I think she really loved him, and she believed he loved her too. Fully. If she'd found out about the affair or let us get more than two words out about it, she'd probably blame Stephanie for seducing her husband."

"She couldn't handle the cognitive dissonance of accepting the man she knew was a few steps away from 'good.'"

"Exactly. This doesn't feel like a crime of passion, unless we're missing something really big hiding in plain sight. The couple had no financial trouble that we could determine. Supportive extended family, decent income for the both of them, fine home in a nice neighborhood. All of that and more, but none of the hallmarks that accompany spousal conflict that would lead one of them to commit murder."

"And the bartender?"

"Stephanie lived in a duplex, a rental in a not-so-nice neighborhood. Low rent and low income as far as the eye can see."

"But she's a victim, so there's no financial motive worth asking about."

"Unless we're still talking about a jilted lover, and this time, it's someone from Stephanie's side of town. But even that doesn't add up, because the roommate confirmed no exes or stalkers, said she knew about the affair, but had good things to say about both Stephanie and Jeff."

"Roommate had an alibi?"

Leo grunted in disgust and slid off the desk, going around to take his seat. "I don't know how we missed asking that. I'll follow up, but I'd honestly be surprised if Jessica Wren… that's the roommate…was involved in this. She was cooperative as can be, and more concerned about finding someone to help her make rent."

"Stephanie making barkeep money, even with tips, can't have been a golden goose in that department. And why kill your roomie if you know you're going to need someone else to catch you up with the landlord?"

Leo tapped a pen against his knee, nodding along in rhythm. "It all goes back to that note. That's our best and, unfortunately, only real lead. Read it to me again? I want to hear the words spoken."

Emma sat up straight, doing her best to adopt an officious tone. "'I am the Way. You are the Lost.' Getting anything, Ambrose?"

He chuckled at her snarky attitude but sat up straight himself. "What if we're dealing with a guy who has a blanket hatred for sin in general? Illicit or at least extramarital sex? The Bible is clear on where that'll get you."

"Pretty sure that's among the 'thou shalt nots.'" Emma clicked away at her keyboard and pulled up the Ten Commandments. "Yep. Number seven. No adultery." She frowned.

Leo frowned too. "What?"

Emma pressed the heels of her hands against her eyes. "This isn't the first time in history that someone has chosen to interpret sacred texts in ways that justify their personal prejudices and violent inclinations. I'm not a follower of any faith, but I still hate seeing someone exploit the Bible, or any religious scripture for that matter, to perpetrate harm. It casts an undeserved shadow over the countless genuine believers who follow their faith with love, compassion, and acceptance."

Leo lifted an eyebrow. "Are you just now getting that people suck?"

Even though she didn't mean to, Emma laughed. She rolled her shoulders to release some of the tension building there. "A small percentage of people suck, but they sure do have a tendency to coat the whole population with their shit."

"Are you off your soapbox yet?"

Emma slumped in her chair. "I guess."

Leo leaned forward, his grin widening and the curls over his brow swaying with his excited nodding. "Let's go back to what you were saying about adultery." He held up one finger and added a second. "Now we add alcohol. The devil's elixir. I'm sure the Bible says it in some other way, but you get where I'm going here."

Emma did another search and came up with an answer. "Ephesians 5:18. 'And be not drunk with wine, wherein is excess; but be filled with the Spirit.' Sounds like you're onto something, if we're correct that our perpetrator not only reads the Christian Bible, but also knows its verses beyond the one he creepily misquoted."

Leo's excitement faltered, and he sat back, frowning. "Fair point. We're just spitballing. But honestly, I think something's twisted in this guy's head. He doesn't feel like a garden-variety religious extremist, misquoted Bible verse or not."

"You're probably right." Emma wrote out *You are the Lost* on her notepad beneath the text of the full verse, going over the pencil lines twice to make it stand out. "Someone super-religious wouldn't make up their own verses."

"It'd be considered sacrilegious, I'd think. I'd call my yaya to ask...my grandmother," he explained when Emma frowned, "but then we'd get a lecture about going to church more often, and neither of us wants that." He grinned. "She'd probably remind us that Jesus also turned water into wine so we should tell our bad guy to cram it."

Emma grinned. "I think I've been to more church in the space of this conversation than I have in my entire life."

"Oh, you are definitely in for it if Yaya ever finds out."

"Fair enough." Emma laughed and twisted open her water bottle, sipping from it as she considered their options. "If we go on this theory, that our guy not only knows the Bible but wants to add his own brand of righteousness into the scriptures, then he must be suffering from some kind of severe psychosis. God-complex stuff."

Leo shifted in his chair, clicking his tongue against his teeth. "Maybe we should start looking into local mental health facilities?"

"I wish it were that easy. This guy doesn't seem like the type who'd get treatment. Worth a check, though, especially since the police or a family member could've admitted him without his consent if he was making threats."

Emma opened a new tab, ready to start searching. It was something to do besides reading blurbs from theologians complaining about biblical clarity.

"If nothing else," she thought out loud as she typed, "we've effectively established this was not a crime of passion. Nobody's found any evidence of a jealous lover running around with a gun."

Leo clutched his chest in exaggeration, pulling his face into a twisted grimace of despair. "And I was so hopeful too. So very, very hopeful."

Emma covered her mouth to avoid spitting out the water she'd just sipped.

He grinned at her and turned on his own computer, whistling as he did.

Emma found that she didn't mind his antics or his bad music.

Leo's more help than a ghost when it comes to figuring out next steps too. Now let's just hope this lead gets us somewhere.

11

"This place look like a post office to you?" Sloan squinted across the street at the clapboard post office of Mooreshire, Virginia. "It's got a wraparound porch."

Mia popped a potato chip into her mouth. "This town only has about two thousand residents. I bet the post office used to be somebody's house, maybe a founding family's that was converted once Mooreshire grew big enough to earn its own zip code."

"You're probably right. It still looks like the kind of place where you'd have better luck getting one of Auntie Em's famous pies instead of postage or packaging."

Mia nearly choked on her chips as she laughed. But she didn't disagree with Sloan's skepticism. The porch was lit by a small electric lantern hanging from a hook. It only furthered the impression that it was someone's dear old aunt's cottage rather than a building where workers conducted official government business.

Sloan sat straighter, pointing at a delivery truck crawling up to the curb.

"Lower the window so we can try to hear." Mia gazed out

the windshield as a portly, balding man in overalls and boots climbed from the front seat and went around to the back of the truck. He lowered the liftgate, levered up the drop-down door, and climbed inside. In another minute, he was back, raising the liftgate. He maneuvered a crate onto it once he had the gate level.

A cold breeze ran through the car as Mia watched the man work. She pulled her scarf tighter and monitored the delivery man's progress as he lowered the liftgate to the ground again. The crate was unmarked, but it was close enough to seven o'clock that this had to be their whiskey delivery.

The front door of the post office slammed open, and a grumpy-looking woman in a worn postal outfit stepped out, arms crossed. "You're late, Barry! How long you think I was gonna wait?"

"Ain't late." Barry bent to hoist the crate and grabbed his back in exaggeration. With a chuckle, he reached into his van box and withdrew a dolly that he brought down to ground level. "I'm just too old for this job. You gonna help me get this stuff onto the porch, Wilma, or am I risking another hernia on account of your local fat cat?"

The postmaster scowled and gestured for him to hurry up. "That's what you got the cart for, old man. Get a move on."

Over the next few minutes, Barry maneuvered the dolly with the whiskey up the stairs. Wilma waved him over to one side of the porch, where he set the crate down. They conferred over a delivery manifest, which Barry had pulled out of a pocket of his overalls. They traded a few words, both of them laughing loudly at the end. Then Wilma reached a hand up to smooth down Barry's wispy hair.

Mia grinned as a comforting warmth spread over her cheeks against the cold night air coming in through the open window. "They're friendly enough. And I'd say she's used to him showing up late."

"Small towns, right?" Sloan tapped a thoughtful finger on the sill of her open window.

"Small towns." Mia brushed her hands of the crumbs from her chips, even gladder than before that they'd followed Sloan's lead into the middle of nowhere. "Let's just hope Ned's boss loves his whiskey as much as we think he does."

Barry and Wilma hugged briefly before he lumbered back down the steps, easily handling his empty dolly.

"You have a good night, Barry."

"You do the same. I'll see you again next time this fella gets thirsty."

Barry closed up his van box and waved to Wilma over his shoulder as he headed back to the cab.

Mia expected the postmaster to go back inside, but Wilma stayed on the porch, looking side to side with the crate of whiskey beside her.

Now she sat up straighter. "She's waiting for someone to show up."

"Maybe a ride?"

"But the whiskey's still outside. She's waiting for whoever's coming to get it. Doesn't the postal service have open and closed hours like every other government agency?"

"They do." Sloan frowned through the windshield. "So why is dear old Aunt Wilma here playing security guard, in her uniform no less?"

"Like you said. 'Small towns, right?' She must know Ned's boss, or whoever he sends out to collect his booze."

"There's no guarantee he's picking it up tonight. One man can only drink so much whiskey." Sloan shook her head, staring off into the darkness. "The delivery was set for today, and this is high-end stuff he's expecting. I've met 'whiskey enthusiasts,' none of whom would leave a package like that sitting around unattended, even with Wilma the Vigilant—"

"Look! Look, look, look!"

An old BMW drove up—too slowly to be planning on passing on by into the heart of Mooreshire—and then angled into the parallel parking space the delivery van had just deserted.

"This has to be our pickup guy."

Sloan reached out to Mia's arm and gripped her tight as a man climbed from the front seat and looked around suspiciously. "Or it's Arthur Roberts himself."

Mia tried not to hope. The man hurrying up the steps to the Mooreshire Post Office was wrapped in a heavy winter coat, his hat pulled low over his face.

Wilma had sprung to attention on seeing him. She and the new arrival exchanged a few words, with a smile growing wider and wider on the postmaster's face, until finally she broke out into a cheer. Her celebration was cut short when the man closed in, lifting a hand as if to quiet Wilma.

She clammed up, her eyes going wide.

The man bent to the crate, pulling an object from his coat pocket. Mia strained to see exactly what he was doing, but the distance made it hard to identify what he held.

"Is that a crowbar?"

"I think so. Look, he's prying it open."

They watched as the man popped the crate open and retrieved a cylindrical object, which he held out to Wilma. Her smile returned, and she accepted the item, giving the man's shoulder a quick squeeze before going back into the post office.

He bent back over the crate and replaced the lid, using his crowbar to set the nails with a series of quick taps. Then he stayed crouched and surveyed the street, lingering there in a hunkered position, as if expecting an army of police officers to swarm him at any moment.

Sloan barely held in a laugh. "Does he think he's on an episode of *Law & Order*?"

"Sure looks that way. I almost want to tell him it's okay. Just your friendly neighborhood federal agents on an unofficial and unsanctioned stakeout tonight. Go about your business, sir."

Wilma was back outside again, locking the door behind her. She carried a tote bag over one shoulder, bulging with what had to be her own private bottle of the good stuff, courtesy of the mystery man. He hefted the crate, releasing a few curses into the night. Wilma let him lead the way down the steps before she followed behind and headed down the street to a white minivan.

The man struggled under his burden, finally reaching the passenger side of his old BMW. He set the crate down, opened the door, then muscled the crate back up and into the car.

Mia and Sloan sank back against their seats, hiding in the shadows as best they could. When the man came around to the driver's side of his vehicle, he gave another suspicious look around the area. His gaze skated right over Sloan and Mia's position.

With a final glance around the street, he slipped into his car like a wanted man on the run. He started the engine, turned on his lights, and pulled away from the curb.

Sloan let him get up the road before starting her Rio and sliding into the street. She turned on the lights when they passed the next intersection, giving Mia a glance. "Any luck, he'll assume we turned onto the road behind him."

Mia could only nod, her heart pounding in her chest as if she'd seen Emma's ghosts rather than some man picking up a delivery.

The woods pressed in around them, putting Mooreshire in their rearview mirror as the man kept driving on into the night, heading into West Virginia on a small country highway. If he was paying attention, he had to know they were following him by now—both women knew it, even if they'd not admitted it out loud—so Mia wasn't surprised when the BMW finally pulled to the side of the road in the middle of nowhere after thirty minutes or so. With no other cars around, there'd been no way to hide their tail.

"We knew it was coming." Mia cursed as she tightened her coat, preparing to go out in the cold. "So here goes everything."

Ahead of them, the driver's side door had already popped open. The man who climbed from the car was hunched, and he hurried around the back of the car to stand there waiting for them, head turned to the ground. He'd left his hat in the car and had his hands buried in his pockets. Mia spotted no sign of a weapon, nor did she sense a threat from him at all. He stood almost relaxed against the back of his car, like he'd expected this as an eventuality.

Sloan climbed from her car, and Mia hurried to follow. This was what they'd been waiting for, one way or another.

His eyes darted up to meet theirs as they approached, and Mia's heart nearly burst from her chest. This was, in fact, Arthur Roberts, Ned's old boss. Just under six feet, with pale skin that nearly glowed in Sloan's headlights and carrot-red hair that was a bit further along in the balding arena than the last picture they'd seen. His eyes jittered between them as he bounced on the balls of his feet, appearing more frightened than threatening.

"What do you want?" he hissed, however softly. "Following me like this? I could call the—"

"We're FBI, Mr. Roberts." Sloan cut him off mid-sentence, holding up her badge within a few inches of his nose. "I'm

Special Agent Sloan Grant, and this is Special Agent Mia Logan. We'd like to ask you some questions."

His eyes narrowed, and his mouth opened as if to argue, but then he only took a slow step back and leaned his ass against his BMW. "I've done nothing wrong."

Mia forced herself to smile, just wide enough that her dimples would show. "We're not saying you have, but we do have questions."

Roberts shrugged as if to say their questions were of no never mind to him, and Sloan stepped forward, closing the distance between them again.

"Why did you decide to pull up stakes in Richmond and relocate here, Mr. Roberts?" Sloan pulled a pad from her pocket, as if to emphasize that they expected answers.

"It's nice up here. I'd been looking to retire."

"In the middle of nowhere?" Mia scoffed, the sound cutting through the night more harshly than she'd expected. "After living in a bustling city and running a major tech start-up?"

His Adam's apple bobbed, and his fists twisted in his pockets. "Personal preference."

"Personal preference to go off the grid?" Sloan lowered her voice. "That's not something innocent men usually do."

"You're FBI." Roberts grunted, the sound echoing more of despair than disgust. "You don't think anyone's innocent."

Mia couldn't help herself. She stepped forward, bringing her face to within six inches of his. "I think your wife was innocent. I think Ned Logan was innocent. What do you say to that, Mr. Roberts?"

His complexion went a shade whiter than white. "My wife was innocent. How dare…wait."

Mia followed the man's gaze as it darted past her shoulder to Sloan. When the other agent offered a thin-lipped smile, he nodded as if to himself.

He focused back on Mia as she took a slight step back, mouthing her last name before clearing his throat, his cheeks going red with either emotion or cold.

"I know who you are." His fist jumped in his pocket, gesturing at Sloan. "We met once at an office gala. I remember thinking you were too pretty to be FBI when Ned introduced you to me."

Sloan sighed, her voice coming out softer when she answered. "I'd say thank you, but I wouldn't mean it."

"And you..." He nodded at Mia. "I remember Ned talking about you all the time. He had a picture of the two of you on his desk, from when you were teenagers. He was a good person."

Sloan seemed to shrink into herself, and Mia wished she could melt into the ground, what with the way emotion roiled in her gut and threatened to spill into sobs of grief.

But instead, she stood taller and willed Roberts to hear her. "Mr. Roberts, we know Ned's death wasn't an accident. And neither was your wife's. We're going to solve the case regardless, but if you help us, maybe you'll be able to avoid taking all the blame. If someone else was responsible, and you know it, it's in your best interest to tell us."

The man breathed in deep, leaning heavier onto his car, but he didn't answer. Arthur Roberts wrung his fists in his pockets and rocked a bit on his heels.

"Whatever you did," Mia flipped open her credentials and hung them in front of Arthur's face where they couldn't be ignored, "I'm sure your actions are worthy of the FBI's attention. And Special Agent Grant and I are very good at what we do. I'm sure we can convince a DA that what you did is worth a hefty prison sentence, particularly when it's in connection to a double homicide."

Sloan straightened, one hand coming up to grip Mia's forearm, playing the good cop for Roberts's benefit. "A little cooperation could go a long way, Mr. Roberts. I don't disagree with my colleague here, but you can help yourself. This is your chance. Maybe your only one, after we've come all the way out here."

"We know where you live now." Mia thought of Ned's face and channeled the image into an angry growl rather than the tears that her memories would've had her spilling. "And we will not stop investigating until we find out exactly what happened."

His eyes looked wider and more conflicted than surprised. He squinted into the woods, not bothering to disagree and then wilted against his car. His keys jangled in his pocket as he shrank in defeat, finally meeting Mia's gaze. "Follow me, all right? I'll tell you. My cabin's just down the road."

Sloan stepped forward this time, releasing her hold on Mia's arm. "We'll follow you. And in case you have plans to attempt to flee, we'll be informing our colleagues in D.C. of your present location and the P.O. box number you had that whiskey shipped to under Ned's name."

Roberts's shock couldn't have been more genuine as he realized just how much the two agents knew about him. "I swear I won't. I swear. I...please, I need a drink, and I'm not about to crack open a bottle out here on the road. I just want to get home."

"You want to get home, and you need a drink? Mia, are we buying this?"

"I am. He's a slippery fish, but I'm ready to take him at his word. Besides, I'll call into D.C. as soon as we're in our car. If he pulls anything, we'll just wait for the cavalry to arrive before taking him down."

12

"This city, son, is a bed of sin. There's little time to be wasted upon human concerns."

Grimacing into my scarf, I pulled it tighter. God's meaning was clear. Human concerns like warmth and food were of little enough worry to Him, but I felt frozen to my bones as I leaned against the wall outside the homeless shelter. And it wasn't as if He'd been clear about where I should focus my next efforts.

I was frustrated with Him telling me we had little time, to hurry out of the homeless shelter and pay attention to Him, but not telling me exactly what I should be doing.

"I'm listening, God. Waiting for your direction."

Though I'd whispered, a couple of old women glanced at me as they passed on the sidewalk. They wore fancy coats and carried expensive handbags. I wondered if maybe He'd tell me to go after them. Make it easy, since they were right here. Maybe they ran an underground gambling den and that was how they afforded their costly attire.

I recited more from 1 Timothy as the women paraded off

down the street, still chattering away. "Let the woman learn in silence with all subjection."

God's voice came to me again as I finished my recitation.

"D.C. is depraved, in need of being cleansed. But you must be more careful when speaking to me, son. You must remain free to do your work, and that means keeping clear of authorities. You do understand that?"

I swallowed down the same promise I'd made over and over again. That I understood. That I was ready.

"I have cleansed these streets of two sinners already, God. Both had enabled others to become drunk on wine and profited from such sin. And they were adulterers, oh Lord. Doubly sinful in their deeds. I am ready, God, for your call."

The image of my hometown church haunted my periphery, looming out of my memory and into the D.C. streetlights. If I found a car, I could be there within hours. "Maybe it's time that I go back to smite those people who bullied me when I was younger. You saw their evil, and surely, for attacking your chosen messenger, they must count as holy diversions."

I thought to mention Father Maxwell in particular but refrained. I hoped God meant for him to be my grand finale, and we weren't there yet.

God's laugh nearly brought me to my knees once more, ringing through the night air along with the swirling winter wind. *"Your work in the city of D.C. is not complete, my son. To quit this soon, the very idea of it is petty. Selfish. You know better, do you not? After all this time?"*

My cheeks warmed with the reminder. He was right. I'd been selfish to think of leaving the city so fast when we'd only just begun. As He'd told me more than once, my time for righting old wrongs done unto me would come. That time with Father Maxwell approached, but not yet. "I'm sorry, God. I'm sorry. I don't know how I could suggest such a thing."

God remained silent, judging me, and I flushed. He couldn't disappear on me now. He wouldn't.

"God, forgive me my sins. It was a momentary stumble. Brought on by the cold and human frailty. I'll do better. My petty squabbles are nothing compared to your divine wrath." I lowered my voice upon seeing a stranger watching me from a bus stop, remembering God's recent warning. "I'm embarrassed over my suggestion. I am sorry. Please, forgive me."

A minute of silence passed, then another. Sweat glided down my spine, building beads on my forehead to make a cold slick of my skin. And then, finally, His sigh came to my ears.

"I forgive you, my son. You are but human, but you are also my son. Only you can do this work. Do not fail me."

I swallowed my panic, knowing God would rather I keep it to myself than spew it into the streets, and only spoke when I could feel my breath evening out. "Thank you, God. You will not regret your faith in me."

"Very well. It's time, son, to move on from simple distractions like liquor. Time to take down people peddling false answers. Walk south, son, away from this shelter. Now."

I began walking before I'd fully processed His directions or how vague they were.

"Walk south, I said. Not north."

I blushed, whirling on my heel and nearly knocking over an elderly man leading a tiny dog on a slim leash. He sneered at me, but I ignored him.

"Tell me what you mean about addressing distractions other than liquor." My whisper seemed to echo ahead of my footsteps, pluming out on the cold air.

"There'll soon be no need for words. I will show you instead. And then, very soon, you will continue with your work."

A grin lifted my lips again, erasing the embarrassment I'd felt over suggesting we leave the city so soon. God cared enough to show me His plan.

Truly, my work was holy, and He was with me.

13

Sloan pulled her hatchback in behind Roberts's BMW, effectively trapping his vehicle between her car and some trees at the front of a gravel driveway. Beside the drive sat a small cabin with a wraparound porch and a glider bench near the front door.

After tapping out a text to Emma, letting her know where they were and what they were doing, Mia climbed from the front seat. She stood in the evening air, somewhat numb with the understanding that they'd found Arthur Roberts after all this time.

A babbling brook ran along the other side of the property, nearly parallel to the driveway, and a little footbridge led from his cabin off into the woods, where she could just glimpse a small shed surrounded by footlights. Big enough for a four-wheeler or a few canoes, she guessed. Maybe a snowmobile or a Jet Ski.

The man had retreated into off-the-grid living, but he hadn't given up his toys or his whiskey.

Mia glanced sideways at Sloan and saw the other woman's face mirroring the disgust she felt.

Roberts has this while his wife, brother, and Ned are long since buried. It's not fair.

The thought was too immature to hold real weight on Mia's tongue, but it settled in her stomach and curdled with the remains of her snacks from earlier. Any flash of sympathy she'd have felt for the man being widowed and alone fell apart before it formed. This guy was more concerned with his drinking habit than with his losses.

Case in point, she and Sloan were being forced to wait while Roberts wrestled his crate of whiskey from his car and up the stairs. Neither woman offered to help, and he didn't embarrass himself by asking for it.

Mia traipsed onto the porch behind him, finding it in herself to be only partially interested in the fact that the man had five locks on his front door. In another case, on another day, she would've been concerned that he was either paranoid or in very real danger.

But with *this* man—who her brother considered a friend, who likely had something to do with his death—she couldn't drum up even an ounce of empathy. From the look on Sloan's rigid face, she felt the same.

With the door finally opened, Roberts shoved the crate inside and left the agents to follow him. Mia moved in first, hand close to her lapel and ready to snap her weapon out should it be necessary. She relaxed only a little on entering.

The door opened onto a tiny foyer at the foot of a staircase that led up to a loft. A spacious living area spread out to each side, leading into a kitchen at the back. Wood grains and deep-cushioned furniture dominated the interior, with a sectional set up around a humongous flat screen to her right. A set of matching chairs surrounded a reading area where a jigsaw puzzle was in the works.

Roberts plopped his hat onto a rack beside the door. His red hair waved at them, static giving it a life of its own.

Sloan closed the door behind her and loosened her coat, but as Roberts reached into his inner coat pocket, she snapped her hand out like a rattlesnake and caught his wrist. "Arthur Roberts. What. Are. You. Doing?"

He blinked. "I need the cat's paw. My crowbar, to open the box." His whine seemed more pitiful than threatening. "I just want a glass of whiskey before you sign my death warrant." His foot nudged the crate behind him as if for emphasis.

Mia reached into his pocket, withdrawing the crowbar herself. Stepping past the man still in Sloan's grip, she shoved the end of the crowbar into the crevice between the crate's top and its side and pushed in hard. The wood cracked.

Roberts yelped for her to be gentle.

She shoved it in farther and levered the top off with a forceful motion. Splintered wood went in a few directions, and she was greeted by five cylinders bearing the Slate House Rye label all nestled into packing foam that divided the crate into six cavities. An empty one showed where Wilma's bottle had been.

"What's with giving one of these away to Wilma?" Mia asked.

"You...you saw that? How long were you watching me?"

"Long enough. Now talk. Why does Wilma rate a whole bottle all to herself?"

He wiped a hand down his face. "She makes sure nothing arrives addressed to me. In my name. Anything that comes for Arthur Roberts either gets shredded or sent back."

"Tampering with the U.S. mail is a federal crime," Sloan reminded him, "and I'd expect a U.S. postmaster to know that."

"She knows, but who's going to care out here?" He waved his free hand around. "Who's going to know? Nobody's being hurt by this, and it's only my mail she handles that way. I've given her permission to do it."

Mia scoffed. "I'm sure Congress would appreciate your self-appointment to the position of postmaster general."

"You can't be serious. How is—"

"Arthur, chill. You wanted a drink, remember? So have one." Standing straight again, Mia smiled sweetly at the extra-pale whiskey aficionado and pointed at the crate. "One drink. *One*. And you talk while you drink."

Sloan groaned, releasing his arm and stepping back a pace. "Do what she said...and fast."

He plucked a cylinder from the crate and took it toward a gleaming bar he'd set up by a gas fireplace. A twist of his wrist brought the flames to light, casting a flickering warmth into the area.

Mia shrugged at her colleague. "If it gets him to talk, it gets him to talk."

"I'll talk." He grunted, opening the bottle and giving himself a generous pour into a tumbler engraved with his initials. "Just give me a second, ladies. Make yourselves at home. And would one of you please lock the door?"

Mia threw the top two dead bolts, figuring that was good enough, even as he whined at her to finish the job. She ignored his pleas and followed Sloan across the room to stand opposite from where he'd just settled on the sectional couch. He took a deep draft of his drink, sighed, and settled back into the cushions.

"Talk, Arthur. We did you the service of following you, even opening your expensive crate for you. It's your turn to do us a favor." Mia frowned as he took another slow drink. "*Now.*"

He huffed. "You're going to get me killed."

"That's all but guaranteed if you don't start talking."

Sloan stepped forward, getting between them just enough

to block Mia if she actually did make a lunge for the man. "Let him finish his last meal at least."

As both agents chuckled, Roberts apparently gave up. He flopped his head back and rested his drink in his lap.

"You want the truth? I got greedy. Some clients led me to understand just how lucrative the drug trade could be, and I decided to take advantage of it."

Sloan took out a notepad. "Drugs as in, what? Opioids?"

"You'd think so, based on my normal clientele, but no. I'm talking about heroin. Cocaine. But I got ahead of myself. I arranged for a shipment of heroin from overseas. It cost me and my associates a pretty penny but would've earned us an almost-four-hundred-percent profit on the street. I was going to retire on it, take my wife on one of those round-the-world vacations."

At the mention of his wife, Roberts's face flushed, and his eyes spilled over with tears.

Mia wanted to shout for him to get to the point but knew that wouldn't get them the answers they needed. "What happened?"

He took a slug from his drink, wiped his eyes, and looked at the agents. "It got seized as soon as it hit port. And it was all my fault. I didn't know how the port authority operated. You hear about stuff coming in on ships all the time, and I… it was my fault. Poor planning. I bit off more than I could chew. Got greedy."

Mia's stomach twisted. She knew the kind of money Ned had earned working for Integra Industries, his tech firm. He hadn't wanted for anything once he landed that job. But even so, his annual salary, even with bonuses, had been a fraction of what this guy made each month. How much cash did one man need?

Roberts swirled his drink, staring into its depths as if thinking the same thing as Mia. "Thanks to my wealthy connections," he swirled some more, "the case was never tied to either me or to them. It was cleared, in fact. I got off scot-free."

A prideful grin curled his mouth but quickly faded as his eyes met Mia's. She clenched her fists and almost snarled. He paled a stitch more and took another sip of his drink before continuing.

"I was lucky. I had my CEO salary to fall back on, but my associates lost everything."

"What was their reaction to learning you'd sunk their operation?"

"They weren't happy about it. To put it mildly. Enraged would be more accurate but still wouldn't paint the full picture."

When he didn't continue immediately, Sloan coughed pointedly.

He finally met both their eyes, training his gaze on each of them in turn.

"If I could take it all back, I would. Hell, I would've taken it back then, even before things got out of hand. If it had been possible, I'd have done anything." He scowled, eyeing his drink before resting it on his knee. "They threatened me for a while, demanding I pay them off. I refused, insisting they'd taken the risks just like I had, and it was just as much their fault for not having kept a safety net for themselves."

"You really are an idiot, Arthur." Mia practically snarled the words. "I'm going to guess your associates aren't the kind of people accustomed to being told off by small-time players like yourself."

"Small-time? Me? Do you have any idea how much I was worth back then? On paper, I had seven figures. Seven!"

"That's just great. How many of those figures are your wife and brother? How many of them are Ned?"

Roberts stared at Mia, his mouth falling open. He blubbered as tears fell anew.

"They killed my wife. My brother. And Ned. They said it was necessary, to make sure I understood that what was owed would be paid. Ned handled all the details, moving all the money around. He didn't know where I got it or what it was for, I swear. I only had him make it look legit on paper, in case the IRS came sniffing around."

"You paid your debt with Ned's blood? You son of a—"

Sloan was in front of her before Mia got one step in Roberts's direction.

He'd cowered against the cushions, holding a hand out as if he could prevent her from driving her fingers into his throat and tearing out his larynx.

With Sloan's hands on her shoulders, holding her back, Mia let loose on the man responsible for her brother's death. "You asshole! Even with all your bank accounts and offshore holdings, I'm betting these associates you keep referring to are somewhere higher than you've ever reached. But you wanted to roll that high too. So you pulled some strings and you worked a deal. You promised them a windfall. You promised they'd get every penny back tenfold."

"Yes, but it was seized. I told you, and there's nothing I could've done—"

"Bullshit! You said it was your fault, because you basically guessed about how the harbormaster's office operates. Your associates came calling for payback, and instead of playing smart, instead of doing the right thing, you turned tail and flipped them the finger as you ran away."

"They killed my wife and brother!"

"And *my* brother!" She jammed a fist into her chest. "They killed Ned. He's gone, and here you are, living it up in this countryside cottage. You're alive and he's not, because you let him pay your way with his life."

"That's not it at all. Mia, I—"

"Agent Logan!" Mia shouted.

"I'm sorry, Agent Logan." Roberts paused, settling back into the cushions again. "I paid them with everything I could spare, cashed out every account I could access without an intermediary involved. They said it wasn't enough. They wanted more. They wanted everything, even though I'd already paid them back twice over. They killed Ned and then my wife and brother in retaliation anyway. As a warning, they said, and they added that I'd be next. So I took off."

Mia retreated from Sloan's grasp, taking a seat on the other end of the sectional. Her blood boiled with rage over what Roberts had done. Her one brother in this world, who'd always been too damn good for it, had died because his employer was a greedy, spineless bastard. "Ned was murdered as a warning. It took that to get you to see the depths of what you'd done. And then you disappeared to live happily ever after."

The whiskey trembled in Roberts's hand as he met her eyes. "This isn't happily ever after. I miss my wife. I regret my actions. I—"

"Save the sob story." Sloan took the whiskey from him, setting it just out of his reach on a nearby table. "This is a hell of a lot happier than the ending Ned or your wife and brother got."

He'd opened his mouth to argue when Sloan took the whiskey away, but now he shrank before them. "I miss them all."

Mia's fists clenched at her sides. Every inch of her burned to drag the man back to D.C. and book him for whatever they could get him on. Stealing Ned's identity. Mail fraud. Anything. Just getting him out in the open, they'd be throwing him to the wolves, who'd surely come for him fast if the men he'd associated with were as deadly as he claimed.

But she and Sloan needed more from him, including potential testimony.

Ned had been stockpiling the man's favored drink, for heaven's sake, and rolling in dough. Partying with his CEO. She shot a glance at Sloan, whose lips were clenched.

She had no way of knowing how clean Ned's hands had been when all was said and done. And, right now, Mia wasn't even sure she wanted to know.

She focused back on Roberts and tapped one of her fingers against Sloan's notepad resting on the couch beside her. "We need names, now, or we're going to make sure that your *associates* get word of where you're holed up."

His eyes narrowed at her. "You can't do that. My case was cleared. You've got nothing on me—"

"Save it." Sloan leaned forward until their noses were only a few inches apart. "You don't think we can pull strings with the media? Even if your case was cleared, there are reporters out there who'd love even the hint of a conspiracy. Give them news about three dead bodies and a CEO who vanished into thin air, and give them his whereabouts, and you'll have a veritable hive of reporters buzzing down your drive. You don't talk to us right here, right now, that's what's going to happen."

Roberts's lower lips trembled. "I—"

"You're going to give us names first." Though he reached for his whiskey, he backed off when Sloan covered it with her hand. "Like Ned Logan's sister, *the federal agent*, just told you." She collected the notepad from the couch.

He closed his eyes, and for a moment, Mia thought he would refuse. After several long moments, he cursed under his breath. "You're looking for Tom Harding and Matthew Spencer. They're the ones responsible for everything, and before you ask, yes, I know where to find them. They took my money and used it to open a nightclub called the Blue River Lounge."

"And where would we find this nightclub?"

"It's in the Golden Triangle, northeast part of D.C. Lots of college kids up there, so they're always packed."

"So we're sure to arrest the right Tom Harding and Matthew Spencer, how about a description of each? Since you're being so forthcoming."

Roberts squirmed where he sat but finally threw his hands in the air. "Fine. Tom's a big, bald fuck. Tall and muscly, like those bodybuilders. He lives at the gym. Matthew is the same, but he's got short, curly hair and wears an earring in his left ear. Diamond stud. They're both mid-forties, no facial hair unless they started growing it after they…after."

As he trailed off and turned his head away, Roberts's chest shook. He put a hand over his eyes and began sobbing.

Mia glanced sideways at Sloan when the other woman finished writing down the information. Sloan's eyes were hooded, her brow lined, as if grief were puckering her face from the inside out, but she nodded.

Re-buttoning her coat, Mia stood and stepped closer to Arthur Roberts, more than aware that she was looming over him, forcing him to look up at her at a steep angle. "Do you have a phone number where we can get in touch with you?"

He mumbled a number through his sobs, which Sloan took down. "It's a burner, but it's all I have. I swear. I don't keep a landline out here and use public Wi-Fi in town. All my bills are paid using a bank account I set up years ago. Please, can you keep me safe? I've told you everything." His words ended on a whimper.

He groaned when Sloan rose and stomped toward the door without responding.

Mia remained where she was, staring down at him. "You better be ready to answer that phone the second we call. If you try to vanish again, we'll put out a BOLO with your full name, photograph," she lifted her phone and took his picture before he could say a word, "and last known location, as well as the make, model, and license plate for your Beamer outside."

Sloan opened the dead bolts and cracked the front door, letting the cold into the room. Mia wasn't sure if she needed to cool off or if she was simply pushing for an end to the conversation. Probably both.

Mia gave the cowering man before her one more look. "Stay here, Arthur. Don't try to run. We found you once, and we'll find you again. Or your associates will."

The man gaped up at Mia like a puffer fish, cheeks blown out with fear, but she spun on her heel before he could say another word. She didn't want to share the same air as the weasel any longer.

The night had grown deeper and colder, and she and Sloan had another stop to make.

14

Emma had been driving the streets near the Lost Highway Tavern for more than an hour, unable to sleep and desperately needing a distraction from staring at the ceiling and wondering what Mia and Sloan had discovered after talking with Arthur Roberts. That they'd found him was good news, but whether or not he'd have useful information remained a question in Emma's mind.

She pulled her Prius to the side of the road when her tank got down to the halfway point. Each tick of her mileage had felt like a judgmental finger wagged in her direction.

Silly Emma, wasting gas on a fool's errand. Give up, already.

"This is ridiculous. What am I even hoping to find? The guy's not going to hit the same spot twice."

She stared out her windshield, down the dark street that led to the bar where Jeff Glanton and Stephanie Jones had taken their last breath. The area remained strung up with crime scene tape, even though Emma couldn't imagine they'd tease any more evidence from the space.

With the owner and primary bartender dead, she had to assume the widowed Mrs. Glanton would hire a crime scene cleaning service at some point. The local PD would probably send out a patrol car to take the tape down soon.

Either way, she'd wasted the bulk of the night so far. Patrolling the area like an anxious beat cop and attempting to put herself in the mind of the killer had gotten her nowhere. She couldn't even focus to really make a solid attempt at profiling the perpetrator, because every time she recalled him from her memory of the video, she kept seeing Ned's headless body instead.

Somewhere near the state border, Mia and Sloan were trying to track down Ned's old boss. They were following up on the clues Emma had provided and some other thing they'd figured out, which had taken them on a late-night drive into the middle of nowhere. As risky as that sounded, it was a damn sight better than staring at the leftovers of a double-homicide crime scene with nobody to talk to.

Is that why I'm out here? I'm just jealous of the fact that they've got a break in their case and would rather be in on the action?

Even knowing that Mia and Sloan had been anxious to get away, Emma had felt duty bound to suggest they all stay late and keep working on the case. Try to find out where the killer was or who he was or something, *anything*, that would help them track him down. She'd been shot down pretty fast.

Vance had, very reasonably, pointed out that D.C. had too many bars for them to even consider what locale their perpetrator might target next, assuming he even went to a bar. Denae, just as reasonably, had reminded Emma they lacked any evidence the killer hadn't specifically targeted either Stephanie or Jeff.

One could've been the intended victim, making the other collateral damage. Without knowing which of the two was the target, or if both had been targeted together, the team couldn't reasonably anticipate where the killer would strike next.

And Leo, though he'd seemed regretful about it, had also calmly argued that, at the end of the day, they were better off being rested for tomorrow rather than chasing their tails around in the dark of night. Jacinda closed the book on it by reminding them all they were essentially out of leads.

Emma was part of a super-reasonable team—she could admit that much—but her gut wouldn't allow her to sleep. Not least of all when she had a friend and teammate out there working through the night.

"Okay, gut, what do you got?" Emma let her eyes glaze over, peering down toward the bar. "It's telling me I agree with Vance, and we can't assume he'll hit a bar next."

Despite the doubts, Emma had started her night out by going to a few dive bars just to check inside and look around. She'd gotten whiffs of gin, puke, and stale popcorn, but no obvious killers. The errand had only led her back in a circle to this street and their one crime scene...because she had nothing else to go on.

Except the scrap of paper with her notes from earlier in the day, scribblings of scripture, with chapter and verse noted beside each line.

It's a good thing I'm alone. Anyone seeing me with these notes might think I'm the unsub.

She clenched her eyes shut, turning off the car and embracing the silence. But unlike at Yoga Map, she pushed herself to think hard. Not to blank out her thoughts and embrace her center, but to go beyond herself and really consider what—if not a bar—this killer might target.

Because of the lack of traffic in the area last night and no sign of headlights shining through in the Lost Highway Tavern's security footage, their team was proceeding on the idea that their perpetrator was on foot. Her and Leo's suspicion that the man was dealing with mental illness went further in suggesting he might be homeless and backed up the on foot theory. Any target, or place of refuge, would have to be nearby.

If not a bar, some other type of business or local establishment.

And hell, even if he did have a car, plenty of killers considered a single zone their hunting ground, so there was more than one reason to keep her focus near the bar. The question was, what sort of territory should she be covering?

As she stared at the Lost Highway Tavern's door, the air chilled around her, growing tighter and closer in the confines of her car. Fighting the urge to lower a window, Emma steadied herself, drawing breath as evenly as she could despite the icy chill racing up and down her spine.

She relaxed her gaze, letting her eyes drift left to right as she waited for whatever the Other was about to reveal.

As she tracked across the neighboring diner's window and the few late-night patrons still enjoying their coffee and pie, Emma caught movement in her periphery. At first, it was nothing but a wispy form, almost mist-like as it emerged through the wall of the bar.

Stephanie Jones stood on the sidewalk. Well, her ghost did anyway. She was still shaking with sobs, arms wrapped around her middle, blood trailing down from one shoulder. Thankfully, she kept her face lowered, so Emma didn't have to see the gory exit wound of the shot that ended her life.

Without lowering a window or opening a door, Emma called to the ghost, hoping she wouldn't scare her away.

"Stephanie? Stephanie, I'm Emma. Can you hear me?"

The ghost stayed where she was, shaking, crying, and dripping with blood. Emma was about to open her car door when Stephanie's head snapped up and her milky-white eyes zeroed in on Emma's face.

"The sign. He wants to conquer in the sign."

Emma froze, one hand on the door release, the other on

her steering wheel. The ghost remained on the sidewalk for a moment before stepping backward into the wall and vanishing.

"Super helpful, Steph. 'The sign.' Thanks. Should be easy enough to figure out what that means."

If these ghosts didn't get their act together soon, Emma was going to file a complaint. With who, she didn't know. But she'd find them, and she'd complain.

For all the good that'll do. Damn ghosts can't even put together a complete sentence half the time. Their management can't be much better.

Emma went back to what she'd been attempting to do before Stephanie so rudely interrupted her.

"So our perpetrator is religious or wants us to believe he is. Anti-alcohol, maybe. Anti-adultery, maybe. Both of which make me think Jeff was the primary target. Although, a zealot might take the whole 'women should be quiet' thing seriously enough to target Stephanie as well."

She continued talking to herself while reading over her scribbled notes and recalling her conversation with Leo. He'd pulled up a page from the online King James Bible and zoomed in on the verse from John that their perpetrator had misquoted.

Emma's eyes shot open wide. The killer was a zealot.

What did zealots attack? *Other faiths.*

Emma fumbled for her phone and began searching for places of worship in the area, focusing on temples, synagogues, and mosques.

Only three blocks from the Lost Highway Tavern, a small neighborhood mosque was celebrating its tenth anniversary that very month. The mosque had educational, service-related, or religious events going on every other night. What better way to greet the organizers in the morning, a killer might think, than with a pair of dead bodies?

Emma's foot hit her gas pedal nearly as quickly as she'd started the engine. She wouldn't call the team yet, but her hands practically vibrated on the wheel, she felt so sure of where she was headed.

When she pulled in across from the Center for Islam Mosque, Emma didn't even bother to zip up her coat before hurrying from her vehicle and beginning her rounds. On all sides of the mosque, the streets were quiet. Plus, no lights shined from within the building, the doors were all locked, and the employee parking spaces were deserted.

Emma circled the building twice. By the time she got back to her Prius and the main entrance, she'd wrapped her scarf tighter around her neck and begun to admit that, just maybe, she really was chasing her tail tonight.

At least you didn't manage to drag along a teammate and keep someone else awake for a goose chase, Emma girl.

But she was onto something...she was sure of it. This particular mosque didn't have anything suspicious going on tonight, but that meant little. The killer could be at another mosque, or synagogue, or temple—nearby or all the way across the city—even as she stood here freezing her heels off.

Emma stretched her fingers in her gloves, ignoring how numb they felt as she stared into the night, loosely focused on the mosque's entrance. What should she do? She couldn't call Jacinda and suggest posting agents or officers at all kinds of non-Christian religious centers in the city.

Even if Jacinda backed her up, the powers that be would never approve it. It would simply involve too many resources when it came to following a hunch, and Emma couldn't exactly say a ghost had given her instruction to look for "the sign." Not that she'd received any indication of which sign was the sign, what it might point to, or how anybody might go about conquering "in" the sign.

Still muttering and recalling parts of her conversation

with Leo, Emma paced toward the front entrance. She'd try it one more time, just to double-check it was locked, and then she'd head to another establishment, extending her patrol just a little longer into the night.

I'll give myself another hour. Not like I'll be able to go home and fall into bed right away anyway. Maybe Mia and Sloan will have called with an update by then.

The door was locked, just like she'd established earlier. But when she turned away from it with a slower step this time, not so intent on reaching the next entrance or scanning the streets, her eye caught on some chalk on the sidewalk.

J146.

Taking a quick picture, Emma checked the time and then sent it on to Jacinda before calling the local precinct. Within a few minutes, she had a *good job* response and a promise that on-duty officers were on the way to keep watch on the mosque through the rest of the night.

Her phone dinged again, Jacinda's picture lighting the screen above a text. *Go home as soon as you're relieved so we can get on this tomorrow. The local cops will cover the scene. Get some rest.*

Emma's thumbs were as tired as she was. *Will do. Good night.*

Their bases were well and truly covered, it seemed.

Driving back to her apartment was uneventful, and with the clock ticking toward eleven, Emma knew the smart thing would be to fall into bed.

That was what she'd come home planning to do...fall into bed and sleep, wake up fresh, and have coffee and a chat with her resident ghost, Mrs. Kellerly.

Her nosy neighbor would ask about Oren, and Emma would blush and be reminded to text him good morning. And then the ghost would disappear before Emma showered and headed off to renew the search for their unsub.

That would be the smart thing.

Instead, Emma sat wide awake in her Prius in the parking lot of her apartment complex, flipping between radio stations and scrolling around the internet on her phone, trying to decipher what "conquering in the sign" might mean. The only things she found were references to a dream a Roman emperor supposedly had before a major battle, right before he named Christianity as a unifying faith across Ancient Rome's empire.

Does our perpetrator want everyone to be Christian, or is he targeting people who clearly aren't Christian? Or fallen Christians, as in Jeff's case?

She snorted.

Chalk one up for the ghosts telling us something we pretty much already knew.

Emma kept one eye on her phone, waiting for an update from Mia, who'd promised she'd alert her whether they were heading into danger or calling off the casework for the night, no matter what time that might be.

15

Mia tugged at the sparkly pink sweater she'd borrowed from Sloan, which was a touch too tight in all the wrong places. Or all the right ones, if the leering men around her in the Blue River Lounge were any gauge. College-aged or not, the guys in the nightclub clearly had one thing on their minds.

Sloan nudged her elbow. "You should hold onto that sweater and wear it for Vance."

"Ha." Mia pulled at the hem again. Still, they were lucky that Sloan practically lived out of her car and kept a veritable wardrobe in her trunk.

Sloan passed Mia and pushed forward through the crowd, waving her glass of ginger ale around like it was a double shot of tequila. Mia followed her lead, holding her purse tight to her chest as she shimmied by a muscle head with a bottle of cheap beer in one hand. His other hand was making a grab for her ass.

"You couldn't own at least one pair of high-waisted jeans?" Mia hissed at Sloan, who just grinned at her in response.

Easy for her. The clothes *fit* her.

The expansive room boasted three bars, each with its own team of bartenders. Colored spotlights cast beams down from the ceiling. They wove around the crowd, picking out women mostly, including the dancers currently occupying a large go-go cage in the center of the floor. Sloan led the way around the cage, catching Mia's outstretched hand as she was almost swallowed by the crowd.

Mia had hoped that they'd waltz inside, be pointed directly toward the lounge owners, and go from there. She was prepared to flirt for information, or maybe just surveil until they had more to go on. But so far, they had no idea when the owners came around or what illicit activities they might be using the lounge to cover.

The first bartender they'd spoken to had only been working there for three nights, and his trainer was too busy serving a group of pretty young things while ignoring Mia and Sloan at every turn.

They couldn't exactly pull out badges and IDs to compel a response, so they'd moved on quickly. The pair tending the next bar, a man and woman, had both been drunk themselves, and overserved every patron who approached.

They headed for the third and final bar.

Did I ever like places like this? What the heck is the appeal? Yuck.

Only a single bartender worked at the final location. Like the others, he wore all black and had his hair kept neatly trimmed off his ears and neck. His mustache, however, could have put Freddie Mercury's to shame.

At least he had fewer customers to interfere with what Mia hoped would be an easy and straightforward conversation. The man poured a beer, wiped down the bar top, and turned to serve a pair of young men. He made quick work of mixing up cocktails for each of them before returning to keeping his bar clean.

"He seems to know what he's doing." Sloan cozied up onto an empty stool.

Mia leaned against the bar beside Sloan, still holding her purse close. She was unwilling to experiment with what the ridiculously low-rise jeans would do if she chose to sit down. "He's too young to be one of Roberts's associates, but I hope he knows something." She forced a disinterested smile for a man who looked to be heading straight for her.

Seemingly sensing the movement, Sloan glanced over her shoulder. The man paused, then kept coming, but in another moment, Sloan stretched one arm around Mia's middle and hugged her closer, like they were a bit more than colleagues.

Biting her lip, Mia just held in a chuckle at the man's wide-eyed look as he skidded to a stop halfway across the dance floor. With a mournful expression, he turned tail and headed to the bar the Drinky Twins were overserving. "Thanks, Sloan."

"Don't mention it." She kept one arm around Mia and waved at the bartender again. "Safety in numbers, yeah?"

Mia blinked, the smoke of a cigarette suddenly getting to her. That was just the sort of thing her brother might have said when they'd been in college, barhopping and hoping to meet special someones.

Finally, the mustached bartender headed their way, and Mia revised her estimation of his age downward. The facial hair gave him an edge on thirty, but up close, she didn't imagine him being over twenty-five. At least he was sober.

"What can I get you ladies?"

"Refill our ginger ales? Just soda." Sloan slid a ten-dollar bill across the bar, promising the tip in return for the cheap drinks, and he grabbed their cups.

"This is a nice place." Mia turned toward the bar, Sloan's arm still hanging around her waist. "How'd it get started?"

The bartender pushed her ginger ale toward her. "Weird question, but I can't help you either way. I'm busy, and the place was here before I moved to D.C."

Sloan reached for her ginger ale, leaning toward him in a way that he couldn't quite bring himself to ignore. "And how about the owners? They around?"

"Not tonight." He frowned, glancing across to the drunk bartenders before his gaze flirted between Mia and Sloan's again. "Technically, I haven't met them. Rosy hired me. She's drunk now, yeah, but during the day, she's a good manager. The owners are around a fair bit, though. They in trouble or something?"

Mia forced a smile, hoping her embarrassment didn't show. This guy had seen through them from a mile away, proving that Rosy was indeed a good manager. "We just want to talk."

Because that sounds less suspicious. Nice.

The guy's nose twitched as if he smelled something bad, and he backed away with a quick wave. "Let me know if you need another drink, ladies."

Mia sighed. "Your clothes might just be too sexy for this place."

"We're not quite the demographic, are we?" Sloan gazed around the lounge, which was surprisingly busy for a Monday night, but mostly with twentysomethings. Sloan looked her thirty-two years, and although Mia was technically among her peers in age, she knew she barely passed for twenty-six on a lucky day, dressed in her professional attire. In Sloan's sweater and jeans, riding low on her hips and threatening to pop at the seams, she barely appeared legal. "Well, let's make the most of it. Everyone can't be as smart as Mr. Mustache."

Mia followed along as Sloan led the way from table to table, skirting the dance floor and chatting up patrons who were, for the large part, inebriated well past the driving point.

One after another, the people they chatted with looked at them as if they were talking gibberish. A few people did indeed know the owners but couldn't offer any information beyond their favorite drinks.

While Sloan chatted up an older-looking man who claimed to have played cards with Tom on a few occasions, Mia felt a tug at her sweater. She turned to find a curly-haired woman with heavy makeup plucking at her. "I love your sweater, doll. Where'd you get it?"

Mia's lips pursed. What was one more question? "At the mall. A little store one of the owners of this place told me about. You know Tom?"

Her brow crinkled. "Well, it's a pretty sweater." In another second, she turned on her heel, about to vanish into the crowd. Mia slipped away from Sloan's arm and sidestepped ahead of her.

"Wait, please. What happened?" Mia lowered her voice as much as the music would accommodate, easing some concern into her voice. "My sister's dating him. Something I should know?"

Please don't let her be sober enough to ask how long my imaginary sister has been with Tom.

The woman licked her lips and took a sip from her cocktail, glancing around as she did. Assuring herself that the owners weren't around, if Mia guessed right.

"I went downstairs with Tom once. I bailed when he started acting like a creep. Thought I was drunker than I was, I guess, and that he could take advantage." She snorted. "Well, he couldn't. I wouldn't even come here anymore if it weren't so close to my place."

"Hey, that means a lot. For my sister, I mean. Thanks. My name's Mindy, by the way." Mia stuck out a hand, hoping they'd get something more than a hearsay statement to go on.

After downing more of her drink, the curly-haired woman gave Mia's hand a limp shake and offered her name. "Debra. Wish I could say it was a pleasure, but thinking about that night has my nerves playing ping-pong. I should head home."

Mia dropped her facade of casual curiosity. "You said something about downstairs, Debra. How do we get downstairs?"

The question could have been a prizefighter's left jab, it sent Debra back a step so fast. Sloan stopped her with a hand to the shoulder. Debra whirled on her heels, coming nose to nose with the agent.

"What…uh, what do you two want? I didn't tell anyone. I swear. Please don't tell Tom I did."

Sloan's lips parted in surprise, but Mia didn't have time to catch her up. She moved her hand down to Debra's elbow, turning her around again and leading her to a nearby table that had just been vacated. "You're not in trouble. Please, just tell us how to get downstairs."

Debra nodded, her drink now forgotten. She let the glass drop a few inches to the table, where it clattered against the surface. Fear had sobered her up fast. She motioned with her chin toward the little hall leading to the restroom at the back of the space.

"The door labeled *Employees Only* goes to a staircase. Stuff goes on down there. You know about it, you can go on down. People who don't know about it walk on by."

Sloan's gaze shot back to the little hallway. They'd given it a quick look earlier, but both had assumed the door led to a private office or storage. "Any guards?"

Their spontaneous informant snorted again. "Anybody down there's too busy to be guarding who's coming and going. But Tom ain't down there." She frowned, her lips going tight again before she continued. "I've never seen him here on a Monday or Tuesday night. Wouldn't be here tonight if I had. He comes around on the weekends. You mind if I go now?"

They both nodded, and Debra spun away, disappearing into the crowd.

Sloan leaned in so only Mia would hear her. "I don't really want to wait 'til the weekend."

"You and me both, sister." They deposited their cups on the table. No longer concerned with the high-riding sweater or the low-riding jeans, Mia made a beeline for the door downstairs.

Sloan kept close on her heels.

At the door, Sloan plucked her badge from a pocket, and Mia slipped one hand into her purse and left it there, resting on her gun.

The stairs were lit well, wide, and carpeted with thick, black fabric. Strands of Christmas lights ran the length of the ceiling and walls, granting an almost romantic or otherworldly light to the otherwise basic staircase.

"Carpeting to hide the sound of footsteps, you think?" Mia's whisper disappeared into the air around them, emphasizing how soundproofed the space actually was. By the time they got midway down, they could barely hear the thumping music from above.

Sloan stopped at the foot of the stairs, lips parted, and Mia heard it too. High-pitched, erratic giggling came from the door to their left, suggesting a woman who was high on more than booze. A long corridor stretched forward in front of them. Moans and other low-pitched voices competed with the giggles for attention. "What the hell is this?"

Swallowing any guesses, Mia bypassed Sloan and tiptoed forward along the carpet that stretched the length of the hall.

She peeked into the first open room and stilled. A young woman was passed out on a bed, skirt and top askew. Her purse was off to one side, and a scattering of white powder decorated the lone table in the room. "Looks like Tom and Matthew are still getting their hands on coke."

Sloan grunted in disgust and moved down the hall. Closed doors hid moaning, and open doors showed beds, some empty and some not. The giggling they'd heard earlier erupted again, this time from a door near the end of the hall.

Mia gestured toward it.

She kept her hand on her gun as they both leaned in. Three voices could be picked out—two women, one of them doing more giggling than talking, and one man.

"Don't you want some more?" The man's voice wheedled, a devil on some girl's shoulder.

"Maybe you could just give me some for later?" The non-giggler sighed loudly, sounding torn. "Jenny's had enough, and if I have more…oh, Petey, stop tickling me!" The non-giggler had erupted in her own little peal of laughter, protest apparently over.

"Come on, Sareene—"

"Federal agents." Sloan held her badge ahead of her, and three sets of eyes landed on her ID rather than on the door she'd just slammed open.

From the side, Mia grimaced at the two half-nude women, both college-aged, but only just. One of them—the giggler, from the high-pitched squeal she let out—had pupils the size of marbles. She dove under the sheets of the bed and hunched there in a fetal position as if to hide. Coked out of her gourd.

The other woman grabbed a corner of the blanket and

held it over her chest as she scooted back to the edge of the bed. "I didn't buy anything from him!"

Sloan waved her badge at their so-called Petey, whose hands had literally gone behind his back. Like the women, he sported eyes as big as saucers, but at least he was fully dressed. Slight of build and with receding brown hair, he broadcast sleazy money as he stood trying to stammer out some form of an excuse. "Cops, I, uh, we're allowed to be here. This is private property. We're not—"

"You're doing coke." Mia took a long step forward so that he backed into the wall. "Working on seducing two girls who are probably half your age and clearly under the influence. You don't think there's anything wrong here?"

Sloan waved her badge again. "I beg you, Petey. Think before you speak."

The girls on the bed whimpered, and Mia suddenly wondered if either of them were even old enough to drink.

Fucking hell, these guys are scumbags.

Mia focused on Petey. "You're done for the night. After you talk to us, you will be accompanying us outside, where you will get into a rideshare, whichever you like, and you will then run away home. Alone. My colleague and I, meanwhile, will get these girls home safe."

The two girls now both had their shirts back on but remained quivering behind the bedsheets. Petey kept his eyes on them, pleading silently that they not say a word. Mia was ready to haul him off on whatever charge she might be able to make stick. But they needed information first, and scumbag or not, Petey was their best chance at getting it.

"Nobody here is in trouble. Yet. But to be clear, you will talk to us, Petey. Or it will be a patrol car you're getting into outside, and instead of going home, you will go into a jail cell. You understand me?"

Beside her, Sloan pulled business cards from her wallet and bent over the bed, talking low to the girls as Mia kept her eyes on Petey.

Trembling, hands still behind his back, he nodded.

Mia kept her hand on her gun but relaxed just a touch. This guy was scum, but he was scared scum. That was what mattered. "What's your full name?"

"Pete Bergan." As if knowing what would come next, he used one hand to fumble his wallet out of a pocket and passed it to Mia. Glancing at it, she ascertained his name, memorized his address for later, and handed it back to him.

"Okay, Pete Bergan. Tell us where we can find the owners of this place."

Sloan stood straight and pointed at her own phone, mouthing, *Cops called*, as she gestured for the two women to get their belongings together.

Point taken.

She'd gotten officers on the way to escort these girls home and, Mia figured, to pick up Bergan as soon as he walked outside. She was under no obligation to keep any promises to this disgusting human, but for now, she'd play it as if he were going to walk away from this a free man. They needed answers.

Bergan swallowed, his slight frame seeming to wobble in front of her. "Sure, sure. I don't know them well, ya know. This is my first time here."

Mia swallowed a snort. "Lie number one. Let's don't make it to two, got it?"

He studied her features for a long moment before hanging his head. "Matthew and Tom, they're big into coke, right? That's why I don't come here often."

Sloan rolled her eyes. No man in the history of the world had ever gone so fast from "first time here" to "don't come here often," and yet, Mia didn't have to fight the urge to remain stone-faced.

The coked-up asshole was standing between her and the guys who'd murdered her brother.

"They got a shipment coming in. Monday nights like clockwork." Bergan clenched his eyes shut, breathing fast. "Don't tell 'em I told you. You gotta protect me, right? They're picking up a shipment in the warehouse district. Tom uses his brother's warehouse...guy's name is Jason Harding. Every Monday. You go to the dockyard, you'll see 'em."

Sloan came up beside him, patting him on the shoulder and nearly making the man jump out of his skin. "Petey? Can I be honest with you? We'd like to make sure these girls get out the front door, and we need to be certain that nobody is going to come up behind us on our way upstairs. How about you stay here and keep watch for us, okay?"

The man grinned, a sheen of sweat on his forehead. "Yes, ma'am, you got it. I got your six, right? Got your back. And I'll never do drugs again. Never. Didn't do 'em tonight, of course, but won't do them again ever."

Sloan slapped him on the shoulder again, hard enough that he sat down on the bed.

The two young women stiffened and shrank away from him, apparently sobering up in lightning time.

Mia motioned for them to follow Sloan out the door. At least Bergan had the smarts to keep quiet as his would-be party partners were escorted away.

At the stairwell, Sloan held up her phone, showing Mia a text. Officers had arrived and were readying to come in the front and the back doors on their go-ahead. "Let's get upstairs and get them outside."

"And then hit the warehouse district."

Upstairs, the dance floor was a chaotic mess of people stumbling to avoid one another as they made for the exits. The lights had all been brought up, the music turned off. Dancers and drinkers alike staggered between tables until a uniformed officer with a bullhorn called for an orderly dispersal. It took a few more tries before everyone got the message.

The incoming lines of officers, some with riot shields and batons at the ready, helped communicate that the night's festivities had reached an end. Mia got one cop's attention and directed him to the stairwell door at the back.

"Peter Bergan is waiting for you in a room back there. Possession at the minimum, possibly contributing to the delinquency of a minor, depending on how old these young ladies are."

The two women both protested they were at least eighteen, but neither of them seemed to recognize that didn't help their situation. They were handed over to the police officer, who rolled his eyes as he escorted them aside.

"Sign on the wall says no persons under twenty-one permitted, ladies. Why don't we start with some ID?"

Outside, Sloan touched base with the sergeant on scene while Mia looked up properties held by Jason Harding. True to Sleazeball Petey's word, she found a warehouse right near the waterfront. They were trotting toward Sloan's car moments later, a new destination in hand.

Mia had her phone out to call Emma even before Sloan's key reached the ignition, and the other woman picked up before a full ring had gone through. "Emma, hey. We got something. We're following another lead, headed to the waterfront."

Emma broke in before she could continue. "Can I help?"

Mia glanced at Sloan. "You good with Emma joining the party?"

Sloan gave the gas pedal another touch. "Just tell her to

make sure she doesn't get there before us. I want to see these guys' faces when they know they're done."

Me too, Sloan. Me too.

Mia swallowed down the emotion building in her throat and told Emma where to go. They were ending this tonight, and she only hoped Ned would be around to watch her do it.

16

Since moving to D.C., Mia had little cause to come down to the warehouse district near the dockyard. And she wished they weren't exploring the area near midnight. Shipping containers and blank-faced warehouses loomed over the streets on each side, with little light to see by. Not wanting to alert their targets, Sloan had turned off the headlights, and now Mia felt as if she were riding along in a dark little phantom mobile, patrolling for ghosts as much as drug dealers.

Emma's Other is getting to me. Here I am thinking of Ned and his buddies in the ghost world instead of focusing on living and breathing criminals.

This part of D.C. might as well be the set for a horror movie. Mia struggled to avoid imagining monsters in the shadows as they approached their destination. She confirmed the address Pete Bergan had given them against property records. The building they were looking for had been registered to Jason Harding since right around the time their whiskey lover disappeared.

"At least everything is laid out in a grid." Sloan inched the vehicle around another corner, leaning forward over the steering wheel. "We'd be a lot worse off if we were looking for a deal going down in some random neighborhood."

Mia glanced at her phone. No word from Emma, who'd promised to patrol the outskirts of the warehouse district.

According to the GPS, their target was right around the corner. An occasional security light cast a halo in front of a door or beside a loading dock. Shadows leaned this way and that, but the night remained still and quiet around them.

"We're close. Next row of buildings up ahead and on the right."

"No lights on that row. Are you sure?"

"It's gotta be close. GPS has us almost on top of the address we have for these guys."

Sloan turned the steering wheel. "I'm going to park here. We'll cover the rest of the distance on foot. Text Emma and drop a pin for her, so she'll know where we are."

"Already doing it." Mia finished messaging Emma and then eyed the crossroads ahead of them. From where Sloan had brought them to a stop, everything looked clear and silent. Just another intersection with mostly dark warehouses on each corner. Every bank of buildings had concrete bollards at the corners and was separated from its neighbors by a narrow fire lane.

Emma's white Prius practically glowed in the dark as she parked behind Sloan's vehicle. Mia and Sloan got out as one unit and quietly closed their doors as Emma emerged from her car.

The trio slipped into their vests and coats. Once they'd all suited up, they edged forward, staying close to the buildings until they reached the intersection. Mia looked around the corner, waving for Sloan and Emma to join her.

Down the street, another warehouse sat with one roll-up door wide open. Light shined within. Near the curb, closest to the open door, sat a sleek black Corvette. Parked just behind it was a gleaming red Jeep Wrangler. A truck parked at the open loading door held a shipping container that faced the warehouse.

Mia's heart beat faster at the sight.

This was it. They were about to get Ned's killers.

Sloan raked her hair back into a ponytail and offered a smile that seemed more sad than anything. "We'll do this together. For Ned."

Mia's throat tightened. "For Ned."

Emma nudged Sloan and Mia. "I'll follow your lead, but we can't just sit here."

Mia watched the street. She'd love it if the three of them could do this on their own, but the scene was too big. Long rows of dark buildings stretched out in every direction, with plenty of hiding places and routes of escape. If they were going to catch these guys, they needed backup.

Around the corner, a lone figure strolled out of the warehouse and toward the shipping container. He moved like he had not a care in the world. He was about to get a surprise.

The man lifted something from the shipping container and carried it back into the building.

Without waiting for Emma or Sloan, Mia ran in a crouch, crossing the street so that she was now on the same side as the warehouse they'd been watching.

Sloan and Emma followed suit and crossed as Mia made her way along the building adjacent to their target, finding cover behind a collection of dumpsters in the fire lane.

Creating a cordon around the warehouse wasn't an option. Not from where they were, let alone with just the three of them in play.

Emma lay down on the ground, peering around the edge of the dumpster from the lower vantage point. "I see four guys unloading the shipping container now. Looks like one directing traffic. Two more standing lookout. No telling how many might be inside. Outside of guesswork, no sign of money, guns, or anything we can peg as outright illegal right now."

Mia frowned. Ideally, they'd verify there were drugs or other illicit activity in play before calling in backup. But getting close enough to confirm such details wasn't possible given how many potential suspects were moving around. They'd have to go on the word of the oh-so-trustworthy Pete Bergan. She'd rather be safe and look like a fool than get one of her friends killed or let one of Ned's killers go free.

Sloan already had her phone out. "I'm contacting D.C. police for backup. Who's calling the Bureau? Mia, you thinking we call Jacinda?"

Mia sighed. "I'll do it." She did *not* relish explaining things to their SSA, but at least Jacinda Hollingsworth was reasonable. With drug dealers right around the corner, she'd back them up first, *then* ask for an explanation.

Before taking out her phone, though, she leaned past Emma, focusing on the lookouts who stood in the illumination coming from inside the warehouse. "Pretty sure our sentries are Matthew Spencer and Tom Harding. I see one bald head and one close-cropped, and lots of muscle. These guys are probably taking steroids. Both are also carrying weapons under their arms. Hanging from tactical slings, I think, and it's possible they're automatic."

Mia swallowed the lump in her throat.

"I'll call Jacinda, and we'll keep an eye on everything until backup arrives. Sloan, if you can get around the dumpster, you can use the side of the building for cover and have an extra vantage. When backup's close, we'll coordinate with them and take point."

Emma unholstered her weapon. "Text Jacinda, don't call. That's quieter, and you know she'll get it and confirm."

Leaving Emma and Sloan to keep an eye out, Mia alerted Jacinda.

As predicted, Jacinda's return text was simple. *Call PD for backup NOW if you haven't already. I'm on my way. Be smartER and be safe.*

On another day, the emphasized "er" might have made Mia laugh. Tonight, there was too much at stake.

Sloan and Emma were positioned at the end of the dumpster near the building. Mia placed herself at the other corner, adjusted her vest, and inhaled a deep breath of cold night air.

Just when she'd prepared to keep her heart rate semi-steady, the plan went to shit.

The first signal was a footstep, followed by a male voice heading in their direction. "Hey, babe, what is it? I told you I'd be late…"

Emma rolled away from the edge of the dumpster, but it was too late. The man's casual patrol had brought him right past her hiding spot, and he was too professional to lose a step.

His phone dropped to the ground even as he raised his gun, already shouting. "Matt! Heads—"

Mia kicked him in the stomach, and his shot went into the pavement. Emma was on him a second later, but a barrage of bullets skimmed the dumpster and the nearby street. All she could do was dive for cover as the man's body jerked with the impact of multiple shots from an automatic weapon.

"So much for backup!"

Mia pulled her badge from her vest and took in a deep breath to scream. It was at least possible they'd drop the guns when they realized their intruders were the Feds rather than snoops or rivals.

"FBI! Put your hands up, all of you! Now!"

Emma echoed the shout, but the bullets kept coming, and

the dead body lying nearby mocked their attempt at peace. Playing nice had ceased to be an option.

Sloan returned fire, and the night turned shrill as all six remaining men made their choices between panicking and firing on the agents. Mia held her aim on the sentries she'd spotted, still believing them to be Tom and Matthew. She sent two rounds in their direction, and the figures dove toward the warehouse entrance.

The four lackeys who'd been carrying crates had dropped them and split, two of them running for the front of the truck. Mia couldn't see the others, but assumed they'd gone into the depths of the warehouse. Most of the gunfire coming her way was originating from that direction.

Bullets impacted on the asphalt, sending chips of it spraying against the dumpster. Mia snapped back behind her cover, checking for Emma and Sloan's position. They remained at the other end, with no signs of injury so far.

More gunfire erupted from the warehouse, punching into the dumpster. Sloan and Emma ducked lower.

They were pinned down, with no easy route of escape that wouldn't put them in the line of fire. Even in the dim light, they'd stand a good chance of being shot in the back if they tried to retreat.

Mia moved to join the other agents, coming up beside Emma as a volley of gunfire split the night. "Any idea how many we're up against?"

Sloan whipped a quick look around the dumpster, all but flinging herself back as shots rang out. Chips of asphalt pattered against their cover as the bullets struck.

"Three guns that I can see. They're all on the side of the doorway closest to us."

"And no cover between us and them."

Sloan snaked her head out and back. "Just the 'Vette and the Jeep. Think they're going to shoot up their shiny cars?"

"They might." Mia swiped away sweat before it could drip into her eyes. "We can't count on that, but we can use them as cover. I'll go for the Jeep. It's farther out from the entrance. Cover me until I get there. When I draw their fire, you two move up."

Emma grunted. "Noted. Count of three, Logan."

Mia's heart did a little tumble. *This is for Ned. For my brother.* She moved back to the other end of the dumpster as Emma began counting.

On Emma's "three," Mia bolted, weapon up, and fired in the direction of the doorway.

Bullets split the night as Mia sprinted across the open ground to the back of the Jeep. Her lungs felt frozen with the night air when she landed against the cold metal of the vehicle, keeping the body of the car between her and the warehouse, positioning herself against the tires so her feet and legs had protection from the warehouse entrance. She gave Emma a thumbs-up that the other woman might or might not have seen.

Drawing her aim around the vehicle's fender, Mia screamed again. "I repeat, this is the FBI! Drop your weapons!"

The truck parked at the loading dock roared to life, followed by a spray of bullets sent in Mia's direction and rattling off the Jeep and pavement. In another moment, the truck fishtailed away from the warehouse, but the driver overcorrected, sending it into a sideways slide. It tipped and scraped down the street before coming to a rest against a concrete bollard. A man climbed from the cab and disappeared down a fire lane between the next two buildings over.

Mia refocused on the warehouse door and spotted Tom Harding's bald head. It glowed beneath the light coming from inside the building. He kept shooting toward the dumpster, focusing on the bullets being directed at him rather than Mia's continued demand that he put down his weapon.

She steadied her aim, sighting on Harding's torso.

Mia fired, and blood spurted from his side. He fell back with a scream.

Two of the lackeys had also appeared with guns, and Mia focused on them, screaming at them to drop their weapons. Raw-throated, a thrill of shock ran through her when one of them actually complied just as sirens split the night. Apparently, that lackey wasn't ready to die to defend Tom and Matthew's cocaine business.

The other lackey made a run for the Corvette. Mia turned as the men in the warehouse and her colleagues exchanged more gunfire.

Emma and Sloan continued to fire from their position at the dumpster. Mia wanted to help them but had to remain focused on the Corvette, waiting for the second lackey to appear. He skidded around the vehicle and landed in her line of sight, spinning to face her. He brought his weapon up as she fired, hitting him in the shoulder.

The lackey fell to one side and attempted to raise his gun again. He changed his mind as Mia tracked her aim to his face.

"FBI. Drop the weapon."

He lowered the gun and finally dropped it. Mia moved forward, planning to kick the gun away from him, but a fresh volley of bullets punched into the Jeep, sending her reeling back for cover. Mia crouched low beside the tires, quickly bringing her aim back to the lackey she'd wounded. He was struggling to get ahold of his gun. With a single shot to his chest, Mia removed the threat and refocused on the warehouse.

Two figures darted back and forth across the entrance. One of them had to be Matthew Spencer. Tom Harding might still be alive, or he might be bleeding out. Right now, all Mia cared about was ensuring her friends stayed alive. She leaned out and took aim on the warehouse doorway, watching for movement. A head popped up and down from behind a stack of crates.

Mia fired in that direction. "Emma, you're clear to move! Go!"

Across the pavement, Emma darted from behind the dumpster as Mia and now Sloan provided covering fire. Emma reached her position beside the Jeep and slid closer to be heard over the continued exchange of gunfire. "Sloan's by herself, but she'll cover our advance. Move up to the Corvette with me?"

Mia was ready to do just that when a new round of gunfire erupted, heavier than before. Two automatic weapons were trained on their position, pinning them down. A third joined the fight, and Mia feared for Sloan when she heard bullets slamming into the dumpster.

The shooting paused but quickly resumed. Mia might've heard running footsteps. The sirens were drawing closer, but they could all be dead by the time police showed up.

With a roar of rage, a man exploded from the warehouse, wielding a rifle that spat continued bursts in Sloan's direction. The shooter ran forward, closing the distance to the dumpster. Mia drew her aim on the running figure and fired.

Her shot caught the man in the ribs, spinning him around so that he hit the side of the warehouse hard. He raised the gun again, pointing to where Sloan had just emerged from cover. Mia and Emma both fired on the man, hitting him several times. His weapon clattered to the ground beside him, and he lay still.

A second weapon rattled against the asphalt, accompanied by a shout of, "I give up!" The fourth and final lackey emerged from the warehouse entrance alongside the first one to surrender.

Without allowing herself time to think, Mia darted around the Jeep and toward the entrance to the warehouse. Just inside the door, she found Tom Harding passed out on his back, arms splayed out, blood pooling around him. She looked to the lackeys who'd surrendered and now knelt on the ground, hands up. One of them sobbed, and the other stared at Mia's gun, which she held at the ready.

A sweeping glance showed no other persons—suspicious or otherwise—anywhere within the warehouse. Before she could make another move, sirens pealed behind her, and an amplified voice announced, "Police! Put your weapons down!"

In moments, uniforms skirted into the entrance behind her, fanning out to clear the space.

Leaving them to it, Mia turned back to the suspect wailing on the ground.

"He hit his head when you shot him. I think he's dead. Fuck, I think Tom's dead. You killed Tom."

Sirens had begun echoing into the night outside as Mia crouched by one of her brother's killers. She felt for his pulse and found it, steady and strong. He might have knocked himself out when he'd fallen backward, but if he died tonight, it would be the concussion and not the bullet she'd put into his side. She wrestled him onto his front, struggling with his muscled bulk, and zip-tied his wrists.

There was no need to call for an ambulance. She could hear their sirens right alongside the screaming noise of local law enforcement.

The lackey—a twentysomething with a goatee so mangy, it belonged on a wolfhound rather than a man—held out his wrists for the next zip tie, still crying about how she'd killed Tom.

She perp-walked him over to a forklift inside the warehouse. Two uniformed officers had brought the other lackey there and had him kneeling on the ground.

Outside, local PD were reading Matthew his rights. He'd survived being shot three times and had nothing but a glare for Mia as she approached. Sloan and Emma stood nearby. Other cops, alongside paramedics, were pulling two more men from the truck that had toppled over while attempting escape.

Mia got the attention of a cop, a woman with sergeant's stripes on her sleeve.

"There was another one. The driver. He took off down that fire lane after the truck went over. And the DOA by the Corvette is my shoot. He had a weapon on me and refused to comply."

The cop nodded. "We got a lieutenant on the way. He'll take over IC and set up the command center. Until then, do you want to secure the location of the shoot? Or I can have a couple of my people do it."

"That'd be great. Thank you."

"No sweat." Her eyes were just a few shades lighter than her dark skin and shined with compassion. "Looks like y'all saw some serious noncompliance from these guys."

Matthew was working on losing his voice as he screamed obscenities at the agents and officers around him, but Sloan only smiled sweetly at him. "You're already in cuffs, sleazeball. Exercise your vocal cords all you want."

Mia stepped in closer to him as the officer finished up, and then knelt down. A paramedic crouched on one side of him, bandaging his gunshots, but she focused on the drug dealer's eyes when she spoke. "You killed my brother, Ned Logan. Now you get to live in prison for the rest of your life. We'll see you in court, friend."

He spit at her, but it didn't come close to hitting her, and the officer and paramedic muscled him onto his back in retaliation. If the man spit again, he'd spit into the air and coat his own damn face in angry saliva.

When Mia faced Emma and Sloan again, the women's smiles had gone a little sadder, a little more serious. Before Mia could find any words, Sloan opened her mouth.

"You two saved my life. If you ever need cover, or *anything*, you say the word."

Mia pulled her into a hug. "You would've been my sister if Ned had lived. He would've gotten his way eventually. You're family, lady."

Sloan hugged her back, and Mia caught Emma's eyes over the woman's shoulder. She mouthed the question scorching her heart. *Ned?*

Emma glanced around before shaking her head in the negative, eyes going hooded in apology.

Sloan's grip tightened around Mia, almost as if the other woman recognized some sudden disappointment, and Mia let herself lean into the hug. The moment was bittersweet, but the weight that had settled in her shoulders over the past weeks was lighter, and wherever Ned was, at least he had some justice now.

And she had her family.

17

After the late night, Emma opted for an extra dose of coffee instead of a run or yoga. Mrs. Kellerly hadn't made an appearance, leaving Emma to her solitude and what she'd hoped would be an easy morning routine.

Oren, however, had other plans. Not that she objected in the slightest when he called her between his first and second classes of the day.

"Emma, hi. Hope I'm not waking you."

She was still groggy but got a charge from Oren's voice in her ear. "No, not at all. I've been awake for…okay, I've been awake for all of twenty minutes. And I'm already on my second cup of coffee. Thank the heavens for latte pods and automatic timers."

Oren laughed, and the sound sent ripples through Emma's stomach. She could imagine him greeting his students, wearing his loose-fitting yoga pants and his not-so-loose-fitting tank top as he stretched into a pose.

"Hey, Oren, I'd love to talk. I mean it, seriously. Just… now's not great. I still have to shower, and I need to be in the office in about twenty minutes."

"That's fine. Totally fine. I just wanted to hear your voice and know that you're doing okay this morning. I'd hoped you would be here, but I understand your schedule isn't always a forgiving one. Maybe tomorrow?"

"Yes!" She hadn't intended to shout, but it happened anyway. "I mean, yes. Yes, I'll be in class tomorrow. Maybe not your early-early class, but I can try for the six-thirty one. I'll be there."

He laughed again. "Okay. That'd be lovely. I'll see you then. I'm looking forward to it."

They said their farewells, and Emma held the phone to her ear for a moment after the call disconnected, as if Oren's laughter might still be echoing through the airwaves.

After downing her second latte, she raced through getting ready and was out the door before a quarter to seven. Jacinda wanted her—and Mia and Sloan—at the office by seven thirty for a debrief, but Emma planned on being there even earlier. She'd show her SSA her devotion to tracking down their gun-toting religious nut by being at her desk and hunting down leads before anyone else arrived.

If nothing else, she could get started checking in with the local cops, making sure there hadn't been any action at the mosque overnight. Or any more tags found at other locations.

But we deserve an early break on a case, Emma girl. Nothing the matter with catching a guy before he can cause more damage.

When she got downstairs, she braced herself for the cold February air. Spring couldn't come fast enough. Through the lobby window of the complex, though, she glimpsed a white-eyed woman in red, lingering along the edge of the parking lot. Her dress all but shined against the cloudy morning, with the sun only beginning to fight off the fog. But with those white eyes against her shiny black skin, she couldn't be mistaken for one of the living.

"So much for starting the day without a visit from the Other. Fantastic."

Emma gritted her teeth, braced herself for more than the cold, and stepped outside. Even before she'd crossed the road, the ghost sidled toward Emma's white Prius, shimmying along in what Emma now took to be an old-style flapper dress and matching kitten heels.

Proof that ghosts didn't feel the cold, if there'd ever been any doubt.

Stopping on the sidewalk, Emma let the ghost come within a few feet of her before speaking. "You're looking for me, I take it?" She dug her hands deeper into her pockets, fighting off the numbness coming along with the cold. The pressure built around her, an almost solid thing as the ghost drew closer.

"I shouldn't be, but yes." The dead flapper swayed ahead of Emma, impervious to the wind. She crossed her long arms elegantly in front of her and leaned forward. Close enough that Emma finally saw signs of an ugly bruise at the side of her temple. Whoever the woman was, she must've died from blunt force trauma. "I'm here to deliver a message. You should look at the bottom of the forgotten place where the memories are stored."

The what now?

"What the heck is that suppo..." Emma's question died on her lips. The ghost disappeared as quickly as she'd spoken.

"Dammit."

Hurrying to her car, Emma threw her bag into the passenger seat and pulled up the notes app on her phone, where she typed in the ghost's warning verbatim. And then, sitting in the cold without even bothering to start her car, she stared at the words.

"Look at the bottom of the forgotten place. How am I supposed to know where that is if it's been forgotten?"

Emma scowled at the message but reread the rest of it before putting down her phone and starting the car. "Okay, so focus on the other part. Where the memories are stored."

What memories?

And was the ghost talking about their perpetrator or about Emma? Or about this wolf she'd been warned to watch for?

Or Mother's? Mine?

Emma got the car moving and decided to proceed as if the ghost were talking about her personally. That only stood to reason, right? The last time she'd had contact with the Other around her apartment, it had come from her mother.

Okay, so, my memories, or my family's memories...being stored.

Not the photo of Mom. I can't forget that, the way it keeps acting. And there are my photo albums, but I don't forget those either.

So where else?

Emma had gotten halfway to the Bureau before she realized what the ghost must've been referencing. Her dad's old storage unit, stuffed full of his things and draining monthly rental payments from Emma's bank account, sat right there in the city, just waiting for her to do something about it. That had to be it. So much for getting to the office earlier than promised.

She made a quick left and headed for the storage facility.

Maybe this detour would be worth the trip, if only to remind her that her father's belongings still awaited her attention.

Fifteen minutes later, Emma typed her father's old code into the storage unit keypad. Her birthday wasn't a hard set of numbers to remember. When her eyes adjusted to the dim interior, she picked out the bulky assortment of boxes and the one or two small pieces of furniture she couldn't bear to leave behind in the family home.

Many of the furnishings she remembered from childhood were still there, covered in dust no doubt. Emma stepped into the storage space, brushing her fingertips across the top of an end table that used to sit beside the couch in her family's home.

Her father had kept it clear of everything except for a pair of family photographs in frames. Emma opened the little drawer a few inches, confirmed the photos were still there, and closed it again. She wasn't here to take a trip down memory lane.

Today's errand was about that ghost's cryptic message and nothing more.

Old photos might be important, but they wouldn't be the ones in the end table. They didn't tug at her, and she felt no chill from the Other around them. Not that she'd feel anything unless a ghost were near, but maybe one was here, just waiting until she found the right picture or old piece of clothing.

It would be a memento, something personal to my parents or me.

Thinking of all the clothes she'd boxed up made her head spin. It would take hours to dig through all of that. She let her gaze wander around the dimly lit space until it landed on her dad's desk.

Emma had to push a stack of boxes aside, and the desk was still obscured by more boxes. But she could reach most of the drawers now. The pencil drawer had nothing but an old legal pad with some names and dates scribbled down—probably left over from one of her dad's last cases as a lawyer—none of which meant anything to her.

The first drawer on the right held nothing but pens, pencils, and highlighters. The drawer beneath it contained stamps, envelopes, and stationery.

Emma turned her focus to the left-hand drawers and

immediately stumbled on a thick manila envelope full of old photographs. As she paged through them, she guessed they were all from the decade leading up to her mom's death. Her parents were featured in many, but most of the other people were strangers to her.

She leafed through pictures of holiday parties, some where she'd attended as her dad's plus-one. Other photos depicted the standard family events like barbecues in backyards and parks or birthday parties for people Emma didn't know.

Only one picture stood out as worth Emma's attention.

In it, her mother stood with two other women, both of whom were strangers to Emma. Their surroundings looked like some wilderness area, maybe a campground or nature preserve. Given the setting and their apparent ages, Emma guessed they might have been college classmates. Maybe the picture had been taken at a reunion picnic or hike. Except none of them wore anything like what Emma would call outdoorsy attire.

All three women wore dresses and were barefoot. One of the unknown women had scarves hanging around her neck and shoulders. The other wore a loose-fitting blouse under a vest.

Emma's mom was dressed much the same, loose clothing and nothing that could be called hiking or camping gear anywhere on her person. She looked about the same as she did in the picture in Emma's room. Smiling, light-blue eyes shining, and not so different from Emma herself except that her hair was much longer and pulled into a braid that stretched well past her neckline.

The other women wore their hair in shaggy layers. They also grinned at the camera without an apparent care in the world.

She flipped the photo over, hoping to find names or

maybe a note about where the photograph was taken. Instead, all she found were three sets of initials and another cryptic message.

GT, CF, MV

Eternally whole.

GT was easy enough to identify, as Taylor was Gina Last's surname before marriage. That still left two women Emma didn't know, and having only initials to go on wasn't that much help. It wasn't like she could google CF or MV and hope to come up with anything useful.

She stared at the photo, wondering who the women were to her mom and what had brought them together under the cryptic notion of being "eternally whole."

Emma cut off the thought, pocketing the photo and grabbing the envelope with the other pictures. She had to head to work and couldn't afford to get caught up in useless conjecture. These women were strangers, and their identities weren't mysteries Emma could explore this morning.

Shaking the door of the storage unit just to be sure it was locked, Emma turned on her heel and hurried toward her car.

"She's watching." Mom was talking about someone when she gave me that warning.

Was it one of the women in the photo? Emma forced the idea aside as she got in her car. The dashboard clock read twenty after seven now. Emma slammed a palm on the steering wheel and whipped the car around to exit the parking lot.

She had a killer to track down. She had work to do that could save people's lives and bring justice to those whose lives had been taken from them.

Still, Emma couldn't help but trace a finger over the photo in her pocket. Perhaps the Other had given her a big clue, and this photo meant something. Or maybe the photo would simply be a reminder to her that she couldn't ignore her mother's warning the way she'd ignored her dad's storage unit.

Maybe the unit's contents weren't what mattered, but that warning was another story.

18

The buzz of the VCU office obliterated Leo's expectations of a quiet morning the second he stepped off the elevator. With no urgent phone calls or texts summoning him to work before sunrise, he'd figured the day would proceed smoothly.

He was wrong.

Stopping at the entrance, he took in the chaos. Vance was typing on his computer with his phone sandwiched between his left ear and shoulder. Denae was on a video call with what looked like five local cops. Beyond the both of them, Jacinda had gathered in the conference room with Mia, Emma, and Sloan, who wasn't even on this case. Door closed.

Denae waved, and he headed to her desk before bothering to take off his coat. She left her video meeting just as he got to her and handed him a coffee. "You're going to need it."

He toasted her with the coffee cup as a thanks before taking a sip. "What the hell's going on here?"

"Mia, Sloan, and Emma went Robin-Hooding last night and caught the men who killed Mia's brother."

"Ned?"

"Yep. He was involved, somehow, with his boss's plans to get into the drug business. And I don't mean over the counter."

A big gulp of coffee scalded Leo's tongue, and he spluttered. "Serious?"

Denae lifted her eyebrows and nodded, making it pretty clear she shared his surprise at the news.

"Yeah, so much for Ned's death being an accident, and so much for thinking you know a person. Mia and Sloan have both had to reevaluate how well they thought they knew him."

"Adding an ass-chewing from the SSA can't be making things any easier." Leo shrugged out of his coat and tossed it onto his chair. "How the hell did I miss so much just by getting a halfway decent night's sleep?"

"Oh, that's just the cake, Leo. Wait for the icing."

Before Leo could ask what Denae meant, Jacinda swung the conference room door open and called them in.

"Okay, everyone, briefing time." The SSA shifted sideways, making a path for Sloan to slip out of the room and toward the VCU entrance, presumably to head back to her own unit.

Leo waited while Denae gathered a notebook from her desk. They moved together toward the conference room.

Vance caught up to them and put a hand on Leo's shoulder. "Hope that coffee was enough to get your brain cells firing. We got a break last night."

Wishing he'd arrived even five minutes earlier, so he could've been brought up to speed, Leo took a seat at the conference table beside Denae.

Jacinda stood at the head of the room and waited only long enough for Vance to sit down before starting the briefing. "Okay, folks, we have a case to get to, but I know everyone's wondering what went down last night. Mia, if you would do the honors? And please, quickly."

Mia grinned, dimples on full show as she stood to address the room. "Short story…last night, Sloan and I got a lead on two local dealers, a Matthew Spencer and Tom Harding. We, rolling in with Emma by that point, caught them smuggling a massive amount of cocaine out of a warehouse near the dockyard, which was destined to be sold at their downtown nightclub, Blue River Lounge. The two men appear single-handedly responsible for the fifty percent uptick of coke that D.C. has seen in the last two years. They were also responsible for my brother Ned's death."

Vance was the first to clap his hands together, and Denae let out a little *whoop* of congratulations.

Jacinda stood and patted Mia on the shoulder as she faced the room once more. "Justice has also been served in the case of another woman and a man that Spencer and Harding killed. All three murders were in retaliation for Ned's old boss, Arthur Roberts, hanging Harding and Spencer out to dry when a drug deal went bad."

Leo lifted a hand. "Ned or his boss was a buyer? Seller? What—"

"We don't know." Mia rested her palms flat on the table, as if trying to ground herself. "We don't know what Ned's role was beyond handling the bookkeeping. His boss was trying to get into the game in a big way, and it went sideways on him because he was an idiot. Ned was killed to teach him a lesson, even though he had no idea what books he was really keeping. Arthur was insistent that Ned was innocent of any direct involvement. As were Arthur's wife and brother."

Vance stretched sideways to hug Mia, whispering something to her that had her blinking back tears. Leo could only raise an eyebrow at Emma, wondering how so much could've gone down in just one night. She only quirked a lip back at him.

Jacinda coughed pointedly, drawing all eyes back to her. "One more thing before we move on. Moonlighting during a case is *not* something to celebrate, and I do not expect it to happen again, let alone become a habit. Agents Logan and Last know my feelings and can now recite chapter and verse from Bureau policy on the matter. I expect the same from all of you. Understood?"

A chorus of agreement rang from around the table.

"All right." Jacinda typed a quick command into her computer, and a photograph appeared on the front board. "Speaking of chapter and verse, I'm guessing we all know what we're looking at here?"

Someone had written *J146* on a sidewalk.

Leo recognized it from the searching he and Emma had done the previous day. "John 14:6. 'I am the Way' again. this killer's signature. Where was this taken?"

"In front of the Lost Highway Tavern. The same signature was found near a mosque three blocks away. Emma discovered it last night, following a grade A hunch as to what our perpetrator's next targets might be. We're proceeding on the suspicion that this killer marks his target locations before he kills. We therefore have a round-the-clock lookout at the mosque. No uniforms or marked cars visible, it goes without saying. Hopefully, we'll catch our guy today before he pulls that gun again."

Leo caught Jacinda's attention with a wave. "Has the signature been spotted anywhere else? Or, rather, do we have other prospective targets right now?"

Jacinda shook her head. "Not as of yet, but Emma's hunch put us on the lookout for activity around other places of non-Christian worship. Local PD has officers visiting non-Christian religious establishments throughout the city, eyes open for any more chalk warnings. Speaking of which, keep your fingers crossed that the weather remains clear. Our perpetrator uses chalk, which will vanish in the first rainfall. Agent Jessup?"

Vance lowered his hand and sat back in his chair, tapping his pen on his knee. "We know what he's going to do, but not necessarily where he's going to do it. Even if he's planning to target this mosque, it still doesn't give us a line on his whereabouts right now."

"Perhaps not. But we do have a radius. We can begin plotting his likely location based on where these markings are found. If we find more of his calling cards, we get more data to work with and can start forming a box to put him in. As for the mosque in question, nobody showed up overnight, but police will monitor the location until this case is closed. I'll send the day's assignments to your phones as soon as I check in with the local chief of police. Dismissed."

Leo stood with the others and filed out of the room, then followed Mia and Emma toward the break room rather than heading to his own desk. "Congratulations." Both women turned back to him, Emma's face going a little bit guarded. Mia's smile dimmed just a touch, and he flinched at how blunt he'd been earlier.

"Sorry, Mia. I could've been more delicate about how I phrased things in there."

"It's okay. I just have to accept that my brother might've had secrets he needed to keep from me, as painful as that is to admit."

"Maybe so, but even if Ned was working with his boss on the deal, he didn't deserve what happened. And I have to ask, how did you make progress so fast? I thought you were barely getting started."

"Oh, it was all Sloan. She had Ned's old laptop and decided to do some digging. His email gave us a lead on his boss's location. From there, we kinda didn't stop to breathe, things happened so fast." Mia glanced at Emma, prodding her to do something more than lurk around like an observant ghost.

Emma nodded. "I couldn't sleep after I found that chalk marking outside the mosque. We'd already agreed they would check in with me, since I knew they were heading out of town and wouldn't be on any official radars. When I heard they had a lead, I was itching to join them."

"Well, that's one case solved. Who's up for making it a double?" Leo glanced between them, wondering whether it'd been luck or real legwork that had won the day last night. Both women grinned and traded fist bumps with him before they each moved off to their assignments.

Leo headed to his desk, wondering if they'd include him next time they needed backup. He'd proved himself by now, hadn't he? With five cases collectively behind them, he sure hoped so.

If not, he had a lot of work to do.

19

God was wise, and He'd proven it to me once more.

By the time I'd walked a mile past the mosque He'd told me to mark, His strength ran in my veins as if it were my own. The city blurred around me. Nothing stood between His wisdom and my path.

True to what I'd been promised, the police had patrolled outside the mosque all night long, nobody suspecting my true intentions. Of course, I'd get to those false prophets eventually, but first, I had a more primal type of holy diversion to defeat.

And nothing, nobody, would stand in my way. Not with God's will and grace powering each of my steps forward. God's wisdom was infinite, and it blessed me.

The blasphemous shop beckoned me from across the street, as it no doubt had beckoned so many others before. But unlike those lost lambs, I would not be swayed by promises of healing and deeper connections to a perverse interpretation of divinity. The little idols and crystals in the shop windows—symbols of heathen worship—helped that business and others like it trade on the goodwill of unsuspecting innocents. It was a den of sin worse than any I'd yet ventured into.

God had made that clear over and over again.

"Do not forget, son, that you are about to confront a heathen evil. One that will seek to trap you if you allow yourself to listen. Do not falter on your path."

I forced a smile at a couple passing by, waiting until they were out of earshot before I answered. "I will not forget myself or forsake you, my God. I *will not*. This next step on the path is one I will relish and honor You with."

His approval came to me as a *hum* that vibrated through my body and bolstered my steps. I barely felt the cold, anointed as I was with His grace.

"The charlatans you will find within are Satan's followers, and they have no other purpose than to draw people away from me with false promises."

I sat on a bench by a bus stop directly across from the shop. The crystals in the shop window reflected the cold winter light, glinting like baubles, attracting the eyes of passersby. These were the people I would protect with my good work, done in His service and for His honor.

An old woman exited the place, tucking a little bag into her pocket. I clenched my fists, fighting the urge to strike now, to tear the bag from her shoulder and throw it to the ground.

She engages in idolatry! Worship of false spirits she believes to be held in the crystals or figurines she has bought.

Even as I raged within myself, God's voice came to me, bringing calm to my mind once again, as His words always did.

"So many have been lured within the charlatan's place of business, my son. But we will not succeed by striking at the branches of their sin, the people who fall prey to the wickedness within those walls."

Even though I wished to shout at the blasphemer walking away from the store, I kept my voice low as I replied, "Tell me how to proceed, oh Lord, that I may honor You and appease You, my God."

"To remove the rot, you must strike the roots, my son. The shopkeeper who operates this den of evil should be your target. Then no more shall my children be lured to their doom this way."

Fishing in my pocket, I found the note I'd scribbled out earlier and examined God's words. *I am the Truth. Through lies, I see.*

The writing was clear. Powerful. Anyone who read it would see the truth here. No greater lie could exist than a false spiritual promise, no greater sin than to actively separate lambs from God's great flock.

Inner Visions, Crystals, & Reiki Massage was a pit of dangerous vipers. A trap built to interrupt God's great works. Struggling, weak-willed souls sought answers and wisdom by going to this vile place, filled with people who fed them lies to conscript them to Satan's army.

Standing, I buttoned my coat and headed across the street. A flashy car honked at me, heedless of my greater purpose, and God egged me on.

"Move, my son. Move, act, and be blessed."

Reaching the sidewalk, I stepped to the side of the door, where the building wall was solid, concealing me from anyone within. I could still see the trinkets in the window display, though, and they all but called my name. I tugged on my ski mask, adjusting it around my neck to make sure my hair was covered.

Taking a deep breath to protect myself against the smells and seductive aromas I knew awaited me inside, I gripped the doorknob and gave it a turn. The small shop reeked of herbs and flowers and scented smokes made to tempt the weak-willed among us. Wooden and metal wind chimes tinkled where they hung from the ceiling beneath vents blasting out heated air.

A young man restocking greeting cards waved at me without looking up. "Welcome to Inner Visions. Let us know if we can help you find anything."

I licked my lips within the mask. He was young, maybe my age.

Behind the counter, a middle-aged Hispanic woman adjusted crystal pendants in a display case, and her brown eyes widened a touch upon seeing me falter in the entrance. The ski mask had that effect on people. I'd just as soon have shown her the face of God's chosen worker, but He'd insisted I cover myself, and I dared not disobey.

Instead, I lifted my gun and aimed it at her. "Come out here, over to your friend."

The man froze where he stood. "Layla, what do we—"

"Shut it!" I waved the gun in his direction, ignoring the fear in his eyes. He looked even younger with panic painted across his face. "Quiet!"

Stay loud. Stay confident. Do not falter on God's path.

The shop owner, who I now knew to be Layla, edged out from behind the counter, inching toward the man. "It's okay, Will."

I'd just allowed myself to relax a touch when she gripped her employee's arm, squeezing. Giving him a signal to run.

But God was on *my* side.

The man stumbled over a floor plant. Layla turned to assist him, her skirt twirling around her feet, almost tripping her.

I couldn't help but laugh now that God's confidence ran in my veins with His clear hand aiding my chore's success. These must be Satanists, requiring vengeance, and we were above them. They deserved my ridicule.

The man was down on his hands and knees, sobbing

aloud with fear. Beside him, Layla the Temptress was tangled in her own skirt, one knee on the ground. The elastic of her garment half pulled down her ass to show lace underwear that was undoubtedly of the devil.

She swallowed, glaring at me, and I gestured with the gun for them to stay down.

"If you stand up and try to run again, I'll shoot. You should be on the ground anyway. You should kneel."

The man raised one hand and swept it through his hair, still facing away from me. "Man, I got a kid—"

"At your age?" I took another step closer, God giving me voice. "And are you married to the woman who gave you such a gift?"

"Married?" His eyes darted back to me over his shoulder. "I'm only twenty-two. I got a whole life—"

I spit on him, and God directed my aim so that the spittle landed on the man's hand on the floor. He flinched and stared down at it.

"Sir," Layla pulled at her skirt, adjusting herself without rising from her knees, "there's been some mistake."

"No mistake." I plucked a crystal wand from a nearby case —an actual, damn *wand*—and waved it above the two of them. Alerting them to their misdeeds. Her eyes followed the instrument of evil in my hand until I threw it to the ground in front of her. "Why do you serve Satan instead of the true God?"

The man-child groaned, hanging his head, but Layla shifted to face me more directly and met my eyes. "You have it all wrong. We don't worship Satan. Far from it. That isn't what this is about. We help people heal themselves through crystals and energy healing, using universal energy and—"

"Don't listen to them, son." God's voice echoed in my ears, blocking out the crystal seller's babbling. *"She's an instrument of the devil."*

"Who are you talking to? Who's an instrument?"

"Shut up! You're trying to confuse me!" I stepped closer and kicked at the man's foot. "You're not a dog. Get on your knees, off your hands."

He mumbled something as he turned around on his knees, keeping his eyes to the carpet even as he faced me, but Layla's voice drowned his. "Please, sir, don't shoot us. I know you don't want to do this."

"Kill the liars, son. If they wish to worship Satan, you must send them straight to Hell."

I smiled back at God's words, letting my gun wander between the two heathens in front of me. My first shot caught the man in the chest, knocking him backward and splattering blood across nearby shelves as well as onto Layla's cheek.

To her credit, she remained silent, as if in acceptance. Tears sparkled on her cheeks, mixing with Will's blood, as I pulled back on the trigger and released God's second bullet of the morning directly into her heart.

I slipped the gun back into my pocket and leaned over the seller of lies and temptations. Her eyes were open, blood speeding out of her wound as if it couldn't flee her sinner's heart fast enough. The man's eyes were closed, but he had no pulse.

They were dead, and I had other work to do. God would be proud.

20

Vance edged the fleet car in close to the curb beside Bucky's Brew and Pastry. He glanced at Emma as he unbuckled his seat belt. "I'll just jump out. You ready for another cup of coffee? Lots of time in the cold still to come."

She was about to tell him she'd come on in with him, but her phone buzzed. A glance downward offered up Oren's grinning face, and she changed her mind. "You don't mind?"

"Not at all. Just be a jiff." Vance hopped out of the car, leaving it running for Emma's benefit. The heat was welcome. They'd already walked around two separate potential targets and just gotten back into the warmth of the vehicle. It looked to be a long morning of foot patrols and Bible-verse searching. She hoped, again, the weather held, as chalk was not the best choice of breadcrumbs.

But first, Oren.

"Hey, handsome." She couldn't help shooting a glance at the coffee shop to make sure Vance had disappeared inside. No need to invite jokes should he get a gander at her softer side.

"Hey, beautiful. Am I interrupting anything?" His deep

baritone just about sent a shiver down her spine, and she only wished she could hear it in person.

"Your timing's perfect. My partner just ran to get us a coffee refill. What are you up to?"

"Oh, just thinking about you again. I mean, thinking about you still. You've been on my mind all morning, and I was wondering…I know we said tomorrow morning for yoga. But that would be business for me and self-care for you."

Emma couldn't hold in a chuckle that was, once again, perilously close to a giggle. "Yeah, that's right. What's wrong with mixing business and self-care?"

He was quiet for a moment, and Emma worried she'd said the wrong thing, maybe put him off from asking what she really hoped he was going to ask.

"Oren, I mean—"

"Will you be available for dinner tonight?"

Emma twisted her hand against her coat, forcing herself to consider the question realistically. He asked. She'd hoped, and then worried, and then hoped some more.

And then…

He. Had. Asked.

"Oren, I—"

"No promises, Emma. Just, as far as you know, do you think you'll be free? Best guess."

I don't deserve this man. Not a bit.

"It's anyone's guess. Just a question of whether we've got real leads or, heaven forbid, new victims." She swallowed down an apology she knew he didn't care about, then gave him one anyway. "Sorry."

His rumble of a chuckle tickled something deep in her belly, and it made her blush.

"No apologies necessary. I'll make plans, and God will either accommodate me or laugh at the attempt." He covered the phone on his end of the line—probably talking to a client—and then came back on the line. "I do understand. Your job is important. Just let me know, okay?"

She leaned her head against the seat back, sighing. "You deserve so much more than this. Wouldn't you be happier dating someone who had more time for a life outside work, and—"

"Don't even start." The seriousness in Oren's voice, the desire in it, warmed her cheeks. "Emma Last, I want you. Whatever else comes along with you, I'll take it. All right? It's that simple. Whatever being with you entails, I'm all in."

Emma's heart swelled. Maybe she'd take a vacation just to spend time with this man. Heaven knew she deserved it. And if *he* wanted *her*...well, she wanted him twofold. Heck, maybe the Other would give her a break and stop short of following her if she wandered far enough. The Caribbean sounded nice, given the D.C. winter outside the window.

"That means a lot to me, Oren. Thank you." Across the sidewalk, Vance appeared from within the coffee shop, balancing two coffees and a bag that most definitely held some fresh scones. "I'll do my best to make tonight happen. Talk later?"

"Talk later." Oren ended the call, and Emma left her phone resting against her ear for another second. His voice echoed in her mind, making her all the more determined to catch the killer. And they were certainly on the right track. Who knew? Maybe she'd even have time to look into that photo of her mom today if things moved along quickly. And then she could meet her man for a nice dinner and perhaps talk Caribbean beaches.

"What are you smiling about?" Vance passed her a coffee and settled the bag of baked goods between them. "Win the lottery while I was gone?"

"Like I buy lottery tickets."

"Avoiding the question." He quirked an eyebrow, not even bothering to buckle himself in just yet. "Seriously, what gives? You look like you got lucky somehow."

Emma had indeed, but being willing to share talk of luck in her love life with Vance was something else entirely. Instead, she only shrugged. "Maybe I'm just happy to be alive?"

Her partner scoffed, but before he could press her further, his phone rang. Jacinda's name lit up the car's Bluetooth screen. He clicked on his display panel to accept the call. "You've got me and Emma."

"We have another shooting, and we were wrong. It wasn't at the mosque."

Emma's gut somersaulted, bitter acid rising in her throat.

Jacinda hadn't said that Emma was wrong, but they'd been proceeding on a clue found via one of *her* hunches.

"I'm sending Emma's phone the address for a shop a few miles from your location. Inner Visions, Crystals, and Reiki Massage. I'm here already, and I'm sure it's our guy. Get here ASAP."

Vance buckled up as he pulled away from the curb. Emma retrieved the address from her messages and typed it into his GPS, not bothering to say anything.

The good feelings that had left her grinning like a besotted teenager were gone, replaced by a bubbling guilt. She'd been the reason they'd had their eyes focused on mosques and other religious establishments.

True, her hunch had led to that writing of the verse outside the mosque…but not the next target. That left one question burning a hole in her gut…

What the hell happened?

21

Inner Visions, Crystals, & Reiki Massage turned out to be a lavender-painted healing center that wasn't more than a few miles from the mosque they'd staked out all night. Emma couldn't help clenching her hands in her pockets as they pulled up outside.

This was the sort of place that could only be run by peaceful, easygoing citizens who cared more about their community than its latest stats on violence. And it was the kind of shop that only added to D.C.'s charm.

You make sure to get these people justice, Emma girl. It's that simple.

Inside, two people lay stretched out amid a chaotic mess of blood, books, jewelry, and plant life. Both had been in a kneeling position when shot, but facing their killer, their legs twisted beneath them. Around them, display cases had been overturned and smashed, leaving crystals and shards of glass scattered everywhere.

Glass crunched underfoot when Jacinda stood up to greet them from where she had been crouched awkwardly next to the murdered young man.

Emma toed a pile of necklaces still attached to their cardboard backing, eyeing the pile of debris leading to the bodies. "Guess this guy really hates crystals."

Jacinda shook her head. "The whole crime scene is a mess. The techs'll be cleaning this up for hours, and the medical examiner's still going to receive two bodies covered in glass."

Vance wrinkled his nose and wafted one hand through the air. "Incense in these places set my head on fire. Are we even sure this is the same guy? All this destruction?"

"You don't like sage and lemongrass?" Emma asked, gaze focused on the little plastic bag Jacinda had plucked from the debris.

"We've got ourselves another note. It's the same guy, Vance." Jacinda angled the bag so they could read it from where they stood.

I am the Truth. Through lies, I see.

Emma snorted. "So another super-clear take on John 14:6. Great."

Vance sneezed, and Jacinda handed him a tissue without comment, but Emma was already gazing around the rest of the space. And she found what she was looking for.

A security camera hung from the ceiling aimed at the center of the shop, as if focused on the carnage. Emma gestured at the device before pointing toward the back. "I'll see if we've got any footage."

Jacinda waved her off with a subdued, "Thank you," and Emma headed back.

She passed through a beaded curtain and into a short hallway lined with doors. Emma poked her head into an empty massage room and then a storage room before finding the main office. Boxes of unopened stock lined one wall, but a neat desk held a laptop and, above that, a monitor showing the front of the shop. Vance appeared in the doorway behind her even as Emma pulled up the security system on the little laptop.

She turned up the volume loud enough to hear the crystals tinkling as the monitor showed their masked murderer entering the shop, one hand in a pocket. He wore the same beat-up coat as before along with that beige ski mask. This security footage was worlds better than the Lost Highway Tavern's, and Emma made out dark slacks, light-colored skin at their perpetrator's neck, and a darting nature to his eyes that suggested the man was unstable.

The woman behind the desk spoke in even tones, but their killer still seemed to become more and more unhinged.

"Sounds like he's having a conversation with himself. Listen." Emma rewound the video and played back the moments just before the shooting occurred. The perpetrator shouted something, and the woman asked him who he was talking to.

"You think he's schizophrenic?" Vance asked.

"Could be. He's got the jerky eye movements and is clearly unstable."

As Emma and Vance observed from the safe distance of time and space, the perpetrator accused the shopkeepers of Satanism before shooting them in cold blood. He then destroyed the shop in a chaotic explosion of gunshots and kicks to every glass surface available. Finally, he tucked the note they'd found into the dead woman's hand, then stood over the victims muttering something unintelligible to himself.

Emma could only stare at the monitor, observing what had been a peaceful, well-kept shop now turned crime scene, two bodies lying dead on the floor among the wreckage. When the man stalked from the store, still masked, she rewound and played the video again.

Behind her, Vance jabbed a finger at the screen when the

man once again began talking of Satanism. "This guy's totally off his rocker. I think crystal healing is bullshit, too, but accusing these people of Satanism?"

Emma tried to force a chuckle in response but couldn't do it. This level of violence was such an escalation. Their perpetrator hadn't done any damage before leaving the Lost Highway Tavern despite the rows of liquor that he could've demolished.

Why go so batshit now? Could he be devolving?

A scary thought, considering that he'd already dropped four bodies in little more than twenty-four hours.

Chimes tinkled as more people entered the main portion of the shop. Emma glanced back at the doorway, and Vance grimaced. "I'll venture back into Scent Hell and see if everyone else is here. Doesn't look like the video's about to give up any of this guy's secrets anyway."

When he'd disappeared from the doorway, Emma rewound the tape yet again, then slowed the footage as the perpetrator began heading for the exit after he was satisfied with the level of destruction. The mask seemed to shift on his face, suggesting his lips must be moving. He was talking to himself again.

She wished Keaton were here to bounce around ideas. At best, she could only hope to guess at what guided the perpetrator's actions. Watching the video, Emma was struck with the scattered and random nature of his behavior. He could be schizophrenic or otherwise out of touch with reality. Whatever was happening with him, his mental health looked to be anything but steady.

Vance's voice echoed into the office. "Rest of the gang's here, Emma, if you're finishing up."

Watching the video play out one more time, Emma pushed herself to her feet before pausing the feed. If anything else was to be gained from the footage, it'd have to be from others who were better trained at analyzing the visual cues of a perpetrator's behavior.

Back in the shop proper, Emma found the rest of her team gathered in the open space behind the shop counter. Mia and Denae were both on the phone, with Vance and Leo glancing into the few drawers left untouched by their killer. As they gathered into more of a circle, Jacinda held up the small note in the baggie again, and Emma leaned in to read the words one more time now that she'd viewed the whole of their perpetrator's destructive rampage.

"I am the Truth. Through lies, I see." Emma sighed. "Super-clear. Great."

"We have the refrain of our perpetrator identifying himself with the truth." Leo gestured at the note, even though his eyes remained on the bodies now guarded by two uniformed officers, both facing the window rather than viewing the bloodied victims. "Guarantees it's the same guy."

"So does the security footage." Emma's eye caught on a certificate for excellence in massage therapy, awarded to a woman named Layla Sanchez. The shopkeepers had been professionals. "One other thing it showed is the guy talking to himself right before he killed them and again as he leaves. Nothing intelligible, but that, plus his jerky eye movements, makes me wonder if he could be schizophrenic."

"It's definitely a possibility." Mia shifted on her feet, her gaze skimming over the crystals hanging from the ceiling. "Also, we have two victims with an apparent age difference. Maybe they were having an affair just like Stephanie and Jeff? I don't see any wedding rings, but—"

"Excuse me." A uniformed officer gestured from the doorway. "I have a man out here who says he's another employee. He was coming in late today and just got here. Some of you folks want to talk to him?"

Emma was already walking around the counter, Leo on her heels, before Jacinda answered in the affirmative.

Outside, Emma found a man leaning against the shop with his hand to his temple, shaking his head. Various symbols that she vaguely recognized as being astrological signs decorated the back of his hand and his neck, long-established tattoos, and his long brown hair covered his face with the wind. "Sir? I'm Agent Emma Last, if I could ask you some questions."

He jolted at the sound of her voice but stood straighter and looked back at her without flinching. "Of course. I can't believe..." He trailed off, frowning at the doorway behind her, past Emma and Leo. "But I don't want to go in there, if it's all the same to you. I don't think I can handle seeing Layla and Will like that."

Emma offered her gentlest smile and gestured the man toward the little alley running alongside the shop. "Of course not. Let's just get out of the wind, okay?"

Because trust me, sir, you're right that you don't want to go inside.

Leo rubbed his hands together, stopping so that he formed a little triangle with Emma and the shop employee. "Can you tell us your name and why you were coming in late today? How long you've worked here, also?"

The man shrugged and jittered a cigarette pack from one pocket. His hands shook, and he was visibly upset, but no more so than the average coworker or friend of a murder victim confronted just after the fact. "Yeah, sure. Name's Alex Wilson. I've worked with Layla for, uh, coming up on three years this April. She'd just hired Will a few months back. He's a good guy, though. They...they were some of the good ones, you know?"

Emma waited for him to take a drag from his cigarette,

then prodded him. "And why were you coming in late today?"

He rolled his eyes, as if by instinct. "My boyfriend's ferret had a vet appointment. Little fucker scratched the shit out of me when I was getting him into the carrier." He rolled up his sleeve and pulled back some gauze that had been taped across his forearm to show a string of deep, raw claw marks stretching over a peace symbol tattoo.

Leo hissed out a breath. "You, uh, should probably go to a doctor for that."

The man shrugged and yanked down his sleeve. "Yeah. I was thinking about doing that, after my shift." His eyes widened, and he jerked where he stood. "Shit. I'd be dead if not for that furry little shit."

The shock was real, and he dropped his cigarette and stomped it beneath his foot as he shook his head.

Emma glanced at Leo, who appeared torn between bemusement and frustration. She rather felt the same. It seemed unlikely that Alex had anything that would help. "Alex, has Layla had trouble with anyone around here recently? Or have you seen any suspicious people hanging out nearby in the last several days?"

Alex shrugged, leaning back against the lavender wall behind him. "No, our customers are always cool. Chill. But yesterday…you're gonna laugh." He frowned, glancing between them.

"No laughing, Alex." Leo lowered his voice, offering that charm that came so easy to him. "That's not what we're here for. We just want to help. What happened yesterday?"

Alex's tongue darted out, wetting his lips, and then he shifted his gaze toward the mouth of the alley. "There was a total, like, dark energy near the place. Got darker as the day went on."

True to his word, Leo didn't laugh, but he did take a step

backward, and Emma caught the line between his eyebrows that signaled frustration.

This wasn't something she could dismiss so easily, though. She stepped closer to Alex, catching his eye. "Can you clarify what you mean? Tell me how it was different than usual?"

For a moment, she thought he'd blow her off, but then he nodded. "Yeah, so usually, there's kind of a lightness to this place. Layla's religious about keeping the sage going and making sure we're welcoming." He glanced at the edge of the alley, where Vance could be seen listening in with a smirk on his face. Lowering his voice, he turned back to Emma. "Lots of skeptics, you know?"

You have no idea, Alex. No. Idea.

She nodded and gestured for him to go on.

"So yesterday, it was, like, unnaturally cold."

Emma felt a small chill in her own gut. She examined Alex's expression, and he appeared both sincere and a bit freaked out. She understood. "How cold is unnatural?"

"Like, not just the winter air, okay? I felt a real cold wind blow against me as I was leaving. Felt like my soul was being sucked out."

Emma stiffened, waiting for the Other to make its presence known, to confirm what Alex was telling her. Nothing came, though, and she began working on a follow-up question. She almost asked it when she felt Leo's perceptive brown eyes focused on her. Suspicious.

Shit.

She bit her tongue, fighting the urge to keep questioning Alex about this energy and what was most certainly some connection to the Other. An ordinary FBI agent would most definitely not take a claim like the one he'd just made at face value. They'd nod, jot some nonsense in their pad to make it appear they cared, and walk away with a straight face until they got far enough off that they could double over in laughter without causing offense.

But Emma wasn't an ordinary FBI agent, and she couldn't just blow off this young man's obvious intuition of the Other's existence.

"Alex, I'm guessing you put a lot of faith in your feelings, and I respect that. Sometimes, your brain identifies a dangerous situation before it happens. Subtle cues get picked up by the subconscious and transmitted into warning feelings. Maybe you'd call them 'bad vibes.'"

"Yeah, that's totally what it felt like yesterday. Like a real bad vibe just hanging around here. I was almost going to call in sick today, but Layla needed help getting Will trained up on crystal healing best practices, so I couldn't."

Emma forced a smile for Alex's benefit and refocused. "What can you tell us about your colleagues? Layla and Will?"

As the man rambled on about his now-deceased friends, Emma forced herself to take notes and listen for anything that might help. When he'd confirmed that the two of them hadn't been romantically involved, she realized she had no more questions except for those that she couldn't ask, given what they'd signal to Leo.

She glanced his way, but he showed no signs of leaving her alone.

And that meant the interview was over.

22

"I just need to know why we killed the boy." In an alley a mile or so from the evil crystal shop, I anchored myself to the frigid wall behind me. My palms on the brick were slick with sweat and cold, but it was grounding. "That bartender was having an affair with her boss, but—"

"Are you questioning me?" God's angry breath stung my face and neck, and I ducked my head down, wishing I still wore my mask.

"No!"

I clenched my eyes shut, but I still saw that young man's face. He'd looked no more than my age, and the farther I got away from the crystal store, the less comfortable I felt with his level of sin and what it had led to. I couldn't pretend otherwise. Why couldn't God tell me what he'd done to be cast aside like that?

God had promised me the people we were killing were devoted to promoting sin. I'd seen that with the bartender even before I'd known of the affair—no godly work was done after midnight on a Sunday—but that employee I'd just killed said he had a son. It was difficult to imagine he was a lost cause.

Hesitating, I chose my words carefully, biting them off one by one. "It's just that he looked innocent. I had a mask on. You said not to spare anyone inside before I went in, but I thought everyone would be bad. Devoted to sin."

"He worked there."

God's argument seemed to end and begin there. But even so, couldn't we have tried to turn the clerk to a righteous path? What if he'd just needed the paycheck? He'd said he had a child, and though he wasn't married and was living in sin, that didn't mean he hadn't planned on getting married. Planned on following a better path.

"Some collateral damage is to be expected from this path of wrath. I thought you understood. Or are you not strong enough to see that?"

I flinched so hard that the back of my head thudded against the brick wall. God's anger was weightier than ever, and those words stung like none before. "I am strong enough."

Doubt filled me, but I couldn't let Him feel it in my words. When He didn't respond to my whispered response, I spoke again, louder.

"I am strong enough, God!"

"You think you can hide your feelings from me?" God's accusation boomed through the alley, buffeting my ears and blowing raw cold against my exposed throat, as if He might strangle me where I stood. *"I am the Creator, boy. I am the Way. I am the Truth. I am the Life. There is no way to Heaven but through Me. You will obey Me, or you will burn."*

My blood froze at the threat.

I fell to my knees, fighting back the tears that I knew God would read as weakness, even as I raised my hands to him in prayer. *He must see that I'm strong enough to complete His mission. He must.*

"I shall obey You, God. I shall." I held my eyes shut, praying He would hear the truth in my words. Not read my hope as doubt of His path. "I only need to know when this will end. That's my one weakness. When will I be able to leave this sinful city? I want to know when I can go home."

The admission shocked me. I'd hoped to flee from that place for so long, but I felt the truth in my words, and I knew God would as well. I wanted revenge, after all, and that was something God could understand.

But the only people deserving of my revenge were back in Woolward. Back home.

God's voice was softer when He spoke again, and I felt His empathy for the first time since I'd killed on His behalf that morning.

"My son, I will only command you to commit one more killing in this city. After that, I will allow you to return home. And when you do, I'll have something for you. A gift for all the righteous work you've done on my behalf."

I lowered my hands but kept them clasped and remained on my knees. "Thank you. I know you have a place for me as Your right hand in Heaven. I breathe for that day."

God's pause before He spoke told me I'd been wrong. *"No, son, this is an earthly gift. One you will enjoy before reaching my side."*

There was no anger in God's voice now. No disappointment. And the promise of a gift warmed me more than any speech about Heaven. God was on my side, still, and I was doing His work.

"Now rise and move forward. You need to rid yourself of the blood of your work."

My eyes shot open, and I gave myself a look at what God must be seeing as I knelt beneath his grace. The dark coat I wore was splattered with the blood of the fallen, and any member of law enforcement who followed man's law above God's law would see it for what it was. There'd been a camera to catch what I wore too.

I tore apart the buttons and tugged my arms out of the coat, standing as I did. With the gun safely in my pants pocket, I looked both ways before kicking the stained cloth into a narrow gap between a dumpster and the building. And I made sure it was crumpled back there good before I turned away.

The alley bordered the Mission of Hope, but it didn't matter. I shouldn't be staying there for another night anyway. Let them find the coat and attempt to locate me.

"God helps those who help themselves." I just had to remember that. God would keep me hidden as long as I helped myself, to the extent that I could. And, together, we would finish this work.

With the coat behind me, I nearly stumbled from the cold as I left the alley, but God had led me back toward the mission for a reason. A man I knew to be a drunk swayed ahead of me, picking through a trash can behind a bus stop. When I got close, I glanced around us, but this was midmorning in a lousy part of town. The mission wouldn't be serving another meal for hours, and we were the only ones around.

"Give me your coat."

The man barely looked at me. "Get your own."

"God commands it!" I pulled the gun from my pocket and tapped it against the man's arm, forcing him to look at me. His breath plumed in the cold, but he wasn't so drunk that he didn't recognize the threat.

In another moment, he'd ripped it from his body and fled in the other direction, leaving behind his grocery cart of nothings. I took my time pulling on the navy-colored puffer coat. More modern than I would have liked and loose on my frame, but even warmer than my old overcoat.

God was looking out for me.

I glanced around as I walked, ensuring I was alone before addressing my Creator once more. "God, who is to be the final smiting? Am I going to another bar? Another crystal shop?"

His silence surrounded me for another dozen steps before He finally answered. *"No. This time, we'll need to make a bigger impact. Perhaps now that the police know the mosque was a distraction from your next target, it will be the perfect time to strike there."*

Just as the coat had warmed me, God's words chilled my blood. I breathed evenly, praying He wouldn't notice my doubt.

But I couldn't believe this could be the path. "But the police." I took a deep breath, forcing my panic back into my coward's belly. "And so many people, all in one place. Surely they'll find me before I can complete Your work."

"Be calm, my son. Be calm. All will be well. You'll see. Wait for the path to become clear, and you will see."

I dug my hands into the coat pockets, anchoring myself in the concrete reality of the gun. With God at my side, the weapon would protect me. It would have to.

And either way, what God willed would be done.

I'd committed to following Him. To obeying Him.

I would not turn away from His path now.

23

Standing in the midst of the crystal shop's destruction, Emma struggled to remain focused. She'd spotted a bulletin board near the counter and noticed a flyer pinned to it with a familiar face smiling back. Oren's flyer that he'd shown her yesterday. Seeing his face calmed her, but she was quickly overcome with guilt. How could she be feeling the giddy happiness of new romance while standing in the middle of a ruined shop with two dead bodies behind her?

Techs had started cataloging the scene, laying out evidence tags and collecting what physical evidence they could. Emma's teammates were conjecturing about what the video told them and where their guy might be headed next. But all of that was a blur.

Rationally, Emma understood that she'd had no way of realizing the chalked verses outside the mosque and tavern had been intended as distractions. Even if they were meant as markers for where their unsub intended to strike, his methods for choosing which target to hit were still unknown. But logic didn't have any effect on the guilt gnawing at her guts, eating her from the inside.

Guilt only told her she should've seen through the ruse, somehow, and been on the alert for any other target.

Mia nudged her elbow. "Step outside with me? Breath of fresh air?"

"Huh?" Emma channeled her inner Oren, forcing a deep breath into her lungs. "Right. Uh, yeah. Let's."

Emma followed her friend outside, thankful the other woman must've seen her thoughts spiraling. Not that she wanted to be that transparent, but there was a reason it paid dividends to have friends as colleagues.

"You know," Mia ushered her away from a couple of uniforms outside, "we were operating on faulty information. I mean, we suspected the verse markings were messages identifying his targets, and we'd found one outside that mosque and that was our best lead. Nobody anticipated him hitting a New Age shop. We couldn't have stopped this."

A breath shuddered from Emma's lungs. "I know. I do." Movement caught her eye from down the road. Beyond a little park, Alex Wilson was hunched against an old junker of a car, speaking into a cell phone.

Maybe I didn't lose my chance for more questions after all.

Feeling her resolve stiffen up to its normal levels, Emma tilted her head toward the shop clerk. "You mind coming along for some additional questioning?"

Mia followed her direction, then grinned. "Alex?"

Emma nodded, already walking.

Mia chuckled. "I wish I could've read Leo's mind when he saw how interested you were in the man's dark cloud of energy. He must've been spinning."

"Clearly, if he mentioned it." Smiling, Emma tried not to think about that. She'd come far too close to revealing her own otherworldly awareness in front of Leo this morning. But at least his presence hadn't forced her into hunting this guy down on her own.

Halfway to the man and his car, Emma's step faltered. Off to the side, clear on the sidewalk, was another chalk marking. *J146.* She pointed at it, and Mia slowed to snap a quick picture while Emma, once again, thanked the weather gods for keeping the rain and snow at bay.

That's one more piece of evidence tying our perpetrator to this crystal shop.

"Mia, can you text Jacinda about that really fast? I need to get Alex before he leaves."

"Sure."

"Alex!" Her shout stopped him from getting into his car. While Mia fired off a quick message to Jacinda, Emma sped up to meet Alex.

"Thought I was free to go." He squinted as she approached. "Everything okay?"

Mia came up beside Emma and held out her hand. "We didn't meet. I'm Special Agent Mia Logan. I'm sorry for your loss."

The man pulled his hair out of his face, knotting it behind his neck. "Nobody can ever be truly lost. Not even in death."

He sounded so sure. Emma was glad they'd caught him. Whether or not this man knew about the Other, he'd sensed something around the shop. She'd known before that she needed to question him further, but his response to Mia's simple comment confirmed it. Meeting his gaze, she nodded what she hoped looked like agreement. "We just have a few follow-up questions."

"Go ahead." He leaned back against his car, glancing between them. "Whatever I can do."

"Could you go into a bit more detail about that dark cloud you mentioned?" He squinted at her, and Emma pushed on. "Was it visible? A physical sensation? Or even just an emotional one?"

Alex's lips twitched in surprise, and he focused on Emma.

He tugged another cigarette from his pocket but didn't bother lighting it. Only twitched it back and forth between his fingers while he held her gaze.

Emma let him examine her face, keeping her expression open and honest. He stared at her for what felt like a full minute. Nervous laughter bubbled up unexpectedly from somewhere inside Emma, and then Alex chuckled too.

For the first time in a long time, Emma felt genuinely at ease with another person. Alex presented no threat or judgment.

He simply was. Alive and present, and…aware. He knew the Other, somehow, just as she did.

"Alex, I think there's something you want to say, and I want you to know I'm here to listen. Whatever it is."

He nodded, and a smile curled his mouth as he replied. "I'm glad you believe me." He kept his gaze on Emma, nodding as if to himself. "I kinda thought you did before."

"I do believe you. Whatever you can tell us might help."

Beside her, Mia agreed.

"I'm glad the people looking into Layla's and Will's deaths are believers." He stood straighter, and then closed his eyes as if to better focus on his words. "Senses aren't really adequate to describe the feeling I got. It was like a spirit was communing with me. Maybe multiple spirits. Giving me a warning. I was going home when I felt it, but if I hadn't already been headed out, I might've left work early. I never do that, but that's how strong the feeling was. How *real* it was."

A deeper cold seeped into the area around them, tightening Emma's lungs. From the direction of the shop, a shifting in the air signaled the change. The ghost of Layla Sanchez, white-eyed and bloody, was approaching from the side.

Mia rested a hand on Alex's elbow. "Alex, if it was that real, why didn't you warn the others? Layla and Will?"

The ghost stilled for a second upon hearing her name, but then she kept coming until she stood as close to Alex as Mia and Emma.

Her focus was on him, and a sudden sadness fell across his features.

"I thought it was just for me. The warning, I mean. I thought about it all night. Didn't sleep. Figured I'd get Starburst to his vet appointment and then come over just to tell Layla I couldn't work here anymore. I knew she'd understand the need to follow energy like that, or to stay away from it. But when I got here, they were..."

He trailed off, but before Emma could come up with an answer, Layla put a hand on his shoulder and leaned forward. She moved so close, Emma couldn't help being shocked the man didn't feel her, even after all she'd seen.

"I forgive you, Alex." The ghost's grip appeared to tighten on his shoulder. "It wasn't your fault."

Alex blinked. Once, and then again, harder. The tension he'd carried left his face, and when he met Emma's eyes again, there was nothing more than simple peace radiating from him. Calm.

Calm like she'd rarely felt.

Layla stepped back, and Alex put his hand on his car door. "Is there anything else?"

Emma shook her head. "No, thank you. Call us if you think of anything else we should know." She pressed her card into his hand.

He was in his car and pulling away just a minute later. Layla remained at their side, though.

"Mia, Layla's here."

Mia's eyes went wide even as Emma turned to focus on

the ghost. There was no reason not to, without their teammates around. "Layla, is there anything you can tell me?"

The ghost reached up and tucked a strand of brown hair behind her ear, either ignorant of or uncaring about the blood trickling along her skin and sparkling against her face. "I went to church when I was a child, but never felt comfortable there. Too much judgment from others. The rules were too rigid."

Emma fought down a sigh, waiting. If the ghost was going to help, she'd do it in her own time. That seemed to be the way of the Other's denizens.

"When I prayed, it never felt like anyone was answering. Anytime I suggested something that didn't align with the church's teachings, I was ridiculed. And then, after that, I had to forge my own path."

The ghost's white gaze turned back to Emma. "Do you understand, Emma Last?"

Emma swallowed. She wanted to ask questions, but none would come. Instead, she simply nodded, then conveyed the ghost's words to Mia before looking back at Layla. "Thank you."

Layla's smile shined brighter than the sun through the clouds, and Emma was suddenly reminded of the peace in her mother's smile that beamed at her from that picture by her bedside. Tears pricked behind her eyes, and she gestured to Mia that they should go. Before the emotion really welled up.

Turning from Layla, Emma led the way back toward the shop.

Layla's gentle voice stopped them on the other side of the street.

Facing the ghost once again, Emma found the woman pointing at her. Pointing, in fact, at her coat pocket.

Mom's picture.

Emma took a step back toward the ghost as she pulled the photograph from her pocket. "This?"

A thin-lipped smile came to the ghost's features.

Emma held it up to Layla. "Do you know them?"

The ghost was all but trembling, shading her sight as if to avoid looking at the photograph. She waved at Emma, gesturing back to her pocket, and Emma realized the ghost would refuse to look directly at it.

"Do you know who they are? The women with my mom?" Emma lowered her voice. "Please, if you know—"

The ghost simply raised her hand in farewell and faded from sight, leaving Emma and Mia standing on the sidewalk with nothing but the killer's chalk message scribbled at their feet.

24

Leo had initially come to the shop window in order to make sure the killer hadn't somehow left another calling card there, maybe on some earlier visit, but the task had been forgotten as he'd seen Emma and Mia approach Alex Wilson.

What could she have left to ask him? She'd seemed satisfied enough with their earlier questioning.

And then the two women had remained in place even after the guy had driven off.

Whatever they were doing out there, it wasn't nothing, but Leo had no ideas beyond that.

Denae coughed behind him just as the two women began walking again, and Leo turned to face her. He gestured over his shoulder with one thumb. "Sorry, I got distracted. Looks like Mia and Emma had some more questions for our shop's one surviving employee."

Denae leaned sideways, raising one eyebrow. "Here's hoping they had luck with that. But hey," she held up the note taken from Layla's hand, "I had a thought. His note says, 'Through lies, I see.'"

The door chimes jingled, and Mia walked in ahead of Emma. Denae waved them over, then repeated what she'd just told Leo.

Ignoring the way Emma was gnawing her lower lip and keeping half her attention on the window rather than their crime scene, Leo refocused on Denae. "Right. You recognize it from somewhere in the Bible?"

"Ha. Me recognize something from the Good Book?" She grinned, and he chuckled at the response. He'd been the one to grow up religious, not her, and they both knew it. "Not a chance. But here's what I'm thinking. Our first crime scene was a bar, right? And he was saying they were lost. Then here, he's saying, basically, that the victims were believing lies."

"Okay, yes, but what does that tell us? I mean, yes, we know that's what he said. But—"

Mia jumped in. "I think I see where you're going, Denae. We have a zealot, right? He's hyper-focused on being right, being the guy who gets it. His notes say as much. 'I am the Truth. I am the Way.' What if he's not just talking to his victims with the accusations, though? What if he's talking to people who go to bars in general? Or people who shop at places like this?"

Leo thought back to how his yaya had railed against alcohol addiction when he'd been growing up. She'd scared him off trying more than a single sip of beer until he'd been of age. "You're saying the notes are intended for larger populations, even though he's targeting specific members of those groups. He's making examples of his few victims, like his intention is to correct a wrong he perceives as being perpetrated by many."

Mia nodded. "Exactly. He believes he's going to fix things by showing other people the error of their ways, and he's using his victims to do that work for him. He can't close down every bar in the city, but he can kill two people who operate one, counting on the knock-on effect to get other bars to close their doors."

Leo put his hands on his hips and shook his head. "He can't honestly believe that's going to happen."

"He does."

Emma's words froze Leo in the middle of a laugh. He met her eyes and motioned for her to continue. The others stood by, quietly observing the two of them like they were watching boxers stepping into the ring.

When Emma didn't offer anything else, Leo cleared his throat and lifted his eyebrows.

"That's it, Emma? 'He does?' I mean, that feels clear, based on the broken glass and blood all over the floor here. But there could be other explanations, and we can't ignore those possibilities. Or can we?"

She stayed silent, looked away, and shook her head. "No, we have to stay open to other options. Even if Mia and I did spot his mark outside."

Looking for that mark might explain why Emma and Mia wandered down the street. But Emma wasn't talking out loud to some chalk on the sidewalk.

And right in front of him, Emma remained silent—maybe thinking on their conversation, maybe not—so Leo raised his voice when he answered. "What about the final part? The 'I am the Life' bit of the equation?"

Emma finally spoke up again, but it was a quick comment. "That's from John 14:6. It's the closing phrase of the verse."

"Does that tell us anything helpful?"

Emma chewed on her thumbnail, saying nothing.

Denae picked up the conversation. "In other words, where will he strike next?"

Before frustration could get the better of him, Leo asked for a recap of what they knew about the perpetrator so far.

Mia began listing facts, starting with the physical qualities they could ascertain from the footage they'd seen. "Then we have his targets. A bar owner and employee, allegedly engaged in an adulterous relationship. And now, a New Age shopkeeper and employee, with no known involvement beyond the workplace."

As Mia continued to run through their facts and findings, Leo couldn't help himself from observing Emma. Even when he'd raised his voice and pointed his comment at her, she'd remained unengaged. Her gaze kept slipping over to the window—over toward where they'd questioned Alex and where he saw her talking to thin air.

She's distracted.

He stepped sideways, obstructing her view of the window and making her refocus on him as he addressed their small group. "I think we just have to keep our minds open to a wide variety of interpretations of the 'I am the Life' bit, and make sure we don't get offtrack. It could mean a lot of things."

Emma flushed, her hands fidgeting in her pockets, and he realized what he'd said.

"Shit, Emma, that's not what I meant."

She shook her head. "I know, Leo. It's okay. You're right, there could be a lot of interpretations."

Though the expression looked forced, Mia smiled. "I think Emma was right earlier. That we could be dealing with someone who's schizophrenic."

Denae frowned. "Which means he really could be talking about anything."

"As people who hear voices do." Leo sighed, lifting a hand to greet Vance as he approached. "You overhear all that?"

"Most of it." Vance stopped beside Mia, gazing unfocused

at the mess of broken glass on the shop floor. "But honestly, I think we need to stick with Emma's hunch from last night. There's obviously some religious bent to this guy's thinking, so I'd say that means we should keep an eye on religious targets as well as local Christian churches."

"Christian churches too?" Leo stared at him for another moment, thinking only of targets, then caught on just as Denae began echoing his own confusion. "Ah, because you think he might be talking to God? And going to church to get closer?"

"Stands to reason." Vance shrugged. "Makes sense he would want to shelter in holy places, too, considering the guy in our security footage looks pretty ratty, like we're looking for someone who's homeless and on foot."

"Could even be a self-described religious leader of sorts," Mia glanced around the group, "either like a street preacher type or someone who's lost his congregation. Plenty of D.C. area churches have shut down over the last few years. If he's feeling adrift or cast aside, he could be taking out his frustrations on what he sees as the reason for losing his community."

Emma's eyebrows knit together, and Leo gestured for her to say whatever she was thinking.

"I still have mixed feelings about putting that stakeout on the mosque last night—"

"You couldn't have known," Leo reached out before he thought about it and gripped her shoulder hard, "and it was a good idea."

She forced a smile too. "That mosque could be a third strike that's coming. Or some other religious spot could be. We might've just been early, or he saw our presence there and changed his priorities, striking here first. For all we know, he could have his targets already mapped out, and is just moving from one to the next based on some schedule we can't anticipate."

Leo gave a hum of doubt. "Would a schizophrenic be that organized?"

"That's what I mean...it might sound organized when we say it, but he could just be marking places on a map in his head with no rational reason for choosing which one to go to."

"But he might have a rational reason for why he chooses to mark them. Is that what you're saying?"

"Yes. I guess. Now that you ask, I'm not sure I know anything about this guy except that he's dangerously violent. But it could be like you said. He could be choosing where to attack based on a set of principles or because the locations have meaning to him."

Vance glanced at his phone. "I think Emma's hunch was solid. Sure, we went to the mosque, and maybe we could've stopped this if we'd known to anticipate him marking this shop as a target. My money's on a religious target being next, or us finding our guy at a religious establishment, be it a church or otherwise."

Mia raised an eyebrow. "Religious *otherwise*?"

He shrugged, but Leo finished the thought. "Lots of places are run or organized by religious groups or churches. Not just churches. You're looking at charities, shelters, even hospitals."

"And we should keep an eye on the streets." Denae pointed out at the gray D.C. morning. "Our guy could be preaching on a street corner right now. Especially if he really is schizophrenic, there's a good chance he's homeless."

Emma frowned. "We need to do some more research. I'm going to look up religious schizophrenia if Jacinda doesn't want me on something else."

With that, Emma turned to hunt down their SSA, who'd

disappeared toward the back office with a police officer. Leo watched her go, still considering the scene he'd observed playing out in the street.

At least Emma being enmeshed in research meant he didn't have to wonder what she could possibly be doing for a few hours. And maybe before the afternoon came, he'd figure out how to ask her what the hell had been so interesting that had her communing with the February air over her own team.

25

Mental health wasn't exactly Emma's specialty, and with their perpetrator devolving, the last thing she wanted was another misstep. But since Jacinda had decided they should all reconvene in the conference room at noon, Emma had been allowed the time to get through the research she'd planned. She'd also checked in with Keaton Holland, her go-to BAU contact, who'd confirmed her suspicions in the end.

By the time her colleagues were gathering around the conference room table, she felt fairly sure of the profile she'd developed. More so than she had since Jacinda had called her and Vance away from their coffee run that morning anyway.

Once the rest of her team was seated around the table, Emma stood back from the board and pointed out the relevant evidence they'd gathered as she began filling everyone in.

"We're all on the same page in thinking our perpetrator is highly influenced by religious texts, given the notes he's left and the chalked references to that particular chapter and verse, John 14:6." Emma paused and thought back over the crime scenes before she continued. "Based off that, and the fact that he's been talking to himself, as seen on video, it's highly likely that our killer has religious delusions related to paranoid schizophrenia."

Jacinda held her hand up for a pause. "And Keaton's in agreement?"

Emma nodded, even as she tried to block out some of her old friend's choicer words.

Hard not to imagine what he'd say about me if he ever caught me talking to ghosts in the middle of the street.

That was something she did not need in her head at the moment, so she hurried on. "He agreed a hundred percent, yes. I have reference cases of criminals who were eventually diagnosed with clinical schizophrenia. They show the same erratic, destructive behavior alongside talking to themselves, generally in relation to religious delusions. The perpetrator accusing our latest victims of being Satanists would also back up this theory."

Leo held up a hand to pause her. "So his behavior is standard M.O. as far as religious schizophrenia goes?"

"There's not really a *standard M.O.* in this case, psychiatrically, but he's showing signs of aggressive behavior—"

"Murder is definitely aggressive behavior…"

"And dysfunctional impulsivity." Emma ignored Leo's interruption. "Which back up the diagnosis we're talking about here when we put all of our evidence together." Emma pointed at Denae's theory from earlier, now written up on the board. "He believes himself to be working on behalf of a larger community, maybe all of humanity. In this thinking, he represents the way to God."

Vance scratched his cheek. "Is this normal?"

Emma lifted a shoulder. "Normal pathology for someone in our perpetrator's condition…to the extent that there is a normal…would show us a man attempting to repent for some unforgivable sin he committed earlier in life. Or, rather, a sin that *he* saw as unforgivable. But when we take into account Denae's theory, which I agree with, what we see isn't that at all."

Mia frowned. "You're right. This guy's too judgmental of others. Self-righteous with a capital 'I am the Way.'"

"Vindictive." Denae shifted in her seat, eyeing the board and then pointing at the photos of his notes. "'You are the Lost?' This guy's concerned about other people's sins, not his own."

Vance piped up. "He thinks he's here to dispense God's wrath."

Emma nodded. "Being deluded about others' relationships with God or religion is a common symptom of religious schizophrenia. His accusations about Satanism, calling people 'lost'…those are pretty clear indicators that he believes he's doing the right thing for the right reasons."

Leo tapped his finger on the table, frowning. "Saint Michael the Archangel. That's who our guy wants to be."

Emma felt her eyebrows raise to her hairline. "Excuse me?"

As everyone turned to him, Leo's cheeks reddened, and Emma realized he'd probably spoken without meaning to. "I grew up in a religious house, sue me. The point is, Saint Michael was regarded as the helper of the church's armies against attacks of the devil. Seems like this guy's trying to follow in his tradition."

Jacinda paused in her note-taking. "Emma, did Keaton say anything about your theory?"

Emma grinned. "He did, indeed, and here's where we might get a clue. He said this type of thing can happen when someone is surrounded by religion at a formative age, so their paranoid delusions morph into what they've been told about the world. It's highly likely that our guy came out of an extremely religious household or community."

Leo groaned. "Like our little town with the axe murderer."

Emma couldn't deny the reference, as much as the case of Little Clementine still left her feeling more sympathy for the killer than her victims. That definitely wasn't the case now. "Basically, yeah. And a small town is especially likely since they not only tend to be more religious in nature but don't generally have resources for mental health. We can't tell from the tapes if our guy has a clear regional accent…he sounds like a preacher if anything…but it's likely enough to keep an ear out for."

Mia leaned forward over the table. "All that said, the piece that really doesn't fit is that our guy seems very organized, considering how long he's evaded capture. If he's suffering delusions strong enough to drive him to commit murders, how do we justify that against them being premeditated murders, with notes at the scene and calling cards left in advance?"

"You're right, Mia. That's not in accordance with everything else we've learned, but there's no denying it. The first possibility in play is that he's being helped by an organized leader or partner. The second is that he has an irregular subset of paranoid schizophrenia that clinicians aren't yet familiar with. The third could be that this is his first spiral into active psychosis."

Denae tapped her pencil on the table, scowling at the board. "All that destruction at the crystal shop, what we saw on the video, that took energy. Young, manic energy, the kind that doesn't know limits because it hasn't been forced to deal with them yet."

Jacinda shut down her tablet. "You're suggesting the

perpetrator is a young man or possibly a teenager? How does that match up with what you've learned, Emma?"

"Pretty well, in fact. Denae's probably nailed it. Men who develop schizophrenia tend to show signs of onset in their late teens or early twenties."

The SSA sighed. "Based on our earlier conversations at the shop, we have cops checking out homeless shelters and churches, starting with those that fall inside our known radius from each crime scene, but it's important we take initiative too. I agree with the profile here, which means it's all the more likely our perpetrator has been seeking refuge in some kind of religious institution, assuming he is young and also homeless. I think the next step is for us to hit the streets."

Mia sat back in her chair. "I agree that his clothing tells us he's living on the street. He's got to be homeless, dressed like that."

"But?" Jacinda asked.

Mia paused before replying, meeting everyone's eyes in turn. "Everyone, we need to keep in mind there are a lot of mentally ill people experiencing homelessness in our city. The vast majority of them are not dangerous, even if their behaviors might be unpredictable. We should be on alert, but also be ready to give people the benefit of the doubt when it comes to their intentions."

Emma nodded. "Same for those with mental health issues. The overwhelming majority of people suffering from delusions wouldn't harm a fly. This individual is an outlier."

"That's a good reminder for all of us. Thank you both." On that note, Jacinda stood up and stretched. "I've ordered us pizza, so we can have a quick lunch. After that, we hit the streets. Emma, you've done great work on this. I'm impressed."

Emma grinned, offering a quick little joke of a bow to

their SSA as the rest of the team echoed her praises. After the guilt of the morning, the compliments felt good. Though they'd feel even better once they caught their guy.

"Before we go, let's take care of assignments." Jacinda glanced around the room, then ticked off pairs with her fingers. "Emma and Leo, you two check out nearby homeless shelters. Prioritize any attached to churches, religious charities, you know the drill. Denae and Vance, the two of you keep looking into mosques and synagogues. Check in with the cops on the mosque that was marked last night and look for any further calling cards. Mia and I will call up some Christian churches and see if that gets us anywhere. Let's catch this guy today, before he has a chance to leave us any more damn notes."

Emma met Leo's gaze across the table, unsurprised that his expression was just as determined. Together, they might just catch this guy in time for her dinner with Oren.

26

My grandpa had used to say that his feet "ached like to fall off" after a day on the job, and I'd always laughed at him.

As much as I didn't want to quote him, my feet ached like to fall off, and God didn't seem too concerned. Perhaps I shouldn't be, either, not with earthly aches when Heaven was waiting, but fear seemed to elevate every one of my pains as I paced behind a thrift store, waiting for an opportune moment.

God was impatient, and with every moment, my brain grew more and more weighed down with threats and fear. I couldn't act right now. I could barely even walk.

"If you do not complete your mission, son, there'll be no place for you beside Me in Heaven."

I ground my teeth together. They might fall out of my mouth before my feet fell off my legs at this rate.

"Failure in great, good deeds sent down from Heaven is akin to one binding himself to Satan. Some deeds, some missions, cannot be finished with anything less than success. You do realize that, don't you?"

Swallowing, I stilled and watched a volunteer disappear into the back of the Second Chance Thrift Store, leaving behind bags upon bags of donations that had been dropped over the weekend and were yet to be sorted through. I tried not to think about what God had just told me, but I understood the implication.

Akin to binding oneself to Satan. If I fail, I am no better than those I have cleansed from the Earth for Him. I get it, God. If I fail, I go to Hell. I forsake my place by Your side, and I go to Hell.

My lips were cracked, but I licked them anyway. Was stealing from a pile of donations a sin? God didn't care, but I'd been taught not to steal. Taught to work for what I needed to live and take only what was owed or given freely.

I swayed on my feet, working up to rocketing forward toward those piles of clothes. It was impossible for me to separate the panic from the fear in my blood now, but both were God-gifted at this point, just like my mission. And it wasn't as if I had any choice about stealing now, whether this would be a sin or not.

The police were looking for someone who looked homeless. The bar might not have had cameras, but the Satan-pushing crystal shop definitely had, which meant my time was limited as long as I looked like I did now. The puffer coat I'd stolen was dirty and smelled of drink, twisting my guts with each breath I took, and my slacks were still blood-spattered if anyone cared to look.

I had to change clothes. To disguise myself again. *Now.*

Before God could make me stumble, or I could lose my nerve, I sprinted forward and tore into a garbage bag by the thrift store's back entrance. Baby clothes erupted around me, scattering over the asphalt alongside some old ball caps. I grabbed one of those and plopped it on my head, but that wasn't enough.

The next bag was tougher to rip open and full of women's

dresses like those I'd seen my grandma wear. God chuckled in my ear, and I darted a glance at the entrance. Still no sign of the volunteer coming back.

I gripped hard and tore open another bag, but this one only offered up more children's clothes, these for toddlers. Then, finally, my perseverance paid off. I ripped into a bag that exploded with men's sweat clothes and t-shirts. Someone had passed away or given up on exercising, or gained or lost weight, and I was the richer for it.

My heart pounded harder and harder, but I grabbed an armful of shirts and sweats, and I ran. A block over, I rested behind a dumpster and sorted through what I'd found. When I stripped out of my dirty clothes and coat, nobody was watching, and the disguise just about fit me well enough to look like the clothes had always been mine.

Clean-ish sweatpants and a sweatshirt over a t-shirt, light gray instead of black and dark blue, and a ball cap that I'd tucked my long hair up into. Nobody would recognize me now.

Before anyone could get a look at what I was doing, I buried the clothes I'd worn and the extra sweats in a nearby dumpster. My shoes would be the same, but they were dark enough that I doubted blood would show anyway.

"Are you done now? Do you feel better?"

God's voice was crueler, less patient, but I tried to ignore His tone. He'd be patient with me once more and welcome me to His side as soon as I proved myself again.

Walking away from the dumpster, I tried to calm my heartbeat before I answered Him. "I'm ready now, so please, if You want me to act quickly, tell me what's next. I'm ready."

"Oh, now you're ready? Only now? On your time and not mine?"

My eyes burned with moisture as well as the wind, but I

shook off the sensation. This wasn't the time. "I'm sorry for my human weakness, God. Please. Tell me what to do."

"Demanding, aren't you? Couldn't simply trust that I would keep you safe and had to stall by seeking out new clothes? A disguise, rather than trusting my Word?"

God let the accusation hang in the air, and my vision blurred. A couple of guys passed by ahead of me, crossing the street at the mouth of the alley I'd just come through, and their faces were familiar.

From Woolward.

Tommy and Graham, bullying me around outside of our high school like they owned the world. Red with power and hate. Eyes narrowed on me like I was a scared fucking rabbit. Arms reaching out to push me backward or take my things and toss them to the ground.

"They called me a shrimpy little weirdo. And I'm not." They'd been older, and I'd grown. They'd never know me now.

A woman passing in front of me glanced sideways and hurried forward as if she were trying to catch up to my childhood bullies.

A cry escaped my lips, and then she all-out ran, and I fell back into the alley.

God was speaking to me, but I couldn't hear him. In my ears, Tommy was telling me I was too weird to live while Graham suggested I just kill myself already before I made anyone else's life miserable. Lies—I'd never made anyone miserable!—but he'd made those lies sound like truth.

Tears burned down my cold, dry cheeks, and I crouched in the stoop of a doorway, willing myself to stop. *Just calm down.* I took a deep breath. *This is my comfort in my affliction: for thy word hath quickened me.*

I repeated Psalms 119:50 to myself. His words had indeed brought me life. I was overreacting. My bullies were nothing.

In the past. And today, I'd finish my mission and attain my rightful place by God's side.

Why am I even thinking of them? God's not a bully, and nothing like those petty teenagers from Woolward. No, He's everything. God would not bully me. Never. He's only doing what's best for me. Pushing me to have more courage.

I swiped an arm across my face once and then again, ridding myself of my earthly tears. This would be the last time I cried. Those evil boys from my past would not destroy my future. Not when I had God by my side. Not when His voice was finally coming through for me again.

"It's only natural to be afraid, son."

I nodded, rocking where I crouched. "I'm sorry, God. It's not that I doubt you—"

"Shh. I know. I know, son. You are only human, and you are doing your best to overcome the evil of your past. I forgive you for thinking of me as a bully."

A protest built in my throat, but the guilt in my belly told me God would see through it. "I'll do better, God."

"I know you will."

God went silent, but I couldn't bring myself to stand just yet. The day was nowhere near gone, but I was exhausted. How much fear had I felt that day? How much love? God's mission was a roller coaster of emotions, and I only wanted the final piece of my mission to be complete. To give me the final *peace* that I so craved.

Licking my lips, I fought down another round of tears, despite knowing that God would understand. Because He would, wouldn't He? God was all about fear and love. And I, as a human, wasn't meant to wrap my mind around God's wisdom. Everything would make sense in the end if I could only hang on.

"And then you'll give me a gift for completing my mission."

I'd whispered that, but of course God heard me.

"I will, my son. An earthly gift you will treasure, followed by eternity at my side, as you've wished for all these long years."

I pushed myself to my feet. My heartbeat was more even now. Tears no longer threatened to undo me, so I stuffed my numb hands into my pockets before I answered. "Okay, my Lord. Please, command me. Tell me how to glorify You, and I will obey."

Now I actually sounded confident, and for the first time since leaving the crystal shop, I was able to smile. God had chosen me for a reason, and I *would* make Him proud.

"I will tell you, my son. The end is nigh. In fact, you've already marked the final sinners for the death they deserve. Walk with me, and you shall finish your mission with all the grace and glory you have earned."

27

Leading the way to the homeless shelter's intake desk, Emma didn't need to tell the volunteer why they were there. Leo already had his badge up.

The young woman offered a quick smile and ducked into a doorway behind her. When she came back, she pulled open the half door by the counter and ushered them past her. "The director just got off a call."

The back office was a chaotic whirlwind of papers, cardboard boxes, and file cabinets, but a thirtysomething man with an easy smile and crow's-feet sat behind a desk and waved them in. "Welcome, Agents. I'm the manager of Lord, My Shepherd. Call me Mike. Caitlin said you have some questions?"

Leo perched on the two-seater couch across from him, and Emma gazed out the window as he filled the manager in, explaining their suspicions as well as their profile. When he finished, Emma turned back around to see the man frowning and shaking his head.

"I can see you have reason to be here, but I'm afraid I can't help you. We don't have the resources here to house anyone who's potentially dangerous, and only the barest resources for the mentally ill. Basic counseling, contacts to visit for specific struggles…that kind of thing. Most of the people we help are healthy folks searching for work, in between homes."

Emma just managed to hold back a sigh. The man appeared to be leveling with them, but that didn't help their case. "And if someone who needs more help than you can offer does come in? What do you do?"

Mike pulled open his middle drawer and took out a card, which he held out to Emma. "We try to nudge them toward Mission of Hope, over on the east side. They have better resources there, including mental health specialists, though it still isn't a perfect option."

Emma took the card, glancing at the logo.

It's something, at least.

"Would you mind if we talked with some of your residents while we're here? Maybe somebody has seen the man we're looking for or has some idea of where he might be if he's not at Mission of Hope."

Mike looked ready to protest but relaxed in posture. "Of course. Please, just be gentle with the people here. If you would. They've suffered greatly, and many are merely doing their best to make it from one day to the next with very little to count on for support."

"We'll be respectful, and we'll keep it short and sweet."

Emma led the way back to the main room, where she and Leo took turns questioning individual residents and some small groups. Most of the residents seemed lost within themselves. More than one stared off into the middle distance. A couple were curled up around their meager possessions. The more lucid residents of the shelter were put off by the presence of federal agents and were reluctant to do more than provide "yes" or "no" as a reply.

By the time Emma and Leo were done, they'd only managed to confirm what Mike had already told them.

At least they still had a business card for Mission of Hope.

Back outside in the Expedition, Leo got behind the wheel and typed the address into the GPS.

"Fingers crossed that the priest's name on the Mission of Hope business card means the place is religious enough to have attracted our guy."

Leo grinned at her as he pulled out of the shelter's parking lot. "One can hope for the Mission of Hope."

Itching to tell him to drive faster, but knowing he wouldn't, Emma settled back in her seat. It was about time they got a break, but the winter day outside seemed darker than before. Even the lack of ghosts couldn't distill her feeling that they were headed for more bodies before they found their unsub. She wouldn't tell Leo that, though.

Someone ought to have some hope left today.

28

The Mission of Hope Homeless Shelter had a parking lot, but a group of three women held hands and swayed in tandem at the entrance, effectively blocking any cars from coming or going. Leo parked the Expedition against the curb across the street, and they hopped out.

Despite being in a hurry, Leo couldn't do anything but stop and stare when he and Emma got within a few feet of them. One had her eyes shut tight, and all three sang the "Hokey Pokey" without making any of the requisite movements. The effect of their slow movement alongside the fast-paced children's song was nothing less than eerie. "A far cry from the other shelter, huh?"

"You're not kidding." Emma glanced toward a couple of older homeless men stumbling back and forth near the entrance. Both were talking, and although their eyes followed each other, neither stopped muttering or speaking in order to *hear* the other. One wore paint-splattered coveralls and had a blanket around his shoulders, whereas the other wore a *Star Trek* uniform and had a hood with cat ears attached.

At the shelter's doorway, Emma waited until the local Trekkie stepped aside before pulling open the door.

Inside, Leo unzipped his coat in the overly warm entrance and focused on a middle-aged woman sitting at a desk. "I'm Special Agent Leo Ambrose, and this is my partner, Special Agent Emma Last. We're hoping to speak to whoever's in charge here."

"That would be Father Jacob Fallar. If you can tell me what this is about, I'll go get him for you."

Emma leaned in close, eyeing a family that sat eating lunch a few feet behind the desk. "We're looking for a murderer who we believe to be living on the street. Time is an issue."

Finally, the desk attendant showed some reaction, blanching a touch and standing quickly enough to knock some papers from the desk. "I'll go get the father. Just a minute."

Leo forced a smile for the benefit of the two parents who'd looked up from their picnic. Then, speaking to Emma from the corner of his mouth, he said, "This place is awfully different on the inside too."

Where the other shelter had been open and somewhat chaotic with people wandering the space inside, conversing and staying out of the cold, this shelter felt like a controlled environment, more clinical than comforting.

The open space they were in was small, with just the desk and a little lobby area of picnic-type tables behind it. Set up for visiting, perhaps. Through a door, Leo saw a veritable maze of cots, most of them empty. An opening to the left showed a cafeteria where small groups of people were scattered in various areas, but the tables were bolted to the floor. Built to stand up to abuse, clearly.

Meanwhile, doors with nameplates on them lined all the outer walls alongside religious posters and motivational messages—the entire display reinforced the atmosphere of clinical oversight.

A portly priest came their way from the door leading to the room full of cots. "Agents, I'm Father Jacob Fallar. If you'll follow me to my office, I'll try to help however I can. Assuming you have identification on you."

After they'd offered up their IDs, the priest led them back to his office. They walked down an aisle bisecting row after row of cots until they reached a glass-fronted door at the back. The space inside was set up for conferences of a sort, with a central round table and chairs, along with cheaper inspirational posters lining the walls.

Even before they'd finished describing their case and the details that led them to Mission of Hope, Leo knew they were in the right place.

The priest's easy smile had fallen away to a thin-lipped expression of disappointment. "I don't know his name," he paused, closing his eyes briefly as if to center himself, "but I think I know who you're looking for. I can't...I can't believe I didn't try to keep him here, to get him help immediately. We might've prevented some of this."

Leo leaned forward. "Don't blame yourself, Father. You couldn't have known. But whatever you can tell us could be of use."

The man sighed, leaning back in his chair and folding his hands over his belly. Despite his size, he seemed to have shrunken in on himself since he'd realized who they were speaking of. "He was here yesterday. That's when I last saw him, at least. As you guessed, he was directed here from another shelter. I knew almost immediately that he was a paranoid schizophrenic...I've been working with such tortured souls for a few decades now...but he showed such clear religious devotion, I didn't suspect him of being a threat. Truly, he seemed harmless."

At Leo's side, Emma had her iPad out, waiting for anything they might use. And she spoke gently when she answered, "We know most paranoid schizophrenics aren't violent."

"That's true." The priest sighed. "Tortured, rather, as this man was. But I admit, some of what he said felt violent and angry. Vengeful, even. He heard voices, as people with his condition often do, but shifted between defending himself against the voices and asking if they'd get revenge. If he'd threatened revenge himself, I would've felt the case to be urgent, but with the man mostly wanting to remain isolated…"

That tracks with schizophrenia, but "appearing harmless" doesn't bode well for him sticking out of a crowd on the street.

"As it was," the priest spread his hands, clearly asking them to understand his position, "I simply hoped to have him speak to a counselor today, but he didn't come back last night. His attitude, the way he seemed so angry at the voice he heard…or maybe even on behalf of it…made me second-guess my earlier assumptions, but I didn't get the chance to confront him. We had a crowd for the meal we offered, and by the time I had a free moment, I only caught a glimpse of him leaving."

"We understand, Father." Leo caught the other man's eye, willing him to hurry on to something they might use. "Can you tell us what he looks like?"

"Right, right. He's in his early twenties, around six feet tall. Average-looking, but with bad posture and good teeth. Light-brown hair that's almost light enough to be called blond, and longish, at his shoulders. He'd probably have a nice smile, though I haven't seen it more than once that I recall."

Leo cataloged the details even as Emma jotted them

down, working to form a picture in his own mind. "And what was he wearing when you saw him?"

"Dark pants, I can tell you. But I saw him throw his coat on the ground this morning before he left. I happened to be looking out one of the windows in the refectory, which faces out toward the back alley. He had on a dark shirt beneath it, but I hope he's found another coat to wear by now, it got so chilly last night."

"We'll look for the coat, Father." Leo glanced at Emma, wondering if her tight-lipped smile hid the same frustration he felt. Just like a priest to worry about whether a murderer was warm enough, and here they sat having come in just a day too late to run right into him. "Is there anything else you can tell us?"

He shrugged, then paused and met Leo's eyes again. "Perhaps. I only spoke to him briefly, and I can't be sure, but he seemed put off by my robes. He treated the women handing out lunch politely enough, but seemed more hostile to me, and I got the impression it was because of my vestments. It would not surprise me if he's had negative interactions with the clergy in the past, though I don't know if that could help you."

Emma stood, handing the priest her card. "If you think of anything else, or if he comes back, please call us right away."

The man took Leo's card also, his lips pursed in concern. "I'll do so. And I'll also pray you find him before anyone else is injured."

Tightening his coat, Leo led the way back out the front entrance and around the corner to the alley. Wadded up against the back of the building, behind a dumpster, was a mass of dark fabric.

"Finally, some fucking luck." Leo put on a pair of gloves, reached down, and gripped the worn overcoat. He tugged it free from where it had been wedged between the dumpster's wheels and the building.

Touching it, even through the gloves, he could feel dried stains that he guessed to be the blood of any of the four victims. On such dark material, the priest might not even have noticed the stains, let alone realized they signaled blood rather than some more innocuous substance.

"Hold it while I go through the pockets, and let's see what we find." Leo shifted the fabric, waiting while Emma popped on gloves herself so she could grip the shoulders.

The inner pockets offered up nothing beyond chewing gum wrappers, but in one of the outer pockets, he found some crumpled papers. Onionskin thickness and tiny, cramped text gave the paper away as having been torn from a Bible.

Emma's eyes narrowed. "Not exactly demonstrating respect for the Good Book."

"We have clear signs of distress, though." Leo did what he could to uncrumple the papers so he could get a decent look at them. "There's writing in the margins. 'Please please please stop stop. I will obey. Death to diversions.'"

"Lovely." Emma grimaced. "I don't guess he left a list of targets there?"

Leo shook his head, gaze still on the sloppy writing scattered through the margins. "Nothing."

Going back to the coat, he dug into the last pocket and came out with a thicker piece of paper. When he pulled it out, he almost whooped out loud in excitement. "But this is something! Look!"

He shoved it in front of Emma's face, and she leaned back to read it. "Shit, that's a bus ticket. Move your thumb?"

Leo grinned and shifted his grip, scanning the ticket for anything they could use. "Ticket was bought in a town called

Woolward. Somewhere in Virginia. He bought it and came to D.C. on Sunday."

Emma bagged the overcoat and pulled out her phone. "Didn't waste any time, did he? I'll call it in. Maybe if we look at arrest records in Woolward, we'll get ourselves a name."

29

Hefting the overcoat, Emma dialed Jacinda as Leo led the way back out of the alley, bagging the Bible pages as he went. Filling Jacinda and Mia in on the new developments, Emma began cataloging the day's finds in her head. They had a description, a bus ticket, and maybe a hometown. That had to lead them somewhere.

By the time she and Leo got settled in the front seat of the Expedition, Emma had her phone on speaker while their colleagues searched.

Back at HQ, Jacinda had assigned herself the job of searching through arrest records while Mia followed the bus ticket back to its origins.

"Woolward is a town about forty-five minutes west of D.C." Mia whistled. "Small as small can be. Population of around a thousand."

Leo pulled it up on his phone, and the first thing he found was an announcement of a church celebrating its bicentennial anniversary. "Just based on what I'm seeing in search results, I'm guessing it's religious."

"You got it." Mia muttered something to herself, then came back more clearly. "I'm looking at records now, and there are a ton of churches, considering the size of the population. Safe to say the place is highly religious."

Emma glanced at Leo, voicing what they were both thinking based on his tight-lipped frown. "You're wondering if it's anything like Little Clementine."

He nodded. "And hoping I'm wrong."

Jacinda's voice pinged through the speaker. "Most of the arrests I'm seeing are for simple issues. Drunk and disorderly. A not-unsurprising number of DUIs for a small and somewhat isolated community. A few cases of domestic violence, some child abuse, and a handful of assaults."

Emma hummed, thinking over the information. "How recent are those assaults, Jacinda?"

"They span the past six years. I searched as far back as ten years. Most recent case involved an Adam Cleaver. Arrested only once, about two years ago, at the age of eighteen."

Emma leaned toward the phone. "That would fall in line with Father Fallar saying our guy's in his early twenties. And with what I read about the general timeline on a first psychotic break in males."

Leo interrupted to brief the others on the description they'd gotten, and Emma added that the shelter personnel had also judged their guy to be a paranoid schizophrenic.

"More reason to think this could be our guy. The details shake out also. He assaulted a group of young men his age with a butcher knife." Jacinda read from the report, going fast. "Nobody was killed or seriously hurt, but listen to this. When Cleaver was arrested, he claimed he did it *to glorify God*. He claimed the local Catholic priest would explain that he was a *warrior of God*. The priest understandably declined. Just said the kid needed treatment."

Emma whistled on reflex. "No question on whether this guy's religious or delusional."

"Okay, reading forward," Jacinda went on, "looks like Adam Cleaver did his time and was released to go back home to his grandfather. He's been out of jail a few months now. We'll have to check with the jail records to see if he was treated for any mental health issues, but that might take some time."

"Either way, this could be our guy." Leo started up the SUV. "Do we have any new targets besides the mosque, or should we head there to keep an eye out?"

"No, head there." Jacinda murmured something unintelligible, probably to Mia. "Mia's getting photos of our guy out to everyone's tablets, and I'll try to contact the grandfather to see if that gets us anywhere. Make sure this guy's not sitting at home watching basketball. But let's not pretend we know everything about our perpetrator. He might still be in D.C., so keep your eye out. You two head to the mosque and call us if you find anything."

Leo pulled into traffic as Emma punched in the address for the mosque their unsub had already tagged. "We have an age and a psychological profile as well as a person of interest."

Emma gazed forward through the windshield as if she might will the man into existence before them. "It's time to bring this bastard down before he hurts anyone else."

Leo shifted his gaze to peer at the photo, which had just pinged Emma's phone, and she held it up for both their viewing.

The man staring back at them had narrow-set eyes and a too-small nose that seemed to hover around a cruel, self-satisfied smirk. He'd been grinning when he'd been arrested, proud of "glorifying God" by way of a butcher knife.

Emma's gut clenched at the pure animosity within the small picture, and then she focused back on the road.

It was time to go find this guy. She had no doubt that he was planning to kill again, and soon.

30

Emma's phone buzzed, and her heart lightened a tiny bit when she glanced down and saw Oren's smiling face. Maybe this wasn't the best time, but they were still five minutes from the mosque.

"Leo, you mind if I take a personal call? I'll keep it quick."

He shrugged. "Might as well."

Emma faced the window as she brought the phone up to her ear. "Oren. It's good to hear from you."

"And how are you?"

Emma's cheeks warmed. His deep voice held such sincerity, all focused on her. She couldn't get enough of it. "I'm fine. You? There must be a reason you called."

He chuckled. "Oh, just wondering how your case is going and what our chances of a nice romantic dinner are."

A vision of Oren's smile all but eclipsed her view out the window, the idea of a romantic dinner with him shined so bright in the winter afternoon.

"I think…they're good." She glanced at Leo, whose focus remained on the road. "We're hoping we're in the final stages of the investigation. Strong suspicions of who our guy is, which means it's a matter of figuring out exactly *where* he is. And while D.C. might be a big city, you'd be surprised how small it becomes when everyone's looking for the same person."

"I'm glad to hear it." Oren cleared his throat, and his voice softened. "There's a lovely little Peruvian place that just opened. The masses haven't discovered it yet, and I think it'd be the perfect spot for us. Perhaps even take your mind off work. I'll make a reservation for seven thirty?"

"Perfect." Emma didn't particularly know what Peruvian food would be like, but she had an easy time picturing her and Oren sitting in a quiet, candlelit corner, stealing kisses and munching on appetizers full of flavors she'd never experienced. "I think I should be able to make it, really. And maybe make up for some of this guilt about abandoning you all the time."

"Oh, no guilt." He hummed to himself, as if teasing her. "But if you insist on making it up to me, I won't argue. Regardless, don't add to the guilt if the case drags on. Worst-case scenario, you'll have cold pizza with your teammates while I have a quiet little dinner to myself, daydreaming about you."

Emma swallowed. Maybe making him wait ten minutes for her wouldn't be the worst thing, if he'd spend them dreaming about her.

But, for now, they were coming up on the mosque, and that meant personal time was over. "Oren, I have to go. I'm—"

"Say no more. I'll see you tonight, love." With that, the phone clicked his goodbye before Emma could say anything more.

She opened and closed her mouth, feeling her blood rise with emotion as his casual words sank in. Him calling her "love" wasn't the same as him saying he loved her, and it was far too early for that, obviously, but the way he'd spoken, she could imagine that coming far too easily.

Get a hold on yourself, Emma girl. Now is not the time to turn into a smitten little schoolgirl.

Leo edged the SUV up to the curb but had one eye on her. "You good?"

"Fantastic." She shook off Oren's voice and the feelings it brought up. "Shall we?"

Out on the sidewalk, Emma stood for a minute with Leo as they took in the broad view of the scene. Unmarked police cars surrounded the area. About ten too many men and women casually sat in their cars, "talking" on phones or with people beside them in the front seat. D.C.'s finest had shown up in force to catch their guy.

The street was otherwise normal as could be. Except, given the weather, a few too many pedestrians littered the sidewalks. Emma watched them carefully, the groups and pairs and several obvious loners. None of them looked suspicious.

Leo jutted his chin forward, and they took off together to do a circle of the block. Despite the cold, Emma still felt warmed by the conversation with Oren. Even the smeared remains of their unsub's chalk marking couldn't deter her optimism.

"You know," Leo shifted toward her, speaking quietly, "you looked a bit like you got asked to the prom back there. Anything you want to share?"

Emma tried to tamp down a smirk. "Ha. If I get asked to a prom at twenty-eight, I'd say you should have some more serious questions for me than that."

"Touché. But you and this yogi you're seeing must be doing pretty well if that blush I saw you wearing is any indication."

Biting her lip, Emma made a show of examining the

windows of the mosque as they turned the next corner around the building. "Okay, investigator. You got me. Things are going well. So can we find this killer so I can make my date?"

Leo glanced at her with a grin, then sped up his steps just a touch as they continued their circle of the block. A few unmarked cars passed by with officers inside, patrolling the streets.

Now that her flirtation with Oren had passed, along with Leo's teasing, Emma was starting to have doubts about the whole stakeout.

"I know Jacinda said this has to be the next stop because of the chalk—"

"I'm having doubts too," Leo said under his breath.

"Let's make a few more circles and then check in with Jacinda. Maybe there's somewhere else for us to be."

He pulled his phone out and began texting—presumably to ask just that rather than wait—while Emma fought down a shiver as a ghost approached from the mosque and passed just behind her and Leo. The ancient, white-eyed man wasn't the first ghost she'd seen around the place, but at least none of them seemed intent on speaking to her while she was with Leo. She only wished they'd keep to themselves rather than making her even colder and the winter air even thicker.

"They still haven't found any more chalk messages," Leo tucked his phone back into one pocket, "aside from the one here and those around the targets he already hit."

Emma grimaced. "So this is our best bet of his next hit right now. Good to know."

Two ghosts stood ahead of them, eyeing an unmarked car.

Emma pulled her gaze away and nudged Leo's elbow, drawing his eye to a woman giving close examination to the *Lost Pet* signs on a lamp post. "Maybe Cleaver got scared off by the police presence. There's an awful lot of activity around here for a Tuesday afternoon, I guess."

"It's possible, but where's he gonna go?" Leo checked his phone, apparently anxious for any update, then tucked it away again. "If we don't have any other leads, this is still the best use of our time right now. And one way or another, he's not going to get away this time."

Emma barely heard her partner as he went on. A white-eyed woman in a fancy cream-colored dress was sashaying down the sidewalk, focused on Emma and pointing at her pocket. Emma responded before she could catch herself. "Not now!"

Leo skidded to a stop and met her eyes. "Who are you talking to?"

Shit.

Emma took a deep breath, wishing she could stop the Other from interfering with her life for one damn day. "Sorry, Leo. I'm just talking to myself." She pointed forward, knowing he had no reason to believe her. "I'm just nervous. Let's keep going, okay?"

And she'd keep her mouth clamped shut as they did.

31

The dumpster seemed to vibrate with the sounds of sirens. They weren't constant, but whenever one passed by, I felt it through my bones. The metal around me was like a cage sent by the devil.

"God, I'm terrified. Please! The mosque is surrounded by police. I've seen them from blocks away. And there must be even more close by. I'm a mile away and keep hearing sirens."

"The siren you just jumped at was a police officer pulling someone over for speeding. You're being paranoid."

But I wasn't. I knew I wasn't. Maybe cops around me were pulling over speeders and grabbing jaywalkers because they were bored, but they were bored because they were in the area waiting for me. The lackeys of the police department were everywhere, even this far from the mosque.

Nearer my target, I could only imagine that detectives and federal agents were walking their dogs and playing chess on the street corners while they awaited my arrival, hiding in plain sight and expecting my disastrous entrance.

I'd never make it into the mosque alive, let alone get in there and pull my gun. Not without being shot dead first.

Thinking of my gun, I drew it from my pocket and checked the cylinder. I had only two bullets left. After killing the bartender and his mistress and the crystal sellers, I'd reloaded with the last two rounds from my supply. When I took my grandpa's gun, it was full, and he'd kept two extra bullets with it.

But he had more ammunition. I just hadn't thought to take it. I knew I should have. Now I only had two bullets to use and the street was full of Satan's assistants, people sent to stop me, to prevent me from completing the work God had arranged for me to do.

How could I ever succeed with two shots against an army of police officers? Might as well have been naked and unarmed.

"Stop hiding, my son. You need to summon your courage and fulfill your destiny."

A rock banged against the outside of the dumpster, kicked by a passerby, and I nearly shat myself. I couldn't do this.

"There's no way." My whisper sounded loud in the confines of the dumpster, and I lowered my voice further. God would hear me if He cared to. And He had to care to. He had to. "God, I'll be stopped if I try. The mission will go unfinished."

God paused before answering, a few beats too long, and the sweat along my back ran even colder.

"Do you dare question my wisdom?"

Clenching my fists together, I leaned back against the inside of the dumpster and willed God to listen. To hear me like I heard Him. "No, God, never. But they must know what I look like by now. They may even know who I am. And I marked that mosque. There's no way to go back. It's over."

"Oh, my son, it is not over until I say it is. And I tell you, you

are Adam. And on this rock, I will build my church, and the gates of Hell shall not prevail against it."

A little thrill ran through me. I knew that verse. Peter's confession of Christ, but God had changed Peter's name to mine. Just for me.

"You must trust in my plan, Adam, my son, and the rewards will be immeasurable."

"God…" I broke off, feeling bile rise in my throat. Now wasn't the time to be sick, but I had to make Him understand. "The forces of Satan are too strong right now. Around that mosque, at least. I cannot go there like You command, not right now. I could do it tomorrow, perhaps? Today, it would be suicide."

God didn't answer, and I let myself slide down the inner wall of the dumpster. I didn't like hiding here, but not because of the smell. It was the feeling of being caged that I couldn't bear. Like when I'd been in jail, having freedom only in God's words to me. And now, even He was frustrated with me. Leaving me alone here, in this new metal trap of the devil.

"All right, my son. A compromise, then."

Tears had begun running down and freezing on my face, but I rubbed my sweatshirt against them, afraid I'd heard Him wrong. "God? A compromise?"

"There is an alternative to the mosque. If you are willing to exterminate another holy diversion, I will still give you your gift. And, perhaps, you might even maintain your freedom once the mission is completed."

"Thank you. Oh, thank you, God." I stood up, remaining bent only low enough to keep my head below the edge of the dumpster. No point in showing myself until God told me where I should be going.

"Look to the ground by the ladder where you climbed up. You

have already seen my message, but your eyes were blind to its importance."

I listened first, but there were no footfalls around. Only the steady sounds of traffic outside the alley. Shoving my fear down, I rose to my full height and peeked over the edge of the dumpster, down to the ground.

A half-crumpled flyer was caught in the lip of a grate, fluttering in the breeze. I'd seen it when I climbed in, but I'd ignored it, thinking it only more of the waste left covering the streets.

Steeling myself, I made sure nobody was watching, then pulled myself up and over the dumpster's edge. As soon as my feet hit the ground, I grabbed the flyer and flattened it out against the side of the building beside me.

Blaze a trail to your inner spirit.

"The Yoga Map." I thought of the small crystal shop and how easy that part of my mission had been. How smoothly it had gone. This yoga studio, pulling people from God's path, would be no different.

And I would tear it down to its studs, just the same.

32

Oren browsed the Peruvian restaurant's website, his mouth watering at the pictures of *tacu tacu* and *ceviches*. He hadn't had tacu tacu since he'd traveled to Peru a decade earlier, and he wondered how Emma would react to the Peruvian version of pan-fried rice. It was one of those dishes that often looked far less appetizing than it tasted.

Perhaps they'd get a few dishes to share, instead, even though the ceviche with mussels might be the perfect aphrodisiac for a romantic night out. Two bowls of that to start, maybe. He thought to send her a few pictures, to make her mouth water like his already did, but she might just curse him for it, considering how far off the dinner hour was.

And yet, as delicious as the food appeared, there was no kidding himself.

He simply wanted to see Emma.

They could've made plans to chow down on oversalted fries and under-seasoned burgers, and his mouth would still have watered for her kiss, if nothing else.

He waved goodbye to his last students of the day, who'd asked permission to remain in the studio and continue their workouts for a few minutes after the day's last class. Their passion for yoga, even as beginners, was a pleasure to see, and he'd gladly given his okay.

Not as if I have anywhere to rush off to at the moment anyway.

He and Emma had only eaten dinner together a few times. He wondered whether she'd be open to sharing multiple dishes rather than an entrée for each of them. She'd mentioned grazing on appetizers with Mia, but that had been a girls' night out, not the night he had planned. No doubt, she'd want a glass of wine to wash the meal down with, though. And dessert.

The question was, would her order tell him anything about what she wanted from the night after dinner? It seemed too early to invite her back to his apartment, but if he rushed home to bake up some special dessert, that might entice her.

Thinking of what he might cook for their dessert, *just in case*, he wandered back to the studio and began cleaning up. Taking care to make sure his students had picked up all their belongings, he checked every cubby near the entrance for any forgotten water bottles or extra blocks and bolsters. He'd found two bottles that morning, and he added those to the five he'd found the day before. Honestly, he should start a water bottle store.

Emma had never left her water bottle behind. And he'd looked, trying to find an excuse to call her up. Instead, Oren had to call her and ask her out directly. Like they were teenagers from the fifties.

Full of warm feelings and excitement at the thought of sharing dinner with Emma Last in a few hours, Oren made fast work of tidying up the rest of the studio. He even emptied the bathroom trash so his cleaner wouldn't have to bother when she came in that night.

The faster she was done, the faster Oren could lock up,

get home to shower, and head to the restaurant to wait for Emma.

Whatever the night brought with her after that, he'd welcome it. She was what he'd been needing in his life, through and through. Even seeing her so little was somewhat welcome. His last girlfriend had hung on his every word. Always seeking his approval before taking any action, almost like a doting puppy rather than a woman with her own mind.

He had no worry of that happening with Emma. She was exciting. A go-getter. Nothing like the hippies he'd so often dated, where things had generally gone stale within a month or two. If Emma, being a different species from him, meant she had to dip out on dates occasionally, he could take that as a fair trade-off. It wasn't as if he'd become incapable of entertaining himself or needing his own quiet time.

The front door of the studio opened, and Oren felt a flicker of annoyance over having forgotten to lock it after those students had left. "I'm sorry, we're closed!" He hurried his movements, switching off the studio lights along the wall before turning to head out front. "The last class of the day is over, but there are some tomorrow morning!"

No answer. Someone who was determined to learn more about the studio even after-hours, then.

Oren moved through the door to the lobby without stopping, grabbing a brochure from the counter before he froze in place. He'd been ready to offer a brochure and a smile, usher the visitor out the door, then hurry home himself. But the vision before him in the little lobby stilled him instead.

A man in a beige ski mask stood in the center of the studio's entryway, a gun in his hand. The gun jittered and jumped in his grip as he muttered something to himself that Oren couldn't understand. He swayed on his feet, then stepped forward.

Finally, Oren moved. He took two steps back, holding

onto the distance between himself and the intruder. His heart pounded faster than it had during any yoga session that day, faster even than when he'd let himself fantasize about Emma that morning.

This was a dangerous city, but he'd never imagined a shooter stumbling into his very own studio. This wasn't a bank or a jewelry store. He sold peace, if anything.

Yet the undercurrent to this man's presence was full of danger. With his angry eyes staring at Oren through his mask's eyeholes, there was no denying it.

My God, I'm going to die today. I'm about to die.

The intruder swayed forward, the gun shifting in his hand, and Oren took another cautious step backward. The gun hadn't been aimed at him yet. Perhaps he had a chance.

"You don't have to do this." Oren waited for an answer, but the man kept muttering to himself. Only when Oren opened his mouth to speak again did the man wave his gun and respond.

"I do. I do. God's making me. I have to do it."

Oh dammit. Dammit, dammit, dammit.

There's no reasoning with him if that's what he's thinking.

The man kept going, apologizing to someone who wasn't present and speaking louder with every moment. He stumbled forward with a jerky step, coming near the lobby desk, and Oren backed up accordingly.

He couldn't talk his way out of this, but perhaps he could run while the man was distracted. Grab his car keys and disappear out the fire exit in the studio.

One, two, three. Go!

Oren lunged forward and grabbed his keys from the lip of the desk, whirling back toward the studio door before he could second-guess himself, but the masked shooter had begun shouting.

"This is God's mission and mine! You will not win the day for Satan!"

A blast like a firework sounded behind Oren, then another, and hammers of pain landed in his back and his shoulder. He spun to the ground, off his feet, and landed face up as his keys flew out of his hand and came to a clanging stop against the wall.

Oren blinked up at the ceiling, pain beginning to steal his breath. An agonizing burn anchored him to the floor, pulling blood from the area of his spine. His shoulder felt as if it had been blasted apart and begun imploding against the ground even as breaths started to stick in his lungs. He coughed, lungs screaming in his chest, and blood burbled up out of his lips to splatter against his cheeks.

In the midst of overwhelming pain, a calming voice echoed in Oren's mind. It was his own voice guiding countless students through relaxation exercises.

"Inhale peace. Exhale fear."

Oren tried to summon the deep, calming breaths he'd taught so many times. He thought of the tranquil faces of his students in meditation, the stillness they achieved.

Don't let Emma be the one to find me.

The shooter loomed over him, staring downward and muttering to himself once more. Oren wanted to say something, but blood came up instead of words, fed upward by the pain building around his heart and lungs.

He remembered the final pose of every yoga class, a pose symbolizing death and rebirth. With immense effort, he stretched his legs out and let his arms fall to his sides, palms facing upward. Savasana, the corpse pose.

The end is only the beginning.

He'd learn what was next for him soon enough.

The shooter leaned out of Oren's view, and keys jangled.

The man's footsteps faded as he stumbled away toward the door again, but Oren was already shutting his eyes.

As darkness enveloped Oren's entire existence, he found a sliver of peace in embracing the pose he'd guided so many through, a pose of surrender and acceptance.

33

Emma stopped in her tracks when her phone shrilled with a call from Jacinda. The SSA would be texting if this weren't big news. She pulled her phone from her pocket and put it on speaker, holding it between herself and Leo. "You've got us both, Jacinda."

"There's been a shooting a couple miles away from your location." Jacinda spoke fast, all business. "At least one fatality, and a witness says the suspect was wearing a ski mask. I'm sending the address to your phones now."

Oh no. No, no, no. How could we have been offtrack again?

"Consider us on the way." Leo began a beeline for the Expedition. "We'll meet officers there."

Trotting down the sidewalk behind her partner, Emma went ahead and clicked open the text with the address. She'd be ready with it as soon as they got to the SUV.

But just the glance she took brought her to a staggering halt.

Twenty feet from their vehicle, she could do nothing but stand still and stare at her phone. She knew that address.

Knew it from memory and from GPS and from a recent flyer.

No, I'm imagining it. I'm wrong.

I've got to be wrong.

From the Expedition, Leo was calling to her, asking her what she was doing, but Emma couldn't even find the air in her lungs to breathe, let alone answer him. She had to check first. Staring wide-eyed at her phone, she pulled up Oren's studio. And then, with that confirmation, her heart stopped for two full seconds, suddenly encased in an ice-steel grip as if she'd been pulled into the Other.

She wasn't wrong. The address was for Yoga Map.

Oren. Please don't let it be Oren.

Leo yelled again, and Emma sprinted for the SUV. "Move, Leo! I'm driving!"

Whatever he heard in her voice, it prevented him from arguing. He landed in the passenger seat just as she slammed the driver's side door shut. With Leo insisting she put her seat belt on, she used one hand to swerve the SUV away from the curb and around a plainclothes detective who cursed at her as she passed.

Lights flashing, she fishtailed a left-hand turn even as Leo typed the address into the GPS, cursing under his breath. All Emma could do was stare out the windshield, teeth clenched against a scream.

"Guess you know where you're going." He flinched as she took a turn faster than even she normally would have, then darted a glance at her. "The way you stopped—"

"It's Oren's studio." She swallowed a ball of air in her throat as Leo cursed beneath his breath. "The Yoga Map."

"Oh, shit. Emma...we couldn't have known." Leo went quiet beside her as he kept one hand on the grab bar and one on the belt across his chest.

She didn't have an answer for him. Maybe the mosque

had been their best guess at their killer's next target, but they'd clearly been wrong. Deathly so.

"Slow down, Emma. Please. We'll get there soon." When she didn't, Leo moved the hand from his belt to the dashboard, bracing himself as she took a hard left. "The mosque was marked. We've had police combing the city, looking for other signals, and haven't come up with anything."

Emma only fought back a scream of helplessness.

Please don't let it be Oren. It could've been anyone. A student. A volunteer picking up flyers to spread around. Oren could have gone out the back. He could be in his car now, chasing after the guy. Calling 911 because he doesn't want to bother me.

Oren wouldn't be alone there, not at this time of day.

It couldn't have been him. He can't be dead.

But even as Emma negotiated with herself, with her own logic, the image of those two victims at the crystal shop remained burned into her mind. The man and woman lying dead-eyed on the ground, blood and broken glass pooling around them as they stared at the ceiling without seeing it. Oren's smiling face looking at her from his flyer on the wall. His face overlaid itself atop the dead man's face on the shop floor.

Emma clenched her eyes shut and shook her head, refusing to entertain the thought.

He can't be dead. It must be one of his students who was shot. Or even someone just stopping in. Not Oren. Don't think like that.

"Emma—"

"Let's focus on how this happened." Her words were too loud, cutting Leo off, but she couldn't bear the sympathy in his voice. "Cleaver's supposed to be escalating, not de-escalating. From a bar, to a Reiki crystal shop, to a yoga studio? How does that make sense?"

Leo's jaw clenched. "We aren't certain this was Adam Cleaver. Not yet. We have—"

"It was fucking Adam Cleaver. Who else could it be?"

"Emma, you're not being reasonable or rational, and I get it. But you have to—"

"I have to get us there, Leo. Now. But why was it Oren's studio? Why would he go there and not the mosque? It doesn't make sense."

A tear made its way down her cheek. She swiped an angry hand across her face, quickly snapping it back to the steering wheel as she raced them down another street, swerving around cars that had pulled as far to the side as traffic would allow.

Leo's hands were still on the dashboard, gripping it as tight as he could. "A mosque would make way more sense. Maybe. But this...shit, Emma, this fits the pattern we've seen. Small businesses, privately owned. Minimal—"

"Minimal what, Leo? Security? Protection?"

"I was going to say staffing. Minimal...just one or two people who run the place."

"Maybe it wasn't Oren." She swallowed, willing herself not to allow tears to come. "Cleaver just followed someone into the studio. Someone off the street he was targeting. He shot that person instead."

"If it was Cleaver, yeah. Maybe he followed someone from the mosque." Leo's whisper barely dented her thoughts. She appreciated the effort, but she could hear the doubt in his words. How far-fetched the thought was, given what they knew of this killer.

Helpless to do anything else, she repeated herself as she swerved around a delivery truck. "Maybe it wasn't Oren."

It can't be Oren. Not him, of all people.

Deep down, though, she felt the falseness to the words. The denial.

She knew what she was going to find, and it was all her fault. She'd told him the flyer looked great. Told him he should put it up all over town. And he had, including at the crystal shop where Cleaver had struck earlier.

Before Leo had gotten his seat belt off, Emma was out the door and running, the door to the Expedition hanging open behind her. A forensic van was parked on the street. Techs carried equipment into the studio. Uniformed officers lingered near the entrance, and they split apart to make way for Emma as she skidded inside.

The Yoga Map's lobby was just as she remembered it. Just as it always was. The wall of cubbies, empty and clean at the end of the day. Everything looked normal. Except for Oren's body lying near the doorway to the back studio, someone from the M.E.'s office standing over him. Camera flashes told of techs recording evidence, but all Emma could focus on was Oren.

She landed on her knees just beside him, hands reaching for his arm before she could stop herself. Blood had dried on his face, leaked from his mouth, but his eyes were shut. Except for the blood, he almost looked peaceful.

Gripping his arm, she shook him before she could stop herself, speaking to the paramedics as she did. "Tell me he's okay. He's going to be okay, right?"

Nobody answered, and Emma finally felt tears spill from her eyes, stinging their way down her face. She bent forward, resting her face against Oren's still arm.

Her fingers hovered over his neck, but she held back from searching for a heartbeat. She knew the truth.

This close, she could smell him—his sweat, his earthy cologne, and his aftershave, but also his blood. His blood above everything.

I shouldn't be touching him. I shouldn't be acting like this. I should be on my feet, finding out exactly what happened. For him.

But even when she heard Leo's voice crack upon saying her name from the doorway and the forensic techs muttering to each other above her, Emma could do nothing but remain kneeling beside Oren. She could feel blood creeping into her hair and clothes from his chest, but it didn't matter.

Leo's boots appeared beside her. "Emma, I'm so sorry—"

"No!" She threw one hand up and slapped him away, even as he tried to grip her shoulder. "Leave me alone, Leo! Get out!"

Above her, Leo told the M.E. to give them space, but Emma only half heard him. Oren was gone, and she could do nothing but remain where she was.

"Emma..." Leo trailed off, and she swallowed the urge to kick him away from her. "He wouldn't want you to fall apart like this. Not over him. Not as strong as you are."

As strong as I am. How many times did Oren mention my strength?

A sob strangled in her throat, and Leo's hand came down lightly on her back. "Emma, come on. Please."

Grief threatened to overtake her, to freeze her muscles, but she clamped her lips shut. Cut off the tears and remained still until she felt them stop running from her eyes. Felt the moisture drying between her face and Oren's sleeve.

Leo was right that Oren wouldn't want her falling apart like this. Not over him, not ever. She was more than this.

Grief would wait. She would *force* it to wait, dammit.

For now, a deep rage was building in her gut, and she welcomed the darkness of something so different from sorrow. This was what she needed now. Right now.

Rage and determination.

She would find the man who had killed Oren. She would find him, and she would make sure he paid.

34

Emma lingered in the doorway between Yoga Map's lobby and studio. A few feet away, the M.E. knelt by Oren's body, near where she herself had fallen at his side upon first seeing him.

Numbness had spread through her, burying the grief in a heavy cloak of anger at the man who'd dared to steal Oren from her. Dared to steal five living, breathing, laughing, loving, beating hearts from their loved ones. Mia had tried speaking to her earlier, but Emma had shrugged her friend off.

Right now, she couldn't allow herself to think about Oren as her boyfriend. Her would-be lover. The man she'd planned on having a romantic dinner with that evening. The man who'd made her think he might be her future, after all was said and done.

And, most of all, the man who'd made her think that a real family was possible.

That, after everything, she could even have a family.

He was my future family. He was.

But that's not who he is right now. He can't be.
Not right now.

Because Oren was also the latest victim who needed justice, and despite the fact that she couldn't move from this spot or look away from him, that had to be the way it was.

"Emma?" Leo's voice was pitched soft. "Emma, look at me."

He stepped between her and Oren, forcing the question, and she finally met his eyes. They were narrowed with concern.

"Emma, you should go. You deserve a chance to process what's happened, and we can take care of this without you having to—"

"Don't you dare!" Emma's shout stilled the room. The M.E. even halted her dictation into the recorder she carried. Emma leaned closer to Leo and spoke more softly. "How dare you suggest I abandon this case now, Leo Ambrose? I'm going to catch this asshole."

Leo's lips flat-lined as he bit down some response, but Emma didn't care. Anger bubbled in her gut. She wanted to hit something. To strike something and make it hurt.

Before she could form another regret, she whirled from Leo and stalked back into the studio. Dim light filtered in through the window, and the air around her cooled just a touch in comparison to the lobby. The same old grouch of a ghost she'd become accustomed to was lurking in the corner, watching her. She snarled at him and stalked toward the bench at the side of the room.

She bent over it, putting her hands on the hard wooden edge, trying to anchor herself in the space and focus her anger.

I'm no good to Oren or my team or anyone else if I'm out of control. I have to harness this rage. Center myself, like Oren would tell me to.

A sound that was half anger and half horror burst out of her throat, and she turned and sat on the wooden bench, barely glancing up at Leo where he lurked in the doorway, having taken a few steps in after her.

"I'll give you a few minutes to decide what you want to do and then check back in with you."

She shook her head and looked up. "I've already decided."

But he was gone. She looked back to her hands, clenched above her knees, the fabric of her pants stained with Oren's blood. Someone had given her wet wipes for her hands, so that they were clean now, but they didn't feel clean.

Not after what she'd allowed to happen.

She stared out the window as the forensic team loaded equipment back into their van. A few of them remained, still collecting evidence, but they, like everyone else, only existed as background noise for Emma. The only thing that mattered to her was the dead man lying in the back studio doorway.

Emma had fully intended to be in that room tomorrow morning, following along as Oren led the class in a series of sun salutations and gentle opening exercises to start the day. She had actually thought to surprise him by showing up before he did and parking her Prius where he usually parked—

His car wasn't on the street. The forensic van was in the spot outside where Oren always parked his red Hyundai hatchback.

Emma stood sharply and went to the window, checking up and down the street. She didn't see Oren's car anywhere on the block. Even when he couldn't park in his usual spot, he always parked within walking distance of his studio.

The air grew thicker around her, colder, and Emma tore her gaze from the street. The elderly ghost who'd all but growled his anger at her, way back on the day she'd met Oren, stood close in front of her. Close enough to shake hands with, if he'd been alive. His white eyes gave away nothing, but his mouth clenched and unclenched with tension.

"What do you want?" she hissed. Grumpy appeared stiff as a board, his sweatshirt and sweatpants even looked starched. She threw up her hands. "Leave me alone, all right? I'll be out of your hair soon."

The white-haired ghost gave no indication of having heard her, his mouth still set in a firm line, but then he raised one hand, pointing outside.

Emma opened her mouth to tell him to get lost, again, that she had already figured out that Oren's car was missing. But the ghost was focused on her. While he'd always growled at her in the past, animosity dripping from him, now he had a stillness to him that suggested something else entirely.

She followed the direction of his finger. He pointed toward the end of the block, where a sign indicated a highway on-ramp at the next intersection.

And that highway ran west.

West toward Woolward.

Emma focused back on the ghost. "Is that the direction the killer went? Is that what you're telling me?"

The ghost didn't nod, but he did the next best thing, considering what their relationship had been in the past. He simply lowered his hand and turned and walked back to his corner where she'd always seen him lurking in the past. He squatted into his customary garland pose, hands held in front of his chest, palms together. Waiting, again, for her to bug off.

The message felt pretty clear, if ever one had.

Leo stepped back into the doorway between the studio and the lobby, an anxious frown on his face. "I'm hoping you've given it some thought and are willing to sit the rest of this one out."

"Seriously? You're still on that track? Forget it." Emma shook out her hands, willing the tension to leave them, and attempted to hide some of the rage boiling in her as she headed his way. "I'm still a part of this team, Leo. Period. And now we have somewhere to go."

She was stepping around him as he gripped her upper arm.

Emma gave a snarl, and he let go, but he kept pace with her as she stormed outside.

"Want to tell me where you think you're going?"

"Woolward. We're looking for a red Hyundai Elantra hatchback, D.C. license beginning Edward-Victor. Tell Jacinda to put out a BOLO for Adam Cleaver driving that vehicle."

She'd reached the Expedition and was climbing inside, cursing herself for not memorizing Oren's license plate fully. But at least she had the first two letters.

Leo was halfway into the passenger seat, the door still hanging open behind him, when Emma fired up the engine and began wheeling them off the curb.

"Dammit, Emma! Will you give me a fucking second?"

Emma ignored the concern in his voice and continued making her U-turn while he fought to stay inside the vehicle. Once they were pointed the right way, she slowed enough to let him buckle in and close the door. The instant it clicked shut, she floored it, letting Leo throw every curse he had in her direction.

Finally, as she turned onto the on-ramp for the highway to Woolward, Leo paused a moment to catch his breath. Emma took the opportunity to confirm her intentions.

"You're right, Leo. I was reckless and could have injured you. I'm sorry. You didn't need to come."

"What the hell is that supposed to mean? Emma, you are

so far out of line right now. If Jacinda were here, you'd be benched, and you know it."

"Then it's a good thing she's not here."

35

Leo risked a sideways glance at Emma, but she sat as rigid as a statue behind the wheel. Still. Foot to the gas, hands affixed to the wheel at nine and three as if to dare him to comment.

By his count, it had been fifteen minutes since she'd spoken. Hell, it might have been fifteen minutes since she'd blinked at this point.

He didn't want a repeat of the "Bonnie and Clyde" cemetery chase, with Emma speeding off on her own, half-cocked and putting herself in danger. But all he'd managed to do was come along for the ride this time. He had texted the SSA, and Jacinda had demanded he rein in Agent Last before she got them both killed.

How he would do that was a mystery. And so far, Emma had ignored every call and text the SSA had sent to her phone.

If she doesn't kill us both, Emma's going to wish she were dead when Jacinda gets ahold of her.

Leo couldn't help flinching as the speedometer inched higher. "Emma, we're no good to anybody dead. If you keep this up, we're going to crash and maybe kill someone else in the process."

Her only response was to veer around a tractor trailer, narrowly scraping by its rear end.

"Please, Emma. I've told you my parents died in a car crash. You've got your foot to the floor like we're speeding out of a burning building. And I'm with you, I understand—"

Finally, she heard him and gave the slightest of nods. The speedometer inched back down a touch. Nowhere near within the speed limit, but down to a point where Leo didn't think his heart might explode.

He'd never seen Emma like this, so wound up in her own rage and grief and laser-focused at the same time, like revenge was the only thing she had the capacity to consider.

Leo willed himself to relax, trying not to let the tension get to him. "There's no way Cleaver makes it to Woolward. The highway patrol's going to find him and bring him down. They know who he is, what he's driving. It's just a matter of time."

"He's one of the luckiest bastards alive. I don't trust the highway patrol to find him. He's slipped around town without anyone paying any attention to him."

I hope she's wrong.

Leo ran his hands along the belt across his chest, grounding himself. He couldn't help being chilled by how cold and flat Emma's voice had sounded. "If we get there, if we find him first, what are you going to do?"

He'd aimed to make his voice even, controlled, but the question hung in the air as if he'd flat-out asked her if she was going to kill him.

Emma didn't answer.

Leo lowered his voice, nearly afraid of his own words. "Emma. You can't just gun him down. No matter how badly you want to."

Emma struck the Expedition's ceiling, slamming her hand into the fabric with a dull thump, and Leo cursed as the vehicle sped forward all the faster and swerved around a car that had just entered the highway from a frontage road.

They passed the next few minutes in silence, Leo forced to listen to his heartbeat thumping in his ears along with the roar of the engine.

At the next intersection with a side road, another tractor trailer was entering, the driver apparently oblivious to the flashing lights and sirens of the Bureau's SUV barreling down the highway.

Emma pulled to the left, eating up the shoulder as she sped past the truck before whipping the Expedition back onto the road.

"I know he hurt you. But you could lose everything. Assuming we even make it there alive."

She nearly sideswiped a sedan as the driver attempted to clear the roadway but pulled to the shoulder too slowly.

When Leo got his breath back, he caught her glaring at him before quickly turning back to focus on the road.

"You think I don't know that?" Her hands were balled into fists against the wheel, white-knuckled. Her words came out like gunfire. "You think I'd throw away my career? For revenge? For nothing?"

Emma was seething with anger built from pain.

And nothing I've said has helped her.

And no matter how much he wanted to be convinced that she had her head on straight, it would do no good to push her. Emma Last was going to do whatever she was going to do.

When the SUV began to slow, relief washed through Leo for the briefest moment until he looked over.

Emma's fingers were running along the edge of the gun in her holster.

Leo sighed but held his tongue, focusing back on the road. He just had to hope that if worse came to worst, he'd be there to help mitigate any disaster before it took over their lives or cost Emma hers.

At this point, that was the only thing to do.

36

Emma searched the highway ahead of them for any sign of Oren's red Hyundai, then double-checked the rearview again. Nothing. GPS put them within ten minutes of Woolward.

Grimacing, she glanced over the side of a bridge as they crossed an exit ramp. "He would have had time to make it home by now."

Leo didn't answer her for a few seconds. "We both think it's where he's headed. Let's not give up until we have reason to."

Despite what he'd said, though, she saw him check his phone in her periphery.

Woolward's sheriff had promised to begin combing the town in search of Adam Cleaver, and he was supposed to call if he found any sign of the man or reports of Oren's vehicle. Their phones still had service but also remained silent. His shoulders slouched a little when he looked back up.

Emma clenched and unclenched her fists against the wheel. She'd hoped, despite her current cynicism, the sheriff would've found Cleaver by now. She wanted to bring him down personally, but she also feared the temptation of being given free rein to do so. Because she wanted to bring the man down for more than justice.

The truth was, Emma wanted Adam Cleaver dead, and the strength of that desire burned in her stomach like acid.

Leo pointed ahead at a sign marking Woolward's city limits just as his phone rang. He turned it toward her as Jacinda's face popped up on the screen. "We just reached Woolward, Jacinda."

"Good. We're about twenty minutes behind you. Agent Last, you are suspended if you do not stop that vehicle this instant. Your driving endangered your and Agent Ambrose's lives, as well as numerous civilians on the highway."

Emma brought them to a stop, pulling over in front of a house with faded and peeling paint and boards over one of the front windows.

Leo leaned over to the phone. "We're stopped, Jacinda."

"Good. Do you have Adam Cleaver's address?"

Emma stared at the GPS pointlessly. "Yep, but hasn't the sheriff already tried it?"

"He did. Nobody was at the house when he went by, but maybe you'll be luckier and catch Cleaver's grandfather. Get out of the driver's seat and let Agent Ambrose take the wheel. When you get there, talk to the grandfather while you wait for us."

"It's on the west side of town. Should be there in five minutes at most, even with Leo driving."

"You're dangerously close to being suspended over the phone, Agent Last. Remember that. And remember I used the word 'wait.' We'll see you soon."

Jacinda ended the call. Emma and Leo switched places, and he wheeled them off the curb. He glanced sideways at Emma as he rolled them down the street, just slightly over the speed limit, Emma noticed.

She forced a smile, hoping it looked less like a threat than a promise. "I'm good, Leo. You don't need to speed on my account."

"Just stay with me, Emma. Okay? I don't want a repeat of the last case, even if you're not driving this time. If we find Adam and he runs, we have to do this the right way."

They pulled up to an overgrown clapboard home that had once been blue but was now mostly peeling paint and vinery, like a majority of the structures they'd seen on their path through town. Bumping into the dirt driveway, Leo cut the engine.

Emma hopped out before he even released his seat belt.

As she jogged down the dirt drive, one hand on her weapon, Leo's footsteps thundered along behind her. "Emma, wait for me. What'd I just say? I'm serious! We do this the right way or not at all."

Slowing just a step, she forced herself to take a deep breath and wasn't entirely surprised when he sped by her, hurrying ahead toward the front door. He banged on the house even before Emma reached the porch. But that was fine. She'd wanted to keep an eye on the sides and windows, just in case Cleaver was inside and about to make a break for it.

Instead, she sensed nothing but empty silence.

Emma frowned at the curtain-covered windows and the barren driveway. "It looks deserted."

Leo banged on the door again. "FBI, Mr. Cleaver! Open the door and come out!" He glanced back at Emma.

Emma gazed along the front of the house. "Let's look out back."

By the time Emma reached the back of the house, stepping through patches of overgrown weeds, she'd begun to smell something more than mildew and wilderness. Leo's hurried footsteps reached her and passed her once more, no doubt aiming to be first inside if that was an option.

He stopped at the back door just above a small stoop. Nose scrunched and eyes hooded, he turned to her. "You smell that too?"

She grimaced. The stench leaking from the back of the property was unmistakable. Rotting fish and sulfurous rotten eggs, feces, and the must of decay. They had a dead body inside, and it wasn't newly dead. The corpse must've been well into decomp.

Too bad our good sheriff didn't come around back.

Leo pulled the top of his turtleneck up over his chin, lips, and nose, then faced the door. "Three, two, one." He kicked out once, hard, and the impact jarred the door in its frame, splintering the edge around the lock.

He pulled his weapon and moved inside, Emma on his heels. The old kitchen they entered held little more than a two-seater table and worn appliances, but the smell of the body was unavoidable. Emma grabbed one chair to prop the back door open as Leo gestured at a doorway off to the right.

The source of the smell. Fantastic.

Leo inched forward and nudged open a door with his boot. Inside, an elderly man with gray hair and a long, willowy beard lay dead on his back in the center of his bed. "Looks like we found the grandfather, Eugene Cleaver."

Nodding, Emma forced herself forward, making herself look at who she guessed was Adam Cleaver's first victim. The man had been shot at close range, blood pooling around his chest and soaking into his bed. His eyes were shut, at least.

A bedside table caught her attention. The top drawer was open. She approached, the stench of the body, thick and shifting, following her movements as if it were a living thing. Its surface held a small reading lamp and a hymnal along with a pair of reading glasses. The drawer was empty except for a tattered paper box of .32 caliber ammunition.

Emma prodded the box with her weapon. It was empty. "He was here, and he has more ammunition. I don't know how much was in the box, but it's empty now."

Leo put a hand over his mouth and nose atop the fabric barrier he'd already constructed. "I can't believe nobody reported this. This man's been dead for days. There must've been a gunshot."

Emma glanced out the window. "Around here, a gunshot might not be out of the norm. People probably hunt for food, whether it's hunting season or not."

Leo backed out of the room, and Emma followed him, weapon still drawn. Clearing the house didn't take long, and when they found themselves in Cleaver's bedroom upstairs, they stood frozen for a beat before either could speak.

A stack of Bibles sat on the nightstand table, but more prominent still, Adam Cleaver had scrawled Bible verses all over the walls of the room. Largest and in red—painted in his own grandfather's blood, if Emma had to guess—was their killer's favorite verse.

Those words positively dripped red down the wall, bleeding into the blankets of his bed and the carpeting beyond the edge of it.

Leo slipped on a pair of gloves before he picked up one of the Bibles and began flipping through it. Emma stepped in close to peer down at the pages with him. Messy handwriting was scattered through the margins, much of it illegible. Other pages had been ripped out entirely.

Emma gloved up as well and selected a second Bible from the stack. She found the same scrawling that couldn't be deciphered as well as missing pages.

"I have to get out of here. I'm gonna head outside and call

this in." Leo snapped a picture of the writing on the wall, then headed out the door without another word.

Emma gave the room one final look before following behind him. There was nothing there but desecrated Bibles and bloody letters, and they had a town to search to find their killer.

At the bottom of the stairs, the atmosphere became thick with more than the smell of Eugene Cleaver, and Emma turned toward the living room rather than the back exit. Standing by the front window, Eugene's ghost peered through. She glanced toward the kitchen, but Leo had already gone outside.

"Eugene?" She stepped toward him, not allowing herself to flinch from the extra cold offered up by the Other.

He turned back to focus on her, blood dripping down his flannel pajamas to his bare feet. Gazing from side to side, as if ensuring they were alone, he took his sweet time settling his white-eyed gaze on her, but he finally did so.

When he stepped closer, the cold of his presence engulfed Emma, but she remained where she stood, focused. If they could get something from this ghost, she aimed to do so.

"Adam was always such a devout boy." The ghost's whisper wavered, and he passed a wrinkled hand through his blood-spattered beard. "Always praying. Always seeking approval, always visiting St. Andrew's and trying to get closer to God, even if his purpose was misguided."

Catholics get closer to God by going to confession. And they confess to priests.

She opened her mouth to speak, and only barely kept herself from gagging on the smell drifting in from the other room. "Thank you, Eugene. We'll find him."

The man dipped a nod at her, then turned back to the window. "He was always a devout boy."

Emma whirled backward, unwilling to hear the ghost

repeat the entirety of his message. The man was pitiful, dead and hurting, but rage covered over any sympathy for him that she might have felt on another day.

Outside, she waved at Leo, who stood a few feet away on his phone. "He's going after the priest at his old church! St. Andrew's! Tell the team and let's get out of here!"

Emma didn't wait for an answer. It was time to take their killer down, one way or another.

37

"This is my final stop," I whispered as I sat parked in front of St. Andrew's Catholic Church. But God heard me.

"And after you receive your gift, it will be your time to take your place in Heaven. As promised."

Opening the door of the little red car I'd stolen, I paused to look up and down the street. "What if they see the car and know I stole it? They must be looking for me."

"It doesn't matter, my son. You don't need much more time."

My hands stilled on the door, but then I stood straight. Grace shifted my concern away, allowing the import of the day to sink in. Finally.

I'd waited so long for this.

Staring up at the broken little church, I felt a thrill run through my blood. If only my grandpa and all my doubters could see me now. I was God's right-hand man. Treasured, valuable, and worthy of His missions like no other. God bringing me back here for my gift, to my sad start that had brought me so far, proved as much.

My gift was waiting for me, then I would have my revenge and stand at God's side.

The floorboards of the front porch creaked beneath my feet, but the heavy entrance door swung open easily. Ahead of me, the well-trod aisle led up to the altar, where a lone figure stood gazing at a legal pad. The middle-aged priest mouthed words silently, probably rehearsing a sermon.

Father Maxwell.

"There is your gift. Enjoy it, my son, for it will be your last earthly pleasure."

I should've known this was my gift had I thought about it. This gray-haired imbecile of a man, who'd called me "mentally disturbed" and attempted to ruin my connection with God. Who should have understood me best but had refused to defend me to the police when I'd been arrested. Who'd convinced my grandpa, my own blood, that I should be treated as a lunatic instead of a warrior of God.

The whole town had been against me, doing the devil's work to sever my soul from God's good Word and good works, but this man had led the charge.

"Maxwell." I wouldn't do the honor of calling him "Father" and signifying his false connection to God. Especially not here in God's house, stolen as it might be by this pawn of the devil.

The priest focused on me, eyes narrowing as if he'd forgotten me already. Of course he would have, the old fool. But that changed nothing.

God's gift to me was the opportunity to kill this man. To take revenge on the person who'd sought to humiliate me and ruin me when I'd still been an impressionable teenager, more in need of God than ever before.

"Thank you, God. Thank you."

Maxwell set his legal pad on the altar and stepped down toward me, lips pursed. And then his eyes went a little wider, one hand fidgeting against a pew as he stepped into the aisle. "Adam? What are you doing here?"

Cool in my pocket, the gun settled into the palm of my hand. Calming.

Moving down the aisle, I let all of God's strength rise into my voice, and I used it. This man would understand what he had done. When he met the devil below, he would see why. "You defied the will of God, Maxwell. You told me it wasn't God's voice in my mind, but it was."

Maxwell stilled in the aisle, hesitating, then shuffled backward a few steps, putting himself halfway between the pews and the altar as I stalked forward, slow and steady. "Adam, God speaks to all of us in different ways, but what you were hearing—"

"*Was* and *is* God's voice!" My shout echoed from the rafters, and I grinned at the sound, reveling in the pain and shock on this old man's face. "You didn't defend me. You knew I was acting upon God's instructions. You must have known. And because of that, I know that you are not a man of God. You are a devil worshipper. It is time that I deliver the fate you deserve, as foretold by God, who still stands with me."

Maxwell's hands fluttered by his sides, his fingers stretching as if searching for the devil's hand to hold.

"Your master has abandoned you, Maxwell. He was false, like you are false."

"Adam...something is wrong with your mind. I am sorry, but that is the truth." He inched backward, to the right of the altar, and I kept in step with him. "What you heard, the voices, those aren't of God. God would never tell you such horrible things, to hurt others. Our Creator is a being of peace and love."

"Love for His followers, like myself." Condescension dripped from my voice, straight from Heaven, and I smiled.

"Now it's time that you stop lying. The time for lies is over. God will deliver my salvation, and I have already delivered six evil souls to God. Only one more remains."

Maxwell sobbed, the sound coming from deep within his throat, and he froze where he stood. "Oh, Adam. What did you do?"

"God's will. It is unstoppable. Don't you remember His will? It will be done. He is the Way. He is the Truth. He is the Life. And His enemies will get what is coming to them."

"Adam, no."

I grinned, taking another step toward the priest as God commended me. *"Well done, my son. You are a brave warrior, indeed. Now shoot!"*

The gun was cold in my grip, filled with the strength of God's will, and I raised it even as Maxwell turned to run. A bullet ricocheted off the altar, two more off the back wall. I kept firing as the pitiful priest ran.

My fourth and fifth bullets pelted the wall near the back exit as the priest flew through it, faster than I could have guessed. I fired again and laughed at the chips of wood flying from the doorframe. On my next shot, my gun clicked empty. No matter. I had collected my grandpa's ammunition when I stopped to say goodbye to him one last time. He'd only had two bullets with the gun where he kept it under his pillow, but the box had several more still inside.

I opened the gun's cylinder and let the casings fall at my feet. As I moved forward, following Maxwell's path, I reloaded from my pocket, taking care to seat each bullet properly. God would not let the old priest escape me.

Maxwell was my gift. Mine.

At the door, I fired once more, watching the priest flee across the patch of dirt behind the building and into the waist-high weeds that filled a narrow field. Beyond that, the woods began. I ran after him. The man was halfway across the little field, headed for the woods. He stumbled, clearly running on feet tangled with the weight of his sins, while I moved surely and easily with God's aid.

I grinned, caressed the trigger, and almost fired at him again. But God stayed my hand.

"Maxwell should be shot close up, face-to-face with the one he has so wronged. That is why you missed him before. Be patient and wait until you can see the sin in his eyes, my son."

God had done me a favor by holding me back from firing. He saved me from running out of ammunition. I would take careful aim for my next shot and wound Maxwell, bringing him to his knees. Then I would complete God's mission and send the man packing to the devil's doorstep, as willed.

38

St. Andrew's Catholic Church loomed up from the side of the road as Emma and Leo arrived. She stared at the plain structure, all white siding and steeple. It was an innocent and peaceful-looking church, but for the red Hyundai parked crookedly on the lawn.

He's here. We've got him.

Rage burned in Emma's gut, but she fought it down even as she pulled the Expedition up to the curb. The team was less than five minutes out by now. She could wait for them, and she had Leo by her side to keep her calm enough to do that.

"Okay, Emma. We found him. Let's secure the perimeter and wait for the team. Just like Jacinda said, right?"

She nodded. "Just like Jacinda—"

Two shots rang out from within the church, and every promise Emma had meant to make went out the window. Leo cursed up a storm before she flew from the Expedition, weapon in hand, sprinting toward the church.

He yelled something, but his words fell on ears that were tuned only to the gunfire coming from inside.

By any means necessary, as soon as possible, Emma was stopping Adam Cleaver. He needed to pay for what he'd done, and she planned to see that it happened on her watch.

By her hand.

She leaped the few stairs to the church's front entrance and slammed open the door. Worry over her own well-being vanished as quickly as it came. A film of red rage covered her vision.

Inside the church, behind the pulpit, Emma caught a flash of movement, a figure outlined by sunlight shining in from a back entrance. The gun fired again, and Emma needed no other proof.

Adam Cleaver.

She bolted down the aisle even as the figure disappeared out the door, firing again. Behind her, Leo's steps thundered into the church. "Emma, wait!"

She flew around the pulpit and out the back door, immediately keying in on the two figures running ahead of her. One—who had to be the parish priest—was at the edge of the woods, just disappearing between two trees, and the other, *Cleaver*, sprinted after him through waist-high weeds. "FBI! Stop!"

Her scream died in the air, neither figure showing any sign of hearing her.

But right now, nothing mattered beyond stopping Adam Cleaver.

Embracing her tunnel vision, Emma shoved herself through the tall weeds behind the church, the figure of Adam Cleaver her only focus. He paused at the tree line and fired, the shot echoing in the late afternoon. Emma barely raised her gun in response. Even in this state, she knew she couldn't chance hitting the priest, and while she couldn't see him, she knew that had to be who Cleaver was hunting.

An innocent man was out there and in Emma's line of

fire. That thought alone stilled her trigger finger as Cleaver darted into the trees. At least that was proof he hadn't yet shot down his prey.

Emma reached the tree line a second later, Leo thundering up behind her through the tall, thick grass.

Ten lunging steps forward, she saw the trees had only been a thin growth of woods at the top of a slope, leading down to a larger field spreading out at the base of a farm. The killer and his prey were in mostly open ground right now, with only a few bits of disused farm equipment littering the field. The priest stumbled forward with Cleaver trailing behind him.

Adam stopped and fired. The priest darted to one side and stumbled but found his feet again and kept moving.

He missed. Now's my chance.

Emma raised her Glock and fired, but Cleaver had moved, making staggering, erratic progress on the priest's trail. Emma's shot went wide, and she corrected just as he ducked behind a rusting tractor.

She held her fire until he reappeared, then shot again. But at this range, his unpredictable movements made it impossible to draw a proper bead on him. She took off in pursuit once more, rushing headlong down the hill leading from the trees onto the farmland.

Behind her, Leo screamed, "FBI! Hold your fire and come out with your hands up!"

Emma sped over the ground, fed by rage and inertia. She was gaining on them. The priest was circling, though, shifting farther to the left for another copse of trees.

Cleaver darted in after him, firing his damn gun once more.

Emma raced after them, branches scraping her face raw as she did. The pain barely touched her, not with the anger she felt driving her on.

Cleaver started yelling at the man he chased, and Emma got close enough to understand his hoarse words sprayed over and alongside his gunfire.

"You cannot run from the Lord, my God! I am His vengeance! I am His destroyer!"

Adam had lost every last shred of sanity, and it spurred Emma on. She had to stop him, and she had to do it now.

He skidded to a stop once more and raised his gun to fire, only twenty feet away from her now, but nothing happened. He'd either run out of bullets, or the gun had jammed. But Emma didn't falter. This man wasn't getting off with a simple cuffing of his wrists. Not after this chase.

Not after Oren.

She slid to a stop and raised her gun. "FBI! Freeze!"

Cleaver spun her way, bringing his gun in line with Emma as he did. She fired, rage burning its way up her throat as she roared at him. The bullet took him in the shoulder, spinning him to the ground against a tree.

Leo, gun trained, breathing heavy, was now at her side.

But Emma remained focused on Adam Cleaver, who lay screaming into the sky and pounding one fist against the dirt beside him. His gun rested useless beside him at the end of a limp arm that hung at an odd angle.

Approaching him, numbness slowed Emma's steps. The broken man ahead of her was wailing in pain, begging God for help with tears streaming down his face and terror in his expression. Like this, she had a hard time seeing him purely as the monster she'd been hunting down only a few seconds ago.

With Leo by her side, however silent, she managed to keep moving forward.

But she'd broken protocol today, seriously. And now she'd shot a man down when she knew he could no longer defend himself with a firearm.

As everything caught up to Emma, her stomach tumbled, and her eyes burned with the same tears she'd shed over Oren's body. She wouldn't let them fall now, but the fact that they stung and that her arm felt positively numb told her the truth of the matter.

Nothing would bring Oren back, and she might have just lost everything else that still mattered to her in this life.

39

Emma stopped and stared, then chose to back away from Adam Cleaver, who had propped himself up against the crooked tree. He'd failed in his mission, and listening to him beg the air for forgiveness—it was all too much.

She couldn't take this anymore. Holding one hand to her temple, fighting the chaotic swim of emotions in her head, she only half observed as Leo secured the man's weapon and bent to speak to him. Maybe to try to calm him or maybe to threaten him. No, that was what she would have done, she corrected herself.

Leo stood straight and caught her eye as Jacinda came sprinting up through the trees, but Emma turned away from him. It was all she could do to hold herself together right now. The mix of sympathy and regret on his face mirrored her own, but it was all too much.

Facing the trees, she allowed herself to embrace the numbness as a chaos of action pushed forward around her, as if to echo the emotions that had been swirling in her own mind.

Mia and Denae went to catch up with the priest, who leaned against a tree sucking in big gulps of air and praying some fifty feet away. Jacinda, Vance, and Leo conferred over Adam Cleaver until two paramedics came trundling up with a stretcher held between them. Cops lurked along the sidelines of the scene, securing the area and holding back a few men who'd wandered over from the direction of the farmhouse.

In the center of it all, Cleaver wailed his misery up to God, who answered only him. Or maybe God had abandoned the man, for his terror certainly suggested he was alone in this world.

Like me. Now. Again.

Emma breathed deeply, thankful the tears that had stung the backs of her eyes earlier had finally retreated. This wasn't the time for crying any more than earlier had been the time for grief. Instead, she had to get herself together and do what she could to salvage her reputation.

When she turned back to face the chaos, Leo's eyes were on her, but she still couldn't face the sympathy yet. A beautiful person, who had nothing but love for the world, had died earlier. Who had nothing but love for her…

She'd just lost her boyfriend, who she'd maybe even been growing to love, and after a life full of losing the people she'd loved, objectivity was the only thing that could save her right now.

Thankfully, something in her gaze communicated that to Leo, and he kept quiet. Moving over to Vance, he left Jacinda to turn her focus on Emma.

The SSA's hair was a storm of red around her face but barely redder than her cheeks. She virtually bled frustration, and Emma braced herself for the brunt of it. "Let's move into the trees, Agent Last."

Silently, Emma followed her supervisor away from the

group, up the little hillock, which she herself had come barreling down with barely a thought in her mind. There, with privacy among the trees, Jacinda stepped as close as she'd ever been to Emma and lowered her voice. "Do you have any idea how reckless you were today?"

Swallowing, Emma nodded her assent.

"At least you've got the intelligence not to argue." Jacinda let out a breath, eyes holding Emma's. "After our last case, I thought you'd learned something about being a member of a team. You were stupidly selfish and could've gotten yourself, your partner, and others killed."

Emma ran her tongue along the bottom of her teeth, fighting the urge to be stupider still by saying anything.

Jacinda held her focus on Emma's gaze. "Do you have anything to say for yourself?"

"I heard shots. He'd already killed too many people, and—"

"And," Jacinda lowered her voice, "you had backup coming. Leo was right there with you, Emma. The whole fucking team was on its way, minutes out, and you ignored protocol because you wanted to play judge, jury, and executioner. Mostly that last one—"

"No! There were shots fired!" Emma's shout died between them, and without checking, Emma knew some of her team members were probably looking their way, but there were some things she couldn't let lie. "I didn't want to kill him, Jacinda. I swear that's not what was on my mind."

"Then *what*, Emma? What was on your mind?"

"Nothing." Emma shook her head. "Nothing was on my mind but those gunshots and saving whoever Adam Cleaver was about to kill next."

Jacinda's expression went flat, and Emma saw her mistake before the other woman spoke. Admitting she had been out for vengeance probably would've been better than thinking of nothing.

"I can see from your face," Jacinda measured her words, "that you know what the problem with that is. Agents can't just run on instinct. On reflex. You got the best training and the best team for a reason, Agent Last, and having *nothing* in your fucking mind is about the worst thing you could be doing when we're looking for a killer."

Emma stared at the ground, embarrassment fraying apart her nerves. The SSA was correct, and they both knew it.

"Do you want to lose your job? You cannot behave like this." Jacinda paced away from her, stared off at the scene, then returned to face her. "You going off half-cocked like that doesn't just put you at risk. It puts your team members at risk. Not to mention innocent lives that could be saved but won't be because everyone is recalibrating a plan and reacting to you rather than thinking through a scene and what makes sense. All because you took it into your head to make the decisions for everyone."

"Yes, ma'am."

"Don't fucking 'yes, ma'am' me, Emma." Jacinda leaned in, closer than close. "How do you think Leo and Mia would've felt if you'd run into that church and been blown away by that killer down there? How do you think the team would've gotten their wits together and managed to save that priest if you were bleeding out on the ground in that church?"

"The priest would have—"

"I don't give a shit about the priest." Jacinda's retort would've been heard by others, had it been a touch louder, but she had far more control than Emma at the moment. "If our team had been split in order to take care of you and go after that killer, he could've gotten away into the woods, and we'd have more dead bodies on our hands soon enough, whether yours was included or not."

Tears burned behind Emma's eyes, but she fought them back. She wouldn't let Jacinda bring her to tears. Not even if the humiliation was what she deserved.

"Get it together, Emma. Get your shit together. Period." Jacinda waited for those words to sink in, then stalked back down through the trees, heading off to where paramedics were treating Cleaver's shoulder.

Emma's world spun around her, numbness spreading through her from her SSA's words.

Down the hill, their paranoid schizophrenic serial killer screamed at his Creator. "I was here for you, God! I was here for you! Why didn't you help me? You said I could have the priest! You said he would be my gift for all I've done. And then you let me run out of bullets before I could eliminate the last sinner. Without my own brimstone for his sins!"

Emma swallowed down her own scream, blocking him out as best she could.

Smoke was clearing from her mind, allowing her to take everything in, but very little of what she saw made sense. How had it come to this?

Emma had lost a loved one, and because of a maniac now left screaming at his God, accusing his Creator of "allowing" him to run out of ammunition at a critical moment. Forsaking him.

She didn't know whether to laugh or scream, to give in to anger or pity.

Emma began the slow walk back to her team, but Leo met her halfway. He stood still in front of her, waiting for her to meet his gaze. Finally, steeling herself, she did. She'd expected sympathy, but his expression was flat with caution, like she might lash out at him now that she'd taken the brunt of Jacinda's anger.

When she didn't say anything, though, he leaned in close to her shoulder, speaking into her ear. "Don't worry about it, okay? Nobody else saw, and nobody's going to believe that screaming idiot. Jacinda will cool off, and it'll all turn out all right."

Bile burned in Emma's throat. She blinked, but the scene swam ahead of her. "Saw what?"

Leo hesitated, but when his answer came, it was even softer. "Saw that he was out of ammo, Emma. He knows it, sure, but that doesn't mean you did in the moment. Nobody else saw that you realized it before you shot him."

Emma's eyes went wide. She hadn't known Leo had seen it too.

Or did I? And I just didn't care?

She shook her head, willing her voice not to shake. "And you're not going to tell anyone?"

"No, Emma, I'm not. Adam Cleaver had his gun pointed at an innocent man, you called for him to freeze, and he aimed the weapon in your direction. You had no way of knowing he was out of bullets."

Emma pulled back and stared at Leo for a few seconds too long. His eyes were focused on her, serious. His mouth a flat line of concern, absent its usual grin.

The tears she'd been holding back so often over the last hour welled in her eyes, and she stepped forward to hug him before she could stop herself. Holding him tight to her, Emma let a few tears sink into his coat.

It took a few seconds 'til his arms came up to embrace her in return. Clinging to him, she let an iota of the grief leak out of her, even as a small part of her wanted to laugh at his shock, which she could hear in Leo's murmurs of comfort.

He'd expected her to explode, and she'd broken apart on him instead.

The seconds lasted too long, and Emma knew it, but Leo held onto her until the explosion of emotion had passed.

When she pulled away and rubbed her face, he gazed off

into the distance as if to give her time. Then he spoke as if nothing had passed between them. "What say we catch up with Denae and Mia and find out what this priest said?"

Some of Emma's nervous tension eased as Leo gestured down the hill, that easy smile she was used to seeing teasing at his lips. "Yeah, let's. I'd say it's about time we find out what the hell happened to shake this man's screws so loose."

Leo led the way back to the team, and Emma followed him. Any urge she'd had to run ahead was long gone.

40

By the time Emma reached her apartment, grief had well and truly sunk into her bones. She ignored the little voice telling her she should calm down and eat something—take care of herself before going to bed—as exhaustion and images of Oren weighed down her every step.

When she managed to stop picturing his dead body, she pictured his smile. And when she managed to block out the rumble of his deep voice, flattering her and telling her she needn't apologize for being too busy with her job, she heard the sounds of sirens speeding toward his studio.

Leo had driven her back to the Bureau, where she sat in her Prius for half an hour at least, just staring at the mostly empty parking garage. Driving home, she'd barely been able to see the road, tears had so taken over her vision. Leo and Mia had both offered to play chauffeur, but she couldn't bear the thought of listening to them trying to tell her it would all be okay. And they would have, because that was what friends did.

So Emma carefully navigated the D.C. streets between the Bureau and her apartment, wiping tears from her eyes every few minutes and narrowly avoiding more than one accident. Wouldn't that have been the cherry on the top of the day? To get in a massive car accident because she wasn't fit to drive?

I would've deserved it. I'm so sick of the ghosts, but maybe they and the Other would leave me the hell alone if I vanished out of this life, just like them. Just like Oren.

She stifled her sobs in her pillow, finally allowing herself to truly break down now that there were no eyes to judge her for it.

The world seemed to be falling in on her, even here in what should've been her safe haven. She was just so tired of the ghosts. Tired of these crimes and the exhausting life that never seemed to stop. Most of all, tired of losing the people she cared about.

Oren had been such a good man. So uncomplicated and accepting.

So interested in her…

And now he's gone.

Oren would be a part of the Other now. Along with her mother and so many others she'd lost. If only she could see him. She knew without gazing around her room that he wasn't there. He would've said something by now.

Just like her mother, he was simply gone. Another ghost who wouldn't speak to her.

Emma's throat ached from crying, but the tears wouldn't stop. Because now that she'd lost Oren, what did she have left? Aside from the scorn of her fellow agents and the possibility of a suspension from the job she'd always loved. The one thing she could call her own. The one thing that normally kept her going, putting one foot in front of the other no matter how grief or the Other assaulted her.

"Oren," she breathed out, raising her voice into the room even as she doubted herself, "if you're here, please, see me. Forgive me."

A moment passed before she forced herself to look up and around at the same familiar features of her bedroom. The weight of her loneliness pressed harder against her chest.

It'd probably be pressing against her forever, now that her hope for a family had disappeared along with Oren and any semblance of happiness.

The thought sent sobs rising into the air again, loud enough to wake every ghost within a one-mile radius, but the raw grief held her frozen against her pillows and bed, shaking until she could barely breathe, barely recognize the sound of her own emotion.

Not after all she'd lost.

When Emma's tears ran dry, she breathed deep into her pillow until her lungs suggested that suffocation might be the next step. Then she rolled over and faced the ceiling.

I need to move. At least take off my coat and put on pajamas so that I have some hope of getting a real night's sleep.

She wasn't kidding herself about not being able to eat dinner. Just the thought of eating brought to mind the romantic Peruvian date she'd been meant to enjoy with Oren that very night and how impossible that now was.

Shoving herself upward, Emma tugged her arms out of her coat and then flung it toward the closet, leaving it to fall where it would. An awkward smack of paper sounded out just before it settled, and Emma glanced down to see the picture she'd found in her father's storage unit. It'd slipped out of the pocket with the force of her toss and now winked at her from the floor.

It seemed like forever ago when she'd cared so much about finding out who those women were in the photo with her mom. Had it really just been that morning when she'd been led to those photos in her father's storage unit?

She just wanted all of it to go away.

Emma picked up the photo and headed across the room to the trash can in her bathroom. She would get the manila envelope from her bag later and toss that out too. But the concrete feeling of the picture in her hand stopped her just before she dropped it into the trash.

"Don't make a decision now." Her voice was hoarse from crying but grounded her enough to realize that it wasn't the time to toss away one of the few things remaining of her parents. Instead, she retreated to her room and tucked the photo into a box of keepsakes at the back of her closet. That one and the other photos would live for another day.

When she closed the closet door, she turned back to face her bed. Her greatest luxury and the comfort she always retreated to at the end of an endless day. Not long ago, she'd entertained fantasies of sharing it with a man she'd been growing to love. Now that seemed no more possible than leprechauns and unicorns materializing out of nowhere.

Her attention landed on her mother's photo—it was on the floor—and she worked to swallow down another round of tears. "I don't care." Her gaze went to the ceiling, then to the window, and she whirled in a circle as she screamed at the air, hoping the Other would hear her. "Do you hear me? Other? Do you hear me? I don't care! I don't want to know anything!"

When her lungs burned with tears, she collapsed near the side of her bed and picked up her mom's photo, gazing into the woman's sky-blue eyes. Just like Emma's own. "I'm sorry, Mom. I can't do this anymore. I just can't."

She put the photo back on the nightstand, placing it face down. Maybe because she couldn't bear to face her mother, or maybe because she didn't want the photo to fall on its own any longer. It didn't really matter either way. She couldn't take the pressure anymore.

Turning away from it, she clenched her eyes shut as more

tears leaked from them. She knew she wouldn't sleep well, but there was nothing else to do.

When her tears had run out a second time, she breathed deeply, willing herself to rest. The slightest of clicks from behind her, at the bare edge of her awareness, told her that she wasn't alone. If she'd had more energy, she'd turn. She guessed that her mother's picture had righted itself. In the morning, she'd remember the moment and wonder.

But for now, for tonight, none of that mattered.

Because Emma Last was alone.

The End
To be continued...

Thank you for reading.
All of the Emma Last Series books can be found on Amazon.

ACKNOWLEDGMENTS

How does one properly thank everyone involved in taking a dream and making it a reality? Let me try.

In addition to my family, whose unending support provided the foundation for me to find the time and energy to put these thoughts on paper, I want to thank the editors who polished my words and made them shine.

Many thanks to my publisher for risking taking on a newbie and giving me the confidence to become a bona fide author.

More than anyone, I want to thank you, my reader, for clicking on a nobody and sharing your most important asset, your time, with this book. I hope with all my heart I made it worthwhile.

Much love,
Mary

ABOUT THE AUTHOR

Mary Stone lives among the majestic Blue Ridge Mountains of East Tennessee with her two dogs, four cats, a couple of energetic boys, and a very patient husband.

As a young girl, she would go to bed every night, wondering what type of creature might be lurking underneath. It wasn't until she was older that she learned that the creatures she needed to most fear were human.

Today, she creates vivid stories with courageous, strong heroines and dastardly villains. She invites you to enter her world of serial killers, FBI agents but never damsels in distress. Her female characters can handle themselves, going toe-to-toe with any male character, protagonist or antagonist.

Discover more about Mary Stone on her website.
www.authormarystone.com

- facebook.com/authormarystone
- x.com/MaryStoneAuthor
- goodreads.com/AuthorMaryStone
- bookbub.com/profile/3378576590
- pinterest.com/MaryStoneAuthor
- instagram.com/marystoneauthor
- tiktok.com/@authormarystone

Printed in Great Britain
by Amazon